INTERVENTION

Intervention

M E GOLESWORTHY

Sospiro Publishing

ISBN: 978-1-8381343-0-3

A CIP catalogue record for this book is available from the British Library

Also by M E Golesworthy:

The Waiter's Game
The Parade
Tea and Moles in Brackenden Green

$$\sim 1 \sim$$

Paris, May 1937

Tom forced a smile as the thin, grey-haired house-keeper stepped aside to let him in.

She glanced at the water dripping from his coat and onto the white marble floor.

'It's not a day for walking, Monsieur Lancaster.' Her voice leaned heavily on the last syllable of his name. She took his hat and broken umbrella before leading him through the grand hallway, and into the library. She didn't offer to take his coat.

It had been raining for months and all of Paris was wet and soggy. Optimists thought spring was just around the corner, Tom wasn't so sure.

The housekeeper went to inform Sir Arthur that his guest had arrived whilst Tom carefully draped his wet coat over one of the leather covered armchairs. Standing in front of the fire, trying to dry himself off, he covered a yawn with his hand, it had been another late night. There had been a lot of them since his return to Paris, but who could blame him for drinking to forget what he'd seen. It was easier to sleep peacefully when you were tight; when you were so tired you couldn't remember your own name. He knew it wasn't a long term solution and at some point he'd have to deal with what had happened in Spain. Agreeing to see Sir Arthur was certainly a first step.

His eyes fell on a healthily stocked drinks cabinet.

On top of this cabinet there was a photo of someone he used to know. He walked over the thick rug, almost hypnotically, towards it.

He remembered when it had been taken; it was one of those happy childhood summer days that had seemed to last forever. Drenched in sunshine and laughter they had refused to go indoors to have their photos taken. In the end a rather grumpy photographer had to come out onto the lawn where Mrs Henderson, the housekeeper, managed to keep them still for long enough for the photos to be taken.

Her name was Bea, and Tom had known her since she was a little girl. They had grown up together like brother and sister and then grown apart as life took them in different directions. Later on in life, in a foreign country, she had died because of him.

He was still staring at the photograph when Sir Arthur appeared in the doorway.

'Tom, it's so good to see you. It's been a long time.' His deep voice boomed as he strode into the room and heartily shook Tom's hand.

'It has. Time just goes too fast.'

'When you get to my age it goes even quicker,' he smiled at Tom. 'It's not too early for a little drink, is it?'

He poured two whiskeys and went over to the armchairs by the fire.

With a deep breath Tom slumped back into one of them and started to relax a little. The drink warmed his throat and he wished the decanter was a little closer.

Sir Arthur relaxed his large frame back in the other armchair and lit a cigar.

His grey receding hair melted into a perfectly trimmed beard, framing his rather round head in an old fashioned Victorian way. As far as Tom could remember, he looked the same now as he did twenty years ago. He felt like a wet tramp next to him and probably looked like one too.

'You're looking better than the last time I saw you.' Sir Arthur said whilst surveying the current state of Tom and sipping his whiskey. 'Considering you weren't really ex-pected to live six months ago, I'd say you're looking rather well.'

His deep familiar voice brought back the feelings of guilt Tom was trying to suppress. He was back here, and living what seemed like a normal life whilst Sir Arthur's only daughter was dead, and he was to blame for it. He'd never said as much, but there was no need to put it in words because how could he not? Tom closed his eyes for a moment to bring himself back under control.

'Thank you. I'm trying to get on with things. I'm looking for work and keeping busy you know.'

Arthur had noticed his moment of imbalance and sighed.

'You have to get back on track, stop the drinking and the late nights. I spoke to your mother yesterday and she's worried about you. We both are, and nothing will get better by feeling sorry for yourself, or worse, blaming yourself for what happened. You have to snap out of it.' The words came out in bursts of assumed positivity.

Tom didn't respond, but instead lit a cigarette and finished what was left of his drink. The crystal tumbler was quite suitable for a residence in this part of town, and as far removed from the harsh drinks in Madrid as you could get. He got up and refilled his glass before sitting back down again.

'Your message said there was something urgent you wanted to discuss.'

'Well, I have been trying to get hold of you for a couple of days but you haven't been home and I have to leave Paris tonight. Dare one ask where you have been?'

'I've stayed with a friend for a couple of nights.'

'Friend, eh?' he raised his eyebrows. 'I'm not sure why you insist on living here when you could be back home in Kent where, funnily enough, the sun has been shining for the last few weeks.' He chuckled to himself. 'You would have family and friends around you.'

'We've been through this before. I'm happy here.'

Tom was 26 years old today and they had had this conversation every time they met since he moved to Paris, almost six years ago.

'You don't look bloody happy to me. Anyway, I have spent the last couple of days with the new ambassador to France, Sir Eric Phipps. I think he will do a good job, and no doubt he's glad to be out of Berlin. It's quite a hot potato these days and needs someone who will pacify Hitler, not antagonize him by referring to him as 'possibly mad''.

'Did Phipps really say that?' Tom smiled reluctantly.

'Oh, he did indeed. Only in his correspondence with London, but I have no doubt it would have found its way to Hitler's ears somewhere along the way. The new ambassador is there to try to keep Germany under control, which will be a lot easier said than done.'

'Yes. Maybe he'll succeed in keeping them out of the Spanish war too. I think Hitler is taking the success of Franco as a personal achievement.' Tom added this with all the acidity he could muster. Sir Arthur was not a fan of the Spanish Republican government, hence his daughter had taken to it with quite a spectacular devotion and energy.

'I'm not going to get into an argument with you about bloody Spanish politics. It'll be over soon enough.' Sir Arthur said condescendingly whilst watching his cigar smoke whirling around in the glow from the fire.

There was a pause in the conversation as Tom held his tongue, and probably Sir Arthur did the same so as not to start an argument. The whiskey had warmed Tom up and just as he was about to start talking about anything at all to stop the silence, Sir Arthur sat up in his chair and leaned forward.

'She's alive.' A smile appeared on his lips before he leaned back again.

'I'm sorry. Who's alive?' Tom asked incredulously, thinking he had misheard.

'Beatrice of course. Come on old chap, who else would I be talking about?' Sir Arthur smiled like a cat that had got that elusive cream.

'What makes you think that?' Tom's heart was sinking fast. He really liked the old man, but his grief had obviously made him mad.

'This is where it gets a little complicated. One of our chaps in Madrid saw her. Only briefly mind, but he insisted it was her and he should know, he used to be engaged to her. Now, that would have been a most unlikely marriage,' he chuckled. 'Anyway, she wore that awful necklace her mother left her. You know the silver one with the blue stone.'

'I know the one you mean. I also know that whoever told you this was mistaken. I'm so sorry Arthur, I was there, I saw her body and she was dead. There is no doubt about it, and if I could change what happened I would, you know I would. I should not have let her come with us, but she did, and that's that. You have to accept it.'

Sir Arthur's grey eyes turned steely and held his. 'You think I'm going mad? Sir Arthur has finally lost the plot. Yes?'

Tom shifted uncomfortably in his chair and was just about to deny the accusation when Sir Arthur continued.

'Well, I tell you young Tom that there is nothing wrong with my head. I had accepted that she was gone and that we would not even find the body. It broke my heart, but I am well aware that these things happen and I had accepted it. There is even a memorial stone in the village cemetery at home, and we had a service for her, and we grieved for her too. Then, a couple of weeks ago, I got a phone call from Charles in Madrid. You remember Charles don't you?'

Tom nodded. Charlie had been his contact at the embassy. He had never mentioned the fact that he was once engaged to Bea even though they'd discussed her often.

'Now that Madrid is under siege the embassy has moved away, but Charles is still there, officially as an embassy representative, but unofficially he keeps our network there going. He said that he'd been walking over to one of the courthouses for something or other and there she was. Hair cut short, but still easily identifiable as Bea and he didn't think she saw him. She was walking alone across Plaza de Colón, but by the time Charles had realised that it was her, she'd disappeared off to some side road and he couldn't find her. He was never one of the brightest sparks our Charles, always best suited for a desk job. Once this is all over, I think we'll grant him his wish and put him back in London.'

'It must have been someone who looked like her. Maybe Charles just wished he'd seen her so much he actually thought he had.'

'Well maybe, but there's more. About ten days ago, I saw a report gathered together for quite a different purpose. It mentions a woman, fair haired, tall and with a blue stone silver necklace. She was trying to sell gold, or rather exchange it for weapons.' He looked at Tom. 'Spanish gold.'

Tom's head started spinning and he stared with disbelief at Sir Arthur.

'The same gold I told you about last year?'

'I don't know what gold it was. Apart from it being Spanish, the report doesn't mention how she came to have it.'

Tom didn't know what to think. Bea was dead, and the gold was what had brought them to the place where she died.

'What do you want from me? She's dead.' He wanted to throw the glass into the fire but restrained himself. 'She's not out buying weapons or selling gold. She's in some grave, somewhere in Spain.'

'Tom pull yourself together. I have seen photos of her.'

'Can I see them?'

'No. They're classified, I'm afraid. You'll just have to take my word for it.'

'She would have let us know if she was alive. You know she would.'

'I don't know if she would. We had quite an argument before she went to Spain and she didn't speak to me again, so no, she would probably not have contacted me in any case.' He shrugged his shoulders. 'Whatever the reason, I want you to go over there. Go to Madrid, find her and bring her home before Franco marches in. Then, we can find out what she's been up to.'

It took a moment or two for this to sink in. Sir Arthur wanted him to go back to Madrid, which was now under siege and had been since November, to find his daughter whom Tom knew was dead. There was nothing he wouldn't do to try to make amends for what had happened, and God knows he wanted to go back. Someone must be masquerading as her. He needed to find this person to stop Sir Arthur believing that she was still alive. All of a sudden, it became important to find this woman. She'd be able to answer a lot of questions.

'I think you'll find that I have somehow offended the Spanish government and they won't let me back in the country.'

Sir Arthur opened his briefcase and took out a large envelope and a small parcel. He moved the glasses to one side and laid the two items on the table between them.

'Your name is Thomas Reid. All you need to go back is in there. Visas from the top, to go anywhere you like. Well, within the Republican territory anyway'

He spoke in a hushed, urgent voice as if he'd never handed over false papers before. Maybe he hadn't, people like Sir Arthur always had other people to do these things for them. Sir Arthur continued. 'You might want to be careful entering the country though as they check and double check people coming and going.'

Tom looked at the envelope and it took only a split second to decide to go. Not because of Bea or Sir Arthur, but this was his one chance to get back to Spain; to get a quiet revenge on behalf of his two friends and to see Maria again.

'You must have hundreds of chaps out in Spain, spying for King and country. Why not ask them to investigate?'

'I'd like to keep this quiet. My position in the government would make it really awkward if she has decided to go fighting for the commies or something like that. Tom, she was trying to buy weapons for God's sake. I wouldn't put anything past her, the girl doesn't have any sense of right and wrong. She never did.'

Tom was just about to interrupt him and argue the point of right and wrong in the Spanish war when Sir Arthur held up his hand to stop him.

'Not now Tom. It's bad enough that she went out there in the first place. Also, I'm sure they would think I'm mad,' he sighed, 'just like you did.' He looked at Tom. 'Like you still do, no doubt. No, no, no. This has to be kept between the two of us. I'm asking you because you've been as much a part of the family as if you were my son. And you're a journalist, which I never thought would be useful, but you can go snooping around anywhere on the Republican side and they won't mind. Just don't upset anyone again.' He paused. 'I am giving you an opportunity to tie up your loose ends.'

He was right of course. The last few months, not knowing how his friends out there were doing, or if somehow they had been suffering for his mistakes had been a bloody nightmare.

It wasn't just Bea who had been killed that day. Tom had spent the last couple of months desperate to go back, reading everything, everywhere about the war and spending his evenings drinking with other journalists and writers who have been over there, trying to get some information on the Café Rosa and its owners.

'Of course I'll go.' He picked up the envelope and the parcel and put it in his pocket. 'I'll go and see Charlie and follow up on his lead. When do I leave?'

'As soon as possible. Charlie has the exit visas for the two of you. And Tom, don't hang around Spain afterwards, if they found you were back they might finish you off properly this time. - And one more thing. There were 100 cases of gold missing when the Russians unloaded the ships at Odessa. I don't need to tell you what some people, or organisations, would do for that amount of gold.'

Tom nodded. The gold story had taken too much from him and he wasn't sure he cared about it anymore.

Sir Arthur put his glass down. 'Right, I have to dash back to London now I'm afraid, but it's been really good to see you again. We'll have a proper birthday party for you when you get back.' He got up from the chair to leave.

'No, no, Tom you stay and finish your drink. Good luck.' He held out his hand which Tom took. 'And take care. I'll give your regards to your mother.'

With this he left the room and Tom sat back down.

Well, isn't it funny how things work out? Madrid had got under his skin, and even with bombs exploding and the blasted bureaucracy that had taken over since the start of the war, it had made him feel more alive than anything ever had.

More than that, it had changed him, like it had changed everyone who was there.

Those last few weeks in Madrid had been the best and the worst of his life. He couldn't wait to get back.

~ 2 ~

'Tom. Tom, wait.'

Emilie's voice nearly drowned on the busy platform at Gare de Lyon. From the front of the train dark sooty steam drifted towards the high glass and metal roof, enveloping the station in its familiar travel aroma. Men, women and children, all going somewhere for a hundred different reasons. Tom was just about to board the early morning train to Perpignan, when he heard his name shouted from further down the platform. He turned around to see Emilie running towards him, pushing other people out of her way as she did so.

'Emilie. What's the matter? What are you doing here?'

'Were you just going to leave without saying goodbye?' Her large blue eyes held his. They made him feel like the coward he'd been for the last few months. He'd had several opportunities to end it, especially now when he should have made a clean break.

'I did send you a note saying that I had to leave urgently. I'm sorry, I should have told you in person but there wasn't time.' Such a shallow excuse. He moved over to the side of the platform to let another couple of passengers on the train.

'You're going back to Spain?'

He hesitated for a moment.

'Yes, but not for long this time,' he promised. 'I'll be back before you know it.'

'You said that last time you went there. Eight bloody months you were gone, and then when you came back I thought you would die. You used to be so much fun and Spain took that away, it took your soul away Tom and it broke you. Why on earth are you going back?'

'I have to. There are things I have to do, and I can't get on with my life until they're taken care of.'

'Well, I'm not waiting for you again.' She put her chin out and continued. 'You stay here with me or we are finished. I mean it this time, I can't do this again.'

Steam filled the air and the conductor blew his whistle loudly to make it heard above the sound of the engine.

'You'll be better off without me.' He lightly brushed away a blonde strand of hair from her face and kissed her cheek. She was an amazing woman and she deserved better than him. 'I'm sorry. I have to go.' He jumped onto the train which started moving with a jolt. Leaning out of the train door window, he waved goodbye to her and to Paris.

'You are a foolish man Tom. She'll be gone by the time you get back.' Aaron Prutzhanski leaned his portly figure back against the thickly padded back rest and put his book down on the seat next to him. He was an easy going young man who was hoping to make his name as a photographer in Spain. He'd been due to go over three weeks earlier with Cloudy MacDonald, a freelance reporter. Unfortunately, Aaron had sprained his ankle whilst jumping out of a first floor window to avoid being caught by his fiancé's father the day before they were due to leave. He could just as easily have hidden under the bed, but admitted he had panicked and more flung himself out of the window than jumped. How true this was Tom didn't know, but Cloudy had gone to Spain on his own and left Aaron to make his own way there.

That had worked out quite well for Tom who thought that it would be easier to get across the Spanish border without too much scrutiny if there were two of them.

Aaron continued, 'I know you don't like to talk about it, but has this sudden departure for Spain got anything to do with your last trip there?'

Tom just shook his head and pulled his fingers through his short brown hair. 'You look rather smart today,' he said changing the subject.

Aaron looked a little annoyed that Tom would still not tell him what had happened, but then he smiled.

'Well, I've never really travelled very far and thought I'd make an effort.'

He was wearing a brown suit which was slightly too long for his height together with his well-worn 'just like Fred Astaire' two tone brogues. 'Jacqueline says I have to make more of an effort with my appearance and I guess she'd know, being a girl....'

'I thought you came from Russia? You must have travelled quite far to get to Paris.'

'I was a baby at the time and I don't think having to leave your home to survive count as travelling.'

'I'm sorry. I didn't know.'

'That's alright. We're doing better now.' He then got on to his favourite subject of Jacqueline Bouvier, his fiancée and Tom felt his spirits falling and stopped listening.

After the change at Avignon, Aaron fell asleep and Tom gazed out over the Provençal landscape as the train moved forward at a slow steady pace along the coast line towards the Pyrenees. The afternoon sun shone on the pastel coloured shutters of the small village houses, and an occasional glimpse of the sea lifted his spirits. He had been wary of telling anyone where he was going, or indeed that he was leaving Paris. Someone didn't want him returning to Spain. He wasn't sure who, but they had gone to a lot of trouble to make sure he wouldn't get back to Spain. Why hadn't they killed him when they had the chance? Why had they shown him mercy and not the others? Maybe they had done. Maybe they had taken them to the edge and then let them live too. Deep inside Tom knew that was not the case. He had been the exception, but he didn't know why.

And what about Maria? Would she still be the same? Madrid had been under siege for over six months and he didn't even know if she was still alive.

He lit a cigarette and closed his eyes. The journey back had begun.

Madrid Prepares For Battle

New Government Posts Declared

From Our Correspondent Thomas Lancaster In Madrid

17 October 1936

Madrid is preparing its defence against the rebel forces who are now less than 30 miles from the city. The rebels captured Mentrida yesterday after a fierce battle with the Government troops, who whilst retreating, demolished the roads as they left. Chapinaria was also taken this morning but with little resistance.

Today is the first day of rationing in Madrid, and although there are still queues for some items the transition has gone well. There is however a lack of food, the water is turned off during night-time and there is no gas for cooking or heating. Once the 11pm curfew sets in, the city plunges in to darkness and the streets that used to be so lively before the war become deserted. The only sounds at night are the occasional shooting of guns as the militia searches for suspects. After General Mola's comment that he would take Madrid by the four columns he had marching on the city and a 5th column of supporters inside, these night-time arrests and shootings have increased. With all this misery the Madrileños still keep going and morale is high.

Since the uprising of the rebel generals on 17th July this year, the Government have re-organised their own militia into *a proper disciplined army enriched with volunteers from all over Europe who have come to Spain's aid in her hour of need. The government is still hoping that the League of Nations led by Britain, will lift the non-intervention agreement and allow the democratically elected government of Spain to purchase food and equipment from other countries.*

I have, with my own eyes, seen German and Italian aeroplanes flying over Madrid, and I find it curious that both these countries are part of the League of Nations but a blind eye is turned to the help they are giving to the fascists.

Also today, the Prime Minister Señor Largo Caballero was appointed Supreme Chief of Military Forces and the Foreign Minister Señor Alvarez del Vayo was appointed General Commissioner of War. Señor del Vayo is to be assisted in his new task by representatives from the Communists, Syndicalists and the Social Unions.

~ 3 ~

Madrid, October 1936

The grass was dry and harsh, still waiting for the autumn rain to come. Tom sat down on the hard mud next to José in the almost empty park and waited. He'd just returned from a two day trip to Valencia where he had tried to get access to some of the fascist prisoners that were held there, but had failed miserably. Now he was glad to be back in Madrid where he'd intended to write up his notes, have a meal and an early night. This was what he would have done if José, his landlady's son, had not asked to have a word with him away from the Pension and dragged him to the park where they were now sitting in silence.

José was only on leave for a couple of days and Tom could hardly say no when his mother, whom everybody knew as Auntie, had been so kind to him since he first arrived. Now José was just sitting there, leaning back against a rock and staring into the trees across the dried up grass patch in front of them.

Approximately thirty miles behind those trees were the enemy. They were advancing rapidly towards Madrid, getting too close to the capital and the Republican army unable to hold them back. How long would it be before the fascists reached Madrid, until they were fighting them off here, on their own streets. How much blood would then flow down those cobbles towards the Manzanares, mixing with the cold clear water, carrying it to the Jarama river, and on to the sea.

Tom knew what had happened in other cities taken by Franco, not just from the propaganda, but from other journalists, friends who had eye witness accounts. How the civilian population had been massacred in Badajoz, and how they had slaughtered the sick and injured in the Toledo hospital by throwing grenades into the wards as they went through the corridors.

There would be no mercy to be had by anyone if they took Madrid.

Enough leaflets had been dropped over the city explaining what would happen if they didn't surrender to make sure that everybody were clear on the subject.

He should be out there fighting them, he really should, but he found himself always coming up with some excuse to delay. Did José and others find him a coward for this? Maybe they just saw him as an outsider, not expecting anything from him. He didn't want to be an outsider, he wanted to be part of the fight, part of his mother's country which he had dreamt of since he was a child.

He'd think about it tomorrow, he was too tired now and for a moment he wondered if José actually wanted to talk to him or if he just wanted some company away from his fussing mother.

'So, why did you drag me down here?' Tom joked, lighting a cigarette. He offered one to Jose which he accepted and lit before speaking.

'I'm going back out tomorrow.'

'Do you know where you're going?' Tom asked.

José shook his head. 'No. We'll see when we get back to the camp. I hope we get sent to the front line. At least you know who you're fighting there. You can see the enemy, and all you have to do is kill as many fascist bastards as you can whilst trying to stay alive to kill some more. You know why you're doing it.'

He stopped for a moment whilst a grandmother walked past with a little girl in one hand and a heavy basket in the other. The little girl was running on her short legs to keep up with her grandmother's long strides. She looked with great interest at Tom and José who both smiled and waved, making her promptly trip over her own feet. Her grandmother's hand stopped her falling over and after a few stern words the little girl was once again keeping her speed up and they disappeared from view.

'Maybe I shouldn't ask this of you. I mean, I don't know you well enough.' His brown eyes looked at Tom through an exhale of smoke, and for a moment he paused as if to decide if he would continue or not.

Tom found himself curious where this conversation was leading and he had to stop himself from pushing José to continue.

'When I'm not here, will you look after my mother and Maria? You see, I wouldn't normally ask but there is nobody else here now, and both of them refuse to leave Madrid?'

'Of course I will. I'll drag them out of here if I have to.' Tom said cheerfully hoping it would not come to that in more ways than one. He would never be able to make them do anything they didn't want to do, but Auntie and Maria had become his Spanish family and even without José's request he would have looked after them.

'There is more to it though that might make you change your mind. I … I think someone is trying to get me arrested. Well, I know someone is. Arrested and shot to make sure I keep quiet.' He paused. 'They might just shoot me anytime now and nobody would think it strange. I don't expect to live forever Tom, but I don't want to be murdered by some thugs who will tell the world that I was a fascist spy. Those lies will be what people actually believe and remember. I just don't know how to stop it.'

Tom, who had not expected this, stubbed his cigarette out on the dry grass and gave José his full attention.

'I'm sorry, you lost me there. You'd better start from the beginning. Why do they want to arrest you?'

José looked around them to make sure that there was nobody close enough to hear what he was saying.

'Some weeks ago, I was part of the regiment guarding the gold reserves on their way down to Cartagena. You know about this?'

Tom nodded, aware of the fact that the gold reserves of Spain had been transported out of Madrid to be kept safe from the enemy. The majority of the gold was destined for Russia to supply the Republic with arms, and to keep the balance of it safe from Franco. These reserves were the fourth largest in the world and the government didn't want it falling into enemy hands.

José leaned his head against the rock behind him and lit another of Tom's cigarettes.

'The gold reached Cartagena without any problems, it was well guarded by a lot of soldiers and even a few Russians pretending to be Spanish and all went fine until one evening. There was a gap of about ten hours between one battalion leaving and the relief one arriving, but it was easily defended where it was. Our Captain sent about twenty of us into the town bar and told us to have an evening off. It did seem a little odd, but nobody was complaining. Why would we? - I'd been feeling ill all day and only had one drink before I decided to go back to camp. - That's when I saw them.'

José's fingers were tapping nervously on his knee.

'I had noticed activity inside the camp as I was walking towards it but I just thought it was the new guys arriving. There weren't many of them, maybe 20. - It was only as they shot one of the guys who'd remained behind, a friend of mine, that I jumped out of sight. They were busy loading the wooden crates containing the gold onto trucks, together with the body of my friend. I was going to run back to the bar to raise the alarm and get the other guys back to camp because I thought they were thieves. Just as I was about to run back, I saw our Captain go up to one of the soldiers and shout at him for not moving the gold quick enough. He then went back into the house with a tall man I'd never seen before. I realised that I couldn't raise the alarm, because now that the Captain was involved, it would be more difficult. I thought the best thing would be to wait until I could report it to someone more senior.' He paused. 'I didn't think that anybody had seen me, and I quickly rushed back to the bar where all the others were and I pretended I hadn't left at all. I guess one of them must have noticed me gone and told someone, because my life has been a bloody nightmare since.'

'Do you know who these people were?'

'No. They had all brand new Russian equipment though. Guns and trucks.'

'Wouldn't the theft be noticed rather easily if you reported it. They must know how many crates there should be.'

'I know. I was going to report the whole thing as soon as I found someone senior enough, but I was ill for a couple of days and by the time I got better, they got the first punch in. They planted fascist material in my bag a couple of days before my leave. Luckily enough I found it before they came to arrest me, and as they didn't find anything incriminating, they had to let me go. They will try again though. Unless I get shot on the front line first.' He rubbed his eyes and looked up to the sky. 'I can't think of a way out of this Tom and I have no idea who I can trust anymore.'

'Have you told anyone else?'

'No. Don't you tell anybody either. I just don't want to be killed off by my own side. Maria and my mother would be so ashamed if it got out that I had been shot as a spy. If they get to me you have to tell them that it's not true. Tell them what I just told you.'

'You have to report it. If you do that, at least they can't just get rid of you without consequences. There is still some law and order in Spain.'

'That's it. I can't report anything now. I have a cloud of suspicion hanging over me.'

'Do you want me to report it for you? Without giving any names.' Tom asked. His head was telling him there was a story there. A story, which if true, would benefit his career enormously, and it was in dire need of a boost. It would also solve José's problem. If the whole world knew about it, they couldn't hide behind lies and intimidation any longer.

'No, but thank you.' José replied to Tom's offer. 'You'd only get into trouble yourself.'

He smiled a little now, and it brought back the younger face of the man who had left Madrid in the summer to fight off the fascists.

'How about a newspaper story?' Tom asked. 'If I knew a few more facts and some evidence to back it up, I could write a piece about it. If thousands of people read it you'd be safe and the people who stole it will at least not be able to pin it on you.'

Tom watched José's face as he mulled the idea over before answering.

'That is not a bad idea. If you are willing to take the risk. It might fuel the worlds vision of the Republic as a madhouse though. Not very good for Spain.'

There was a glimmer of excitement in José's eyes now which had not been there before.

'I do know the name of one of the men that were there that night. He was involved in the transport of the gold from Madrid. They called him Blackstone but I don't know anything else about him. Someone told me he was an American banker but I'm not sure I believe that.'

Tom was going to ask him why but stopped mid-sentence as Maria came walking towards them.

Her dark hair was tied into a plat and her large brown eyes smiled at them both when she informed them that they were in trouble for being late for dinner.

'We'll talk more later.' José got up and smilingly hugged his cousin, lifting her off the ground.

'Come on, let's go back home.'

Two days later the afternoon sun warmed Tom's back as he ran down the wide pavements of the Gran Via. He was late as usual for his regular catch up with Bea and Maria at one of the few restaurants that were still open in Madrid. He wished he'd left the press office sooner.

The beautiful imposing buildings of the Gran Via never failed to impress him. The road itself had been agreed for construction in the middle of the previous century but only completed seven years earlier. Before the war there had been shops and cafes everywhere, now most of them were closed and militiamen from various unions and parties were hanging around in their dark blue monos and red, or red and black, scarves, depending on their political direction. They were mostly unshaven, and with their guns slung over their shoulders, they looked rather intimidating as they demanded to see your papers for any random reason they could think of.

The propaganda poured out all over town through loudspeakers urging people to arm themselves and be on the lookout for fifth columnists. There was also the inspiring

¡NO PASARAN!, they shall not pass, between every bit of propaganda, plastered on walls and sun faded banners blowing in the wind between buildings. Madrid was after all going to be the tomb of fascism.

Tom had got himself caught up in all of this largely by accident but his heart and soul now belonged to the Republic and he didn't want to be anywhere else. Spain had turned into an air tight bubble and it was becoming more and more difficult to relate to the outside world, if indeed the thought of it ever entered one's mind. All that mattered was the victory of the Republic.

What he could not understand though was why Bea had chosen to come to Spain. A London society girl who had never liked to get her hands dirty, she'd arrived in Madrid like a whirlwind in a sweltering August, full of enthusiasm for the cause and raring to go.

The day before her arrival, her father had sent word via the embassy to warn Tom of her imminent arrival and left him with the responsibility of looking after her. Very quickly she'd moved out of the Pension where Tom was staying and into a rented flat near the hospital, leaving him to trawl all the way there on a regular basis to check up on her. Generally, apart from her newly acquired membership in the communist party, he had to admit that there were no major problems.

Maybe she had finally grown up.

For Maria there was never the option of moving out of the Pension. When she wasn't helping out at the hospital she was helping her auntie with the running of the Café Pension Rosa. Bea and Maria were like chalk and cheese, but they had become good friends in the madness of those early days.

The restaurant was full of International Volunteers on leave, journalists and prostitutes. It had seen better days, but somehow it fitted in and agreed with its clientele's appearance.

The girls had not yet arrived and Tom wiped his forehead as he entered the bar area of the restaurant where the atmosphere was stuffy and warm. Being in the basement there wasn't much fresh air coming in to disperse the cigarette smoke which curled around the low ceiling with nowhere else to go.

He caught the bartenders attention and ordered a drink for himself and one for his friend Alex Pearson who was standing by the bar looking miserable.

The drinks arrived and he lit a cigarette, offering one to Alex.

'Cheers,' he said as he accepted it together with the fresh drink. 'Bloody riffraff in here as usual. Not sure why I keep on coming back.' Alex looked around.

With his white shirt unbuttoned at the top and his grey hat still on, he looked morosely at Tom who was a good head shorter than him. Before Tom had a chance to respond, he felt an arm on his shoulders.

'What's with the sad faces, eh?' The familiar voice of his friend and neighbour Eduardo appeared behind them and Tom grinned as he turned around.

'What are you doing here? I thought you despised this place.'

'I don't know. It just happened. A friend of mine had a baby boy, he's out fighting somewhere so he can't celebrate properly. I'm a good friend, so I'm doing it for him. Actually, I'm not sure he knows yet. Come on my friends, have a drink with me.' He turned to the bar and tried to get the attention of the bar man. He was ignored until he loudly banged his fists on the bar and with a yawn ordered the drinks.

'To the Republic.' He held his glass up and they clinked it with theirs whilst repeating the toast. Tom smiled because he usually did, and Alex didn't for the same reason.

'I'm glad you guys are happy,' Alex said morosely.

'Oh come on Alex, you have got to enjoy yourself sometimes,' Tom said. 'Anyway, Franco is making his way closer to Madrid every day. I expect, one way or another, it'll be over soon.'

'Bloody hell. Don't talk like that. Madrid won't fall, it can't be allowed to fall.' He took a glug of the drink Eduardo had just put in front of him before continuing. 'I've joined up you know. Going to Madrigueras for training within the next few days. I won't be sitting on the side watching anymore.'

Tom thought he'd been more glum than normal and he guessed this was the reason why. He also had a feeling that last remark was aimed at him.

'Oh, well done.' Not knowing what else to say, Tom continued. 'I have been thinking of it myself recently.' His trouble was that he enjoyed his life here in the city too much and kept on telling himself that his writing actually helped the Republic more than his non existing soldiering skills.

'You should. There are enough people writing about what is happening, we need more soldiers to make it happen.'

'You're joining up?' Eduardo asked looking rather stunned and bemused at Tom.

'Why are you looking so shocked?'

'I'm not shocked, I just can't imagine you as a soldier. Stranger things have happened I guess.' He shrugged his shoulders. 'Before you do anything, you have to know what you are letting yourself in for.'

'I'm not expecting it to be a walk in the park but I want to help.'

'There are other ways you can do that. Winter is coming and the militia are lacking proper clothing and equipment. It's going to be grim.'

'Well, if I said I'd join them in the spring when the weather is better, what would that make me? Don't you think I'm up to it?'

'Of course I do, but you don't take life very seriously and you bring laughter to all of us. I'd hate to see that replaced with,' he glanced at Alex, 'misery. It is admirable and God knows we need all the people we can get, but if you really want to help, come and do some writing and fundraising with us.'

Eduardo worked as a photographer for the CNT union paper.

'Well, I will join up, but just not right now. Too much work on at the moment.'

'Really, you do surprise me,' Alex muttered under his breath.

'Good. You'd just end up with fleas and Auntie would never let you back into the pension.'

Tom laughed.

'You think I'm joking?'

'Not at all. That's why I'm laughing.'

"Well, I have to make my way home or I'll be in trouble. Tom, could you pop over to see me tomorrow morning. I may have some news for you.'

Tom said he would, and Eduardo held up his glass. 'Viva la Republica, and Pedro Junior'

They joined him in his toast before he made his way out on slightly unsteady legs.

'Don't listen to your friend there. Those anarchists are all the same. If it was up to them, soldiers would be fighting only when they had the spare time to do so. "Ten soldiers wisely led will beat a hundred without a head." Euripides. That is what they don't understand.'

Tom nodded and looked around for a reason to leave when luckily he saw Bea come in together with a tall dark haired chap in uniform. It was too loud and crowded for them to notice Tom at the far end of the bar, but it was hard not to notice her. She wore a 'just below the knee' softly lilac dress and her neatly styled blond hair and green eyes drew the attention of the men in the place, as she always did. He turned his attention back to Alex who had also noticed their entrance.

'Come and join us.' Tom offered

'No thanks, I won't if it's all the same to you. Tell Bea she should choose her friends more carefully.' He snarled his lips and turned back to the bar.

'Why, who is he?' Tom asked curiously.

'Russian. A nefarious sod you don't want your friend seeing.'

Tom tried to get him to expand on his comment, but his friend had gone back to his previously melancholy state of mind. He said goodbye and made his way over to Bea.

'I'm not interrupting anything am I?'

'Not at all darling,' she replied.

Tom very noisily pulled out a chair and sat next to her whilst wondering what this man had done to deserve the description of nefarious.

'Tom, I'd like you to meet Pietr, and Pietr, this is my darling friend Tom.'

Pietr stood up to shake his hand and his piercing blue eyes seemed to evaluate Tom's character in moments. He smiled warmly before sitting back down.

'I've heard so much about you Tom that I feel like I know you already. Every other sentence Bea speaks is of you.' He looked back at Bea and his face softened as he seemed to drown in her. Tom wasn't surprised, he'd seen it all before.

'Well, she hasn't mentioned you.' Tom lit a cigarette and eyed him suspiciously.

'Oh Tom, don't be so rude,' Bea said. 'And wipe that disapproving look of your face, it's all very tiring.'

'I'm just surprised that's all. Anyway, I need another drink after the day I've had. Anyone else?' He asked whilst trying to get the attention of Alfonso, the useless waiter, who was obviously just ignoring him.

They both shook their heads. Tom raised his eyebrows before turning back towards Alfonso and finally getting his attention, he ordered wine.

'How was your week at the hospital?'

'Just the usual blood, sweat and tears, darling. Let's not ruin a perfectly good evening by talking about it. I long for an evening without war talk. Just witty conversation and good food. Is that possible these days?'

'I think for one of those evenings you'd have to go back to London. I'd settle for some good food. It seems like a lifetime ago I ate something for the pleasure of eating it, not just to stay alive.' Tom said longingly.

'Revolutions are always difficult in the beginning. At least you have food to sustain you. There are a lot of people worse off than us.' Pietr added making Tom feel embarrassed.

He wanted to know what Pietr did here in Madrid but didn't want to ask; it was obvious he was part of the influential Russian contingent and with Alex's words still fresh in his mind, he thought it best to leave it.

Pietr glanced over to the bar where a man in a dove grey uniform stood on his own looking over towards their table.

'Would you please excuse me for one moment, there is someone I need to have a word with.'

Once he was gone Bea's face lit up and she smiled like she used to.

'Where did you two meet?' Tom asked her.

'At the hospital last month. He just wouldn't take no for an answer and here we are. He is a sweetie, but it is nothing serious. How have you been?'

'Hungry.' Tom grinned and she laughed

'You should be used to it by now. At least you have Auntie looking after you. Although how you can justify letting an old woman do your queueing and cooking for you is beyond me.' Her voice carried memories of their childhood and another life which he still found very strange to hear in these surroundings.

'I remember you not minding an old woman cooking for you. Poor Mrs Henderson, she must have been 70 if she was a day, and she was running after you, cooking and cleaning. Besides, Auntie's not that old, she's probably just in her 50s.'

'Yes, that's what I said. Old. Mrs Henderson on the other hand, wanted to continue working, she liked looking after us. Well, sometimes anyway. Do you remember when we snuck on to the train in the village and got all the way to Tunbridge Wells? We can't have been more than 10 years old, and I can still see her red face in front of me now when we were delivered back home by the police.' Bea laughed. 'The poor woman. - She died only a few months before I came over here you know. Well, you did know and you didn't come back home for her funeral.'

'I'm sorry. You know I only got the telegram after it had taken place,' Tom said guiltily.

'I know. It's ok. You are my only family now Tom. The only one that matters anyway. I miss those simple days and wish I could bring them back. Life is so very complicated here don't you find.' The laughter all gone and replaced with a sad smile which she hid behind her coffee cup.

'Bea, stop being so melodramatic. You have your father and my mother who both love you to bits.'

'Yes, that's what I used to think, but it turns out it was all lies. All of it.'

'I don't understand. Is this to do with the argument with your father?'

'It wasn't an argument. I found out something that he, and probably your mother, had lied to me about since I was little. When people that are supposed to love and look after you do that, well... it changes you, it changes everything.'

'So go on, what did they lie about?' Tom couldn't see what could possibly be so bad. She had been loved and spoilt her whole life by everybody from her father and Tom's mother to the staff at Orrington Manor.

'It doesn't matter. Forget I said anything.' She smiled and squeezed his hand. 'Look, there's Maria' She pointed over to the door as Maria came in and waved to her.

'Hello darling,' she said as Maria sat down on the chair next to Tom's and helped herself to some water. Pietr had returned from the bar and the person he'd spoken to had disappeared.

Tom was curious about the lies that Bea had mentioned and made a mental note to ask his mother; she would know. Sir Arthur confided everything in her.

'Hola. I'm sorry I'm late, but something came up.' Her soft English had a strong Spanish edge, especially when she felt stressed or under pressure.

'What? Do tell us.' Bea said and the sadness that only moments ago had made her vulnerable was all gone and replaced with a broad smile put on for Maria's and Pietr's benefit. 'I'm intrigued. You're never late for anything.'

Maria shrugged her shoulders. 'It was nothing in particular and definitely nothing to be intrigued about. Now, what have I missed?' She looked over towards Pietr, waiting for an introduction.

'Oh, I'm sorry. This is Pietr. Pietr, this is Maria, we work together at the hospital. There, that's the introduction done. Do you know what, I think I'll have a small glass of wine filled to the brim after all.'

Pietr poured her a glass and then he turned towards Maria. 'So you work at the hospital too?'

'Yes, but not as much as I would like.' She paused. 'I have to help my aunt with her café too.'

'Her aunt has the Café Rosa on Calle Mayor.' Tom added for Pietr's benefit.

'Ah, I know it. I haven't been in, but I walk past it often.'

'You should go in darling, she still serves the best coffee in Madrid. Is that not so Tom?'

'She does,' he replied and decided to change the subject as Maria looked uncomfortable and rather annoyed at Bea describing her as a 'work colleague' only. 'Shall we order some food before it is all gone. At this rate we won't have time to eat it before having to go home.'

'Yes, lets. I'm on a very early shift tomorrow,' Bea added.

'Well, I'm off to Cartagena in the morning,' Tom said and immediately wished he hadn't. He'd promised Jose not to mention the story to anyone.

'What's in Cartagena?' Pietr asked.

'A large naval base,' Tom joked. 'It's just a little errand I'm running for someone.'

He was rescued from having to expand on his reasons for going there by the waiter coming over to take their order. It was not really a difficult choice Fabada a la riojana con chorizo was on the menu again and even though the chorizo only flavored the beans in the stew, it was a more attractive option than the fish that Pietr ordered. Tom knew. He'd had it before.

'Pietr has been my knight in shining armor today. He rescued me from the hospital and took me out to the countryside for a lovely drive.' She looked up at Pietr who briefly looked worryingly at her before she continued 'It is strange, but when you go just behind the hills where there are no people and no noise, it is so peaceful, the war could be a million miles away.'

The waiter came over and the stilted conversation died off a little. Tom picked it up again by talking politics.

'Well, it's a damned disgrace that England's not only withholding their own help to a democratically elected government threatened by mad generals, but convincing the rest of The League of Nations to do the same is just ignorant and cruel.' Tom added the old chestnut of the Non-Intervention agreement. It was a safe bet as everyone liked to complain about the agreement between the League of Nations members not to help any side of Spain in any way, and to block her purchasing anything at all from any other country, including arms and food. Despite this, Germany and Italy were both helping the Nationalist side, everybody knew it, but the two countries continued to deny it, and the League of Nations choose to believe them.

It was a lie easily swallowed by the United Kingdom and France which made it easier for them to keep up the pretense that the war in Spain was an issue for Spain alone, when clearly it was bleeding into the rest of Europe every day.

Maria shook her head. 'They will help us when they find out what Franco has done. Throwing grenades into the Toledo hospital wards, killing all the injured and sick people in there. That alone must be against some international law and then all the thousands of people in Badajoz in August, just machine gunned down in the bullring. Women and children too. It makes me feel sick thinking about it.'

'Well, don't think about it then.' Bea snapped. 'This conversation bores me now. I came out to get away from it all for a few hours. Go on, eat your food,' she said rather brusquely to Maria before taking a bite of her own food which had just arrived.

'Don't tell me what to do. It is not your country that is being destroyed,' Maria continued slightly agitated now. 'And I will think about it. And I will choose who I spend my time with.' She got up from her chair, hesitated for a moment and then turned and walked out of the restaurant without looking back.

'Maria, come back. I didn't mean anything by it.' Bea put her cutlery down and started getting up from the table to go after her.

'I'll go,' Tom said and got up. He didn't want her to walk home on her own.

Maria was halfway up the road already when Tom came running out of the restaurant and she only stopped when he shouted after her.

Outside it was very quiet and after the day's sunshine there was a distinct autumn chill in the air. He pulled his jacket tighter and walked briskly towards her.

As she turned around he could see tears overflowing and gently rolling down her cheeks.

'I'm sorry. I don't know what came over me,' she whispered quietly. 'I'm not normally like this.'

Standing there with tears in her dark eyes in an almost deserted Gran Via she looked so forlorn. Tom had never seen her cry before. He wanted to comfort her and tell her that everything would be fine, but he couldn't, because it would be a lie.

'You know that Bea always speaks before she thinks. She didn't mean anything by it,' he said instead.

'I know that. It's not her. It's everything,' she looked up at the sky where the large moon shone on a sky full of stars. Slowly she put her head on his shoulder, and he wrapped his arms around her and felt her warm breath on his neck.

It made his whole body tingle and he held her tighter for just a moment.

'It will all get better soon. Everything will be fine. I'll make sure it is,' he said quietly as much to himself as to Maria.

Out of the corner of his eye he noticed Bea and Pietr walking up the road towards them and he reluctantly had to let her go.

'I'm so sorry,' Bea said. 'I didn't mean to upset you. It's just that sometimes everything gets on top of me too. Besides, you were wrong. We are in this together, and I'm not leaving until we've won or until Franco is chasing me down the Gran Via with a fork in his hand.'

Maria looked up at her and a small smile formed on her lips

'No, I'm sorry. I'm not sure what's wrong with me. I've been feeling down all day and shouldn't have left the Pension. I could be a danger to other people's morale.' She laughed a forced little laugh.

'Are you ok now?' Bea asked as she looked at Maria's hand still holding Tom's.

'Yes. I'm fine. I'll see you tomorrow at the hospital.'

Bea nodded. 'Well, goodnight then.'

'Goodnight.'

Maria and Tom walked on along the Gran Via chatting easily to each other in Spanish.

Tom had had quite a few drinks that evening and it hadn't felt wrong to say that he would make sure everything would be ok, but the disturbing part of the evening had been the effect her soft breath had on him, and how he couldn't forget about it.

$$\sim 5 \sim$$

Later that night Pietr was finding his way carefully forward through a grass covered field, along a path he knew was there but could only just see. The moon came and went through the low broken clouds, showing the sharp outlines of the hill side trees ahead of him.

It was towards those trees he was moving as quickly as he could, constantly aware that when the moon was out he could easily be spotted. Every dry straw of grass seemed to Pietr to echo between the hills in the silence. He subconsciously checked his belt for the gun he had brought with him from Russia. It was like an old friend and he'd put his trust in an old chum rather than a new one any day of the week.

He would be able to get himself past soldiers easily enough but he didn't want to encounter any unreasonable anarchists or farmers who would probably shoot him before asking questions. He was driven by an overwhelming desire for the right side to win and a nice little cash balance for him to live on afterwards. And they would win, there was no question of that, only how long it would take and how difficult it would be for him to stay alive until then. The staying alive part had become more difficult, but at least he was safe in Madrid for the moment and doing a good job too. Hopefully a good enough job to keep him there until the end.

Whatever happened, they would have to shoot him before he went back to Russia voluntarily. All that was waiting for him there was a miserable wife, a mad dog of a leader and if anything went wrong, probably a bullet. In Spain he could look forward to Bea, the most beautiful woman he had ever met and a nice pile of cash to retire on. He had no intention of losing either. When he realised he was smiling to himself he stopped the daydreaming and concentrated on reaching the barn.

The abandoned building was old and unused, he guessed since the beginning of the war. The smell of manure, rotting feed and hay from the cattle still lingered and he took a deep breath of the fresh night air before entering. There was a stone hearth on the opposite wall and signs of a bed where someone would have slept on the nights that the animals needed additional attention.

He shut the door behind him quickly and walked back and forth from the far wall to the door getting angrier by the minute. Enrique was late and Pietr kept on getting more and more annoyed until he was just about to leave the barn and keep what they wanted for himself. This was when the door creaked open and he could see the long face of Enrique and the moonlight lighting up the whole bloody barn before he closed it behind him. Pietr did not have much time now, he was due back in Madrid in a couple of hours.

Once Enrique had shut the crumbling wooden door which hung precariously on its hinges, he lit a torch and shone it into the corners of the barn. It finally landed on Pietr who had so far been standing very quietly behind him, worrying that this was the person to whom he was supposed to tell his secrets. When the light settled on him, his hands flew up to protect his eyes and a stream of abuse came out in Russian.

'Put it away for fucks sake,' Pietr hissed. 'If you don't blind me with it, you'll attract every guard in the area.'

Enrique lowered the torch and spat at Pietr.

'There is nobody here to see us. Door is closed and there are no windows. If I didn't have to be nice to you I would shoot you right now.'

'You could always try you fucking coward.'

'Do not insult me. You should show me the respect I am due.'

'That was not an insult, that was the truth. Now, let's get on with it. I've only got a few minutes.'

Enrique stared for a couple of seconds at Pietr before sitting himself down on some old hay. He arranged the torch so that it would give as much light as possible whilst pointing away from the door. He then gestured for Pietr to join him. Pietr who had no intention to sit down on a floor that smelled that badly remained standing, and anyway, he wasn't going to stay long.

'So tell me what news you have,' Enrique said.

Pietr spoke for a couple of minutes, giving only the highlights of events since their last meeting. If the stupid man had been on time there would have been more but he seemed happy enough.

'You are a mine of information.' He took a deep breath 'Now let us get to the important part. Where is the gold?'

'It's safe for now. You tell me where you want it delivered to.' Pietr had no intention of giving this stupid man any indication of where the gold was kept. He didn't trust him. Besides, he hadn't yet had time to move his own part of the gold away from the main stash. It wouldn't do to have this rough looking peasant noticing there was more than he told them there was. Pietr knew he held the trump card, and he would play it his way.

Enrique scratched his head pretending to think the matter over before shaking his head slowly.

'That is not good for us. We need to get the gold over the line quickly before the theft is noticed. Because, they will notice, and when they do, the gold has to be safe. I also think that the missing gold can be quite easily traced to you my friend. In fact, I know there is someone in Madrid looking into it as we speak.'

'How do you know.' Pietr was sure that nobody knew and that Enrique was lying. 'And who is this 'someone'?'

'I do not know his name, but I would be very careful if I was you. You need to tell us where it is kept now so that we can remove the evidence.'

'Well, the quicker you tell me where to take it, the quicker it will be safe. Now why would you want me to tell you where it is kept now?' Pietr squatted down to Enrique's level. His narrow, piercing eyes burrowed in to Enrique's. 'You wouldn't want it to get lost somewhere on-route would you.'

Enrique looked away first. 'I will have to report this. In the meantime I have no choice but to do it your way,' he said resignedly. Pietr stood back up and brushed a few pieces of hay from his trousers.

'I'll expect a message from you in a day or so,' Pietr said as he walked towards the door and left Enrique sitting there by the torch, seething that his orders were not followed. If he hadn't wished the worst things on earth onto Pietr, he would have warned him that he had been followed up to the main road and then shaken them off on the other side of the hill. That was the reason why he had been late. He sighed, turned the torch off and left the way he came, all the while hoping that somebody would shoot Pietr Alexandrow.

~ 6 ~

'Look, all I'm asking is that you keep your ears alert to the name Blackstone.' Tom looked at Charles' uninterested face and wanted to use his college left hook to make it show some kind of emotion. His heart must be somewhere, there was nobody in Spain who had not taken sides with either the Republic or with Franco, but Charles was seriously on the one true side - the British one.

Tom's morning had started badly as it was. His car had not started and he didn't know what was wrong with it. That meant that the planned trip to Cartagena had to be put back a couple of days but that was ok because he still needed more information about this American banker Jose had heard called Blackstone. And he needed to know if the gold had been reported missing.

'No I haven't. Is there a particular reason you're asking this? Who is he?'

'I don't know. That's why I'm asking. I think he went with the gold to Cartagena.' Tom gave a general outline of what Jose had told him. 'I know it's got nothing to do with us but I thought I'd mention it anyway. Also, I thought that was what you wanted me to do, you know, letting you know what I hear,' he said with a hint of sarcasm whilst perched on the side of a brown, worn, leather armchair.

Charles could be so bloody stuck up and obstinate sometimes that he wondered why he kept coming back. It was no skin of his nose if he wasn't interested in what Jose had told him, in fact he had been in two minds whether to tell him at all and wished he hadn't bothered now.

Charles did look very British, getting slightly podgy with embassy food and dressed in what used to be a well-fitting, well cut suite and tie in the middle of revolutionary Spain.

Tom looked at him sitting behind his small clear and tidy desk, his fair receding hair neatly cut and quite suitable for a diplomatic bureaucrat like himself. He was tapping his short, clean fingernails on the desk next to a small photo of an elderly woman. The likeness wasn't there, but Tom had always assumed it must be his mother. One day he'd ask him.

Charles sighed. 'We do know what Negrin is doing with the gold, it's not a big secret. The security, or lack of security, is also down to them. If there was a robbery of a jewelry shop in Hatton Gardens, would you get involved or would you leave it to the police?' He stood up to indicate that the meeting was over. 'Don't get involved Tom. We can't help you if you get into trouble here. In fact, I think it would be wise if you went back home, just for a while.

It would benefit everybody. I'm sure Bea would follow you and we have all got her best interest at heart.'

'The theft is not the issue. If it was, there would be people out looking for the thieves.' Tom persisted, ignoring Charles' friendly advice. Let him take Bea back home.

Charles walked over to the door and held it open. 'Tom, I am ordering you to leave this alone. If true, it really is a matter for the Spanish police or militia, no matter how useless they are these days. Rather than thanking you they will probably shoot you. Whoever told you this was just pulling your leg or he was drunk, or both.'

'You're ordering me?' Tom raised his eyebrows and tried not to laugh.

'I am.'

'Well, of course, I won't get involved.' Tom smiled at him 'Don't work too hard Charles. Hasta la Vista'

'Bye Tom. Take care.'

He went down the stairs whistling loudly, attracting frowning glances from embassy employees and a smile from a typist who was just visible through an open door. She was a very attractive girl and he toyed with the idea of popping his head around the door, but decided against it as he was liable to get thrown out.

He had to admit that at least Charles had cheered him up a little. Ordering him to stay out of it! Charles couldn't order him to do anything.

He smiled at Miss Spencer, the receptionist, who handed him his post before promptly turning away from him with a frown. He wasn't sure why she disliked him, but he was pretty sure he had never been rude to her. In fact he'd never really spoken to her, yet this is how she acted every time he collected his post.

There was only one letter and it was from his mother. He put it in his pocket and left the embassy building.

The wide Paseo de Castellana was surrounded by imposing buildings and he strolled leisurely along it towards the centre of the city. To imagine that he could have ended up like Charlie, tucked behind a desk and getting more and more resentful each day for a life passing him by and not being part of it.

Thank God he had stood up to them all, and thank God for Paris.

~ 7 ~

The building was tall and imposing, but not handsome enough to draw the attention of the Government or in a location where refugees would go. Most of the windows had been broken and their frames scuffed where stones had been thrown or guns fired.

This was the house where his mother's family had lived until the beginning of the uprising. Only this morning had Eduardo shown him the records from the orphanage where his mother had been left as a baby. Tom's grandmother's name had been Teresa Orzana, living at this address. That was all Eduardo had found from the records he'd searched through at the now abandoned orphanage. From the government records he had found out that they had been on the side of the generals and managed to get out of Madrid very quickly after the uprising. Who knew where they were now.

Wasn't that typical. Tom had been searching for them since he came to Spain, and until July they had lived only 20 minutes up the road from the Pension.

The street was quiet even though there was a main road bustling with life only around the corner and Tom was a little weary of anybody seeing him there. He walked up the cracked brown tiled stairs to the door and knocked on the heavy wood. The house may well have been taken over by some other family or militias and he needed to be careful as his enquiry may draw unwanted attention. Why would he be looking for a fascist family? At that moment in time, in Madrid, people had got themselves into a lot of trouble for less. That was a good enough reason to keep your wits about you and ensure nobody was watching.

There was no answer, and when he tried to open the door, it was locked. He looked up at the building again but there was no sign of life anywhere, only darkness behind the broken dirty windows.

Disappointed he walked back down the steps, and with a last glance, he decided that he would return later with a penknife to open the door.

Back at the Pension Rosa, He popped in to his little room on the first floor and was disappointed to find only some stale bread and tomatoes. He really had to go and get some food, but the queues put him off and they were full of women who looked at him and whispered. Last time one woman had even asked if he wanted her to collect his food for him. It had been jolly nice of her, but he'd declined and gone back on his staple diet of bread and tomatoes for lunch and breakfast and a meal out somewhere in the evening.

He was lucky that his allowance from his mother paid more than his wages from the paper, because even though living in Madrid was a lot cheaper than his lifestyle in Paris, he somehow went through the money very quickly.

His room wasn't much to look at, but it was situated in the centre of Madrid and the four story townhouse with its iron balconies overlooked a small square to the side and the Calle Mayor in front. The faded blue flowered wall paper was starting to peel of the walls and the red tiled floor not quite as clean as it could be. He figured that there was such a small amount of space in the room that wasn't taken up with wash stand, bed, wardrobe or his possessions, it didn't matter too much. He didn't spend that much time in there.

He put the bread back in its box and went downstairs to the café. It was one of the best loved cafes in Madrid, mainly because they had something that resembled coffee in their drinks, and of course Auntie to listen to their problems and hand out advice accordingly. Both Maria and her auntie were under strict instructions from Maria's mother to leave everything and go back to the village if the fighting came too close, but the enemy was now almost within sight of Madrid and they showed no sign of leaving, they just carried on like they always had.

The walls were tiled from top to bottom in white and dark green ceramic tiles and there were a handful of tables as well as a couple of small wooden benches in the window recesses, overlooking the little square.

Through one of the windows he saw Maria washing up behind the counter and stopped for a moment. For the last eight months he had not thought of her as anything more than a friend or his land lady's niece. Now that moment on Saturday night came back to him again and again.

He had a girl already. He kept on forgetting about Emilie and hoped somehow that she had done the same, but he knew from the letters he received that she had not forgotten at all. He put Saturday night away and decided that in a couple of days he'd be back to normal.

He went in to the café through the large old carved oak doors and Auntie, who was sitting at one of the tables with a pile of papers in front of her, looked up and smiled.

'Hola Tom. ¿Cómo estás?

'I'm very well, Auntie. How are you?'

'It's always a struggle, but we mustn't complain. Must we, Maria?' she looked over to the bar where Maria was washing up. Was this the tail end of an argument he had walked into? The cafe was unusually empty but still smelled of the coffee and cleaning liquid which he now associated with 'home'.

'No auntie,' she replied behind her auntie's back, raising her eyebrows and rolled her eyes briefly to the ceiling. 'Hello Tom.'

Before he got a chance to respond, her auntie had pulled out a chair for him.

'Come on, sit down and talk to an old woman for a minute.' She tapped her hand on the table.

'Is that from your mother?' She looked at the letter Tom had collected at the embassy and now held in his hand.

'Yes. I just picked it up today.'

'Well, open it and tell us how she is and how life is in England.'

Tom laughed and did as he was asked.

Auntie had never met his mother, but seeing him as an extension to her own family must make his mother some kind of relative whose health and happiness interested her. It was lucky Tom didn't have a lot of secrets, as it would have been impossible to keep anything private.

He started reading.

'She says that she is well and hopes that I am too. She wishes that I'd come back home soon as she is reading a lot of horror stories about Spain in the papers.' He looked up at Auntie. 'She always says that.' He continued, 'Her back is getting better and the garden has gone into hibernation for the winter. It continues to say that I am a very bad son for not writing to her more, but Bea's father updates her from time to time.' He looked at Auntie 'Well, I wonder what he has to say on matters. I hardly ever speak to him myself, so I can only assume that he tells my mother all is well so that she doesn't worry.'

'That's very good of him. Does it say anything else?'

'Just that there are Christmas decorations up in Fortnum's already and that she is inundated with invites for New Year's eve and can't decide which ones to accept.' He shook his head. 'It's difficult to remember there is an outside world sometimes, don't you think Auntie. It all seems so far removed from here, and it's only when you get a letter or speak to someone who has just arrived, that you remember that there are places in the world outside Spain.'

'Ahh, I remember the Christmases we used to have before my husband died. We never made it back home to my village, but Honesto's family were all in Madrid. We would prepare lots of food for the whole family in the morning and then dress up to go to midnight mass, because in those days you had to go to church or they would...' She made a cutting gesture across her throat and raised her eyebrows. It was a little dramatic but when she saw that Tom got the picture she continued. 'When we got home, we'd drink and eat the food which would be done by then. - This will be the first Christmas at war. I wonder what it will be like.'

'Christmas is what you make it Auntie. You can still see Honesto's family and you have Maria here.'

'Yes, but if we have no heating or if we are still not allowed lights, we'll be in bed at seven, keeping warm under blankets.'

'I'm sure it will be fine.' Tom wanted to add that he'd be here too but couldn't guarantee it so kept quiet.

The rebels were so close to Madrid that they might well join them for Christmas dinner, and the closer they got, the more Tom felt the need to pick up a gun and go out to shoot them.

'Maybe Franco will be dead by Christmas,' she smiled. 'There are still too many people dying, and now my Jose is back out there.' She crossed herself and looked around to see if anyone had seen her. Old habits die hard. 'Yes, when will it all end. Good boys dying and women and families too. Did I tell you that Señora Calera, you know her, yes, from down the road, her daughter died on the Aragon front just a couple of weeks ago. She was a lovely girl. I remember her running around in here when she was a little girl, always singing. Always singing.' Her eyes disappeared briefly into the past.

Maria came over and sat down.

'Auntie, we all wish it would end but we didn't start all this.' She took her auntie's hand.

'I'm just a silly old woman who doesn't like change. Ignore me.' Auntie went up to the bar. 'I will make you both a good cup of coffee.'

She was blinking back the tears.

Maria had spent so long with her auntie that she had become the daughter she never had and now, here in Madrid they really only had each other to rely on.

Auntie was Maria's mother's sister and had grown up in the house where Maria's family still lived. It had never been an easy life and Maria's mother and most of her family had never left the village. They sent Maria to Madrid to help her auntie when Honesto had died unexpectedly a few years earlier.

She had helped with the café and the pension whilst also taken the opportunity to study and learning how to read and write. She'd learnt English from an old Kentish woman who used to stay at the pension prior to the war. The war had put her studying on hold and she had started helping out at the hospital instead. The Kentish woman had gone back home soon after the rebellion had started as advised by the British Embassy. Now Maria was practicing her English on Tom.

Auntie brought the coffees over and went back to serve a customer who had just come in and was chatting away loudly to her across the counter.

'I thought you were off to Cartagena this morning.'

'The car broke down and I need some help to fix it.'

She nodded. 'So what have you been up to today?'

'I popped in to see Eduardo for a bit, and then got my pass to the western front for tomorrow morning - from Pietr of all people. I'm getting a lift there by a Captain something or other and we leave at 6am.' He rubbed his eyes at the thought of getting up that early and smiled at her.

Her long dark hair was tied with a red ribbon and hung heavily down her back and her eyes shimmered in the sunshine that broke in through the long windows. They were beautiful eyes and it wasn't like him to not have noticed them before.

'I'm glad for you. Make sure you don't get shot or captured,' she said before taking a sip of her coffee.

'I'll be fine. It's only for the day and anyway, the Captain should at least know where the battle lines are.'

There had been a few cases where both soldiers and journalists had quite unintentionally wandered into enemy territory and got themselves captured or shot.

'Today is the birthday of Señora Antonia so auntie has decided we are closing the cafe early and taking something to eat over to her. I can leave some food here for you Tom, unless you want to come with us.'

'Don't worry about me, I'm going out for a drink or two but it won't be a late evening. The car leaves so early to-morrow I'll need an early night. It is unlucky really, I got a special night pass so that I can get to where I'm being picked up before the car leaves which also allows me to stay out longer than 11pm of course. Just a shame I have to get up so early.'

'Even if you have a pass, the militia will stop you and make your life difficult. Probably better to get home before you need the pass. Yes?'

'I wouldn't be home later than the curfew anyway. I wouldn't be able to find my way back here in the dark'

There were more customers coming in now and Auntie asked Maria to come and help.

'How long will you be gone?'

'It's just a day trip.'

'Well, you take care. We'd like you back home safe and sound,' she said as she went over to the counter.

It was nice of her to worry about him.

8

Tom hid briefly around the corner, until a couple of militias had wandered past. He heard their chatter receding as they disappeared down the street and around a corner. As soon as the coast was clear he quickly went up the stairs to the front door and inserted the penknife between the lock and frame and tried to push the latch down.

He needn't have bothered as it was already open. Maybe he hadn't pushed hard enough earlier in the day. The door squeaked and slowly opened to reveal a long, high ceilinged hallway where the late sunlight streamed in from the large windows on either side of the door. There were a couple of rooms coming off it and a large oak staircase at the end.

The front door shut loudly behind him and in the eerie silence he looked around the rooms that had been looted at some point. Now only lighter terracotta coloured tiles showed where once large rugs had covered them and a couple of broken chairs and old newspapers lay scattered on the floor. The papers showed the early war cries of the generals and Tom's heart sank at the sight of them. He had deep down hoped that they had left for some other reason, but it would seem that Eduardo's research had been correct. They had fled the city as fascists. How far had they got? Were they safe in Franco territory or had they been caught and killed somewhere on route.

It had only been three months since they'd left. Such a short period of time. If only the records had been freely available prior to July he would have found them in time. Would he ever see them now, he wondered? And if he had found them earlier, would he have had to run too? Even though the windows were broken and letting in fresh air, there was a smell of sewage lingering. He quickly made his way up the rubbish littered stairs and had a look around.

The rooms were empty of everything apart from dust and the odd piece of broken furniture.

Disappointed, he turned around and went back to the stairs where he sat down on the top step and sighed. Nothing supplied any clue as to who they really were, and he had come such a long way to find out. It was like a swarm of termites had made their way through the house and taken not just physical items, but also taken the soul of the house and its former occupants.

The place was unnerving him and he was just about to go downstairs when he heard one of the floor boards below creak. He told himself it was just one of those noises old houses make, but nonetheless he picked up a long piece of wood from one of the steps and cautiously walked down the stairs.

Once on the ground floor he walked over to the front door, throwing one last look at what had once been the home of his grandmother and her family, the family she had actually wanted.

He put down the piece of wood and tried to pull the front door open, but somehow it had locked itself. He scrambled around in the now nearly dark hallway for his penknife which had hidden itself deep in his pocket. A floorboard somewhere behind him creaked once again and he forced himself to turn around. He still couldn't see anybody. He was just about to turn around and have another go at the lock, when he caught the movement of something in the corner of his eye.

'Hello, who's there?' he shouted as a man stepped forward from behind the staircase. The sun had now nearly disappeared from the windows and Tom could not see him properly.

'That should be my question to you.' His voice was raspy and in the semi darkness his face seemed thin and white with large dark eyes focusing on Tom. 'There is nothing else to take from this house.'

'I'm sorry, compañero. I didn't know anybody was here. I was just leaving but the door is locked.'

The man seemed to have something he wanted to say but remained silent.

'I can't leave unless you open the door for me.' Tom tried again, feeling braver as he could certainly take this old man if he had to.

The old man remained silent and Tom was starting to lose his patience.

'What's your name?' the old man finally asked.

'It's Tom, Compañero. What's yours.'

'You have given me a problem now... Tom. Maybe I caused it myself, but you will have to solve it. Come with me.' He beckoned Tom to come with him, turned around and went back behind the stairs.

Did the old man really expect him to follow? Tom's curiosity had always got in the way of his common sense, and from a professional point that was good.

Tom followed him towards the back of the stairs, and as he peered around the corner, the man had disappeared. There was a small door slightly ajar on the other side of the staircase and a very faint light came from within it.

He very nearly fell down the steep stairs hidden in the gloom just inside the door. He managed to grab hold of the door frame and got his balance back. His eyes adjusted themselves to the dim light and he wished he could say the same for his nose. The rank sewage smell that had been faint upstairs was now intense and he had to force himself forwards. Once he reached the bottom he could see the old man again, sitting at a small table surrounded by religious artifacts.

What Tom had not noticed upstairs was that he was wearing a priest's cassock. Worn and dirty, frayed at the ends, it was still that, a priest's outfit. His stomach knotted itself. There were not a lot of priests anymore in Madrid.

There was no room for religion in the Republic. Any priests that had not run away to join Franco or managed to persuade the people that they were not against them, had been killed by mobs of revolutionaries in the beginning of the war. There were still some priests in Spain who were on the side of the people but they didn't hide away in grimy, foul smelling basements like this one.

If this priest was found he would be thrown into prison, tortured and then probably shot. Tom could see his problem now. It was him.

The one candle burning in the darkness was on the table in front of the priest. The flame was low and its wax dripping slowly onto the base of the bottle holding it. It threw dancing shadows onto the walls and their faces. When he asked Tom to sit down, he did so.

Another thing he had not noticed before was the small dirty gun the priest held in his hand. He now placed it on the table before him whilst pouring two drinks from a nondescript old bottle.

'Are you surprised?' he asked and Tom nodded. 'You now see my problem, yes?'

'I do. How long have you been down here?'

'Since you burned down my church on St Hope's day,' he looked up at Tom. 'Compañero.' The last bit was added with venom. His skin was sallow and his eyes were cold as they held Tom's gaze without flinching. Finally he let go and Tom drained his glass of the liquid, hoping to gain courage. The foul tasting liquid burned his throat and made his eyes water, but this was not unusual for Spanish alcohol, he had it quite regularly.

'You still haven't told me why you are here.' The priest continued

'I'm looking for my family. I think that my grandmother, Teresa Orzana used to live in this house before the war.'

Tom had decided that telling him wouldn't cause any problems as he was most unlikely to go to the authorities and report him. Tom's main concern was to find out a little more about the priest and then get out of there with his body and soul intact.

If Tom's revelation surprised him he didn't show it. Instead he refilled their glasses and waited for Tom to continue.

'My mother was brought up by the nuns at The Sacred Heart and I have traced her mother to this house. Did you know the family that used to live here?'

'El pecado se paga con la muerte. The wage of the sinner is death. The devil is working his way through Spain and the only way I can stop him is to stay alive and pray for the righteous to come to our rescue. I'm sure it won't be long now. - Franco is very close, is that not so?'

Tom ignored this just like the priest had ignored his question and silence ensued.

'Is your mother still a good Catholic?' he finally asked.

Tom nodded.

That wasn't an outright lie as he knew deep inside that she was, she just didn't go to church as frequently as she always wished she did. He also noted the 'still' in his question. He must have known about her, he must have known Teresa.

'I'm glad for that at least. Teresa paid for her sin and has been working tirelessly for the church her whole life. She found someone willing to marry her, and her children are all good Catholics too.'

'How did you know them?'

The priest smiled sadly now and that hint of humanity changed his face.

'I am her son.'

Tom again emptied the glass in front of him. This was his long lost family. His uncle, his mother's brother she didn't know she had. The tables had turned. She was living the sweet life in London and here was her brother, hidden away in a filthy cellar in Madrid waiting for liberty or death.

'You are my uncle?'

'No,' he answered quickly and with certainty. 'Your mother was born out of wedlock, therefore I am not her brother. She was the sin of my mother and she paid dearly for her weakness. I hope your mother paid too.'

Tom looked at him and shook his head in disbelief. How could he say that, the mean minded old sod. He didn't know her, his beautiful, sweet mother who would never hurt a fly. Sitting here rotting away in this basement, he deserved every minute of it.

Keeping his ever growing anger under control, Tom decided that this might be the last chance he ever had of finding out a little more about them.

'Is Teresa still alive?' he asked

'She was when they left and it will take more than this to kill her. She is old of course, and I am under no illusion that their journey would have been easy.'

'Where did they go?'

'They went to stay with my brother in Seville. It would not have been too difficult for them to get there, although I haven't heard from them.'

He saw the question on Tom's lips before it was asked.

'There are others like me. I believe you call us fifth columnists, although I have no intention of fighting. The faithful still in Madrid, hiding from you, have to have someone to turn to and I could not, would not, abandon them. Jesus' pain and punishment was worse than what I have to put up with and he didn't leave his flock.'

Shit, Tom though, he had really walked into a lion's den. Fifth columnists! If he didn't inform the authorities that he was hiding here and someone found out that he knew, he would be shot before he could say Hail Mary, and if he did tell them, he would have the blood of his uncle on his hands. Arsehole as he was he didn't wish him dead. These thoughts breezed through his mind as he was sure they were the priest's.

He needed to get out of there.

If this priest wasn't mad before the war, he would have become so after months in this small room surrounded by all these relics, foul air and mulling over the wickedness of the Republic again and again.

'Shall I expect the devil to come as you leave?' he asked calmly.

Tom shook his head.

'If they find you, it won't be because of me. No matter what you say or think, you are my uncle, and I won't have your blood on my hands.' Tom said as he went over to the stairs and looked back at his uncle sitting at the table, and was sure that this sight would stay with him forever. This sad, broken priest from the old days of Spain, locked in this dark damp room waiting for his release.

One day it would come to him, one way or another.

He was at first silent, then nodded his head to show he believed him.

'There is a catch at the bottom of the front door. Pull that and it will open.'

Tom stood on the creaking old stairs for a few moments, slightly reluctant to leave. Maybe this was it, this was all he would ever find. All of a sudden the priest banged his fists on the table, making his heart jump, and shouted.

'Go, go, go. Don't come back here.'

Tom did leave and heard him praying in Latin as he shut the door behind him.

The city streets were dark as Tom walked slightly unsteady on his feet towards Calle Mayor and the neighbourhood he now knew so well. He'd had a few drinks after leaving the priest and had bumped into his friend and colleague Silke. An American journalist who had, in his heyday, been right on top of his game until ill health stopped him in his tracks. This was his 'come back' and he always knew what was going on. Tom was sure that if this Blackstone existed, Silke could find him.

It was still almost an hour until curfew and he decided he would go to see Eduardo before going back home. His house was only a couple of doors from the Pension, but he worked funny hours and Tom had no idea if he would be there.

The light of the city had to be off when darkness hit to ensure no help was given to enemy aircraft to navigate. It was now a danger walking around, not just from criminals or militia, but also from the uneven cobbles, pavements and streetlights. Most people stayed indoors after dark, but if you were a single man living in a pension trying to make a living as a journalist that was not an option.

His life had until last week been simple enough and he'd liked it that way. All of a sudden, Jose is in trouble, gold has been stolen, he can't stop thinking of Maria in this new and slightly worrying way and now he'd found his uncle. And what an uncle he turned out to be.

There was a light on in Eduardo's house and Tom knocked on the wonky front door. It was opened by the man himself carrying the new baby and Tom was invited in. They sat down by the kitchen table and he wondered where Eduardo's wife, Pabla, was.

'She went next door to help the old Señora to bed. She'll be back in a minute as I have to go to work.' He said this as he tickled the baby's stomach with his beard which caused it to laugh almost hysterically.

Tom decided that it was probably best not to mention his visit to the house yet. Not just because it was difficult to get a word in edgeways, but also because Eduardo's sense of duty would make him report the priest. He couldn't help smiling at the scene as Pabla came in and hurled a stream of carefully chosen words at her husband for exciting the baby at bedtime.

'Buenas tardes, Tom.' she said smilingly as she grabbed the still laughing baby away from his father.

'Tardes, Pabla. Como esta?'

'If I had a husband that was more sensitive to what a child needs I would be fine.' She ruffled the hair on Eduardo's head. 'Now I have to get this little one to bed.'

'She's a fine woman, my Pabla.' Eduardo said as he leaned back in his chair and stretched his neck to catch a last sight of her as she went up the stairs.

'You are a lucky man.' Tom agreed.

'What made you pop in?'

'Not sure really. I think I just needed to see a sane person'

'You should have gone to the mental asylum, there are no sane people here.'

Tom hesitated for a moment and then mentioned that he went to the house.

'I thought you might. Should be alright, it was empty yes?'

'It was. And it had been looted of course.'

'That was only to be expected. If they are alive, you can always find them again once we have won. Now you have their names it should be easier.'

'Mmm..., I will.' Upstairs, Pabla was singing the baby to sleep whilst the usual militia sirens were echoing around the streets and the occasional gunshot could be heard from across the town.

'Let's have a quick drink and then I have to go back to work.'

A couple of drinks later Eduardo went upstairs to say goodbye to Pabla and then he left with Tom.

Tom got back to the pension just before the curfew started and said goodbye to Eduardo by the front door. Still convinced that Tom was going to join up his parting words were, on a serious note, for him to reconsider his decision. Tom shut the door and turned around to find Maria sitting on the wooden stairs, in the dark, waiting for him.

'Why are you sitting there in the dark?' he smiled.

The stairs creaked as he sat down on the step right next to her. She had a blue dress on that he hadn't seen before and her hair was piled up on top of her head, held up with a dark Spanish comb and gentle curls framing her face. He guessed she had dressed up for the birthday party they had been to.

She had her hands on her lap and smilingly whispered.

'Auntie has just gone to bed so speak quietly.'

'Ok,' he whispered back. He was rather tight and it felt very intimate sitting there in the dark, so closely together. Tom found himself wishing she'd put her head back on his shoulder so he could hold her again, with no interruption, just the two of them, there in the dark.

'You smell of drink.'

This pulled him back into reality and he moved away a little.

'I'm sorry. It's the friends I keep. Always drink, drink, drink. Don't like the stuff myself, but I don't want to be rude.'

'I think the bad influence is you'

'Ah, sweet Maria, you know me so well'

'I just wanted to say goodbye before you go but wished I hadn't bothered.' She smiled, pretending to be offended by the couple of drinks he'd had.

'Sorry.'

'It's ok' She looked at him curiously. 'So, are you going to tell me'

'Tell you what?'

'I heard you at the door. You're going to join up'

Tom sighed and looked down at the stairs in front of him.

'I haven't decided yet, but yes, I probably will at some point. Not right now, but if things don't change soon I will have to do something. You understand don't you.'

'Of course I do. I'm Spanish, I know what has to be done, but I don't want you to go. I just mean.... I'll miss you.'

Tom slowly moved his gaze from the floor to her eyes.

At that moment he was sure he saw in her what she surely must have seen in his. He slid his hand into her soft hair and moved her towards him, and as his heart was pounding, he kissed her. It can't have lasted for more than a few seconds, but is seemed like forever until he fully realised what he was doing and slowly pulled away from her.

What had he done? Nothing would be the same again.

He had a girl in Paris and even if he had been known to stray from her path occasionally it had never meant anything. Maria did mean a lot to him and she deserved better.

'I'm sorry, I shouldn't have done that.'

A hurt look came over her face briefly. 'It's fine. Really, don't worry about it.'

He stood up and the floorboards seemed to creak louder now and all of a sudden he felt very sober and grateful for the darkness which hid the guilt showing on his face.

'You should go to bed Maria,' he said and rubbed his eyes.

She stood up.

'That's it?' She looked at him 'Maria, you should go to bed?'

'I'm sorry.'

'Fine. I'll see you when you get back.'

She turned and started walking back up the stairs to the rooms set aside for her and her auntie on the top floor.

'Maybe.' She added on her way up without turning around.

Tom also went up the stairs, but stopped at his room on the first floor. He sat down on the bed with his head in his hands.

How could it have gone from feeling so good, to so bad, so quickly?

9

Whilst Tom was feeling bad about the way he'd treated Maria, Pietr had no such worries about having taken advantage of Bea. They now lay in his bed smoking a French cigarette and finishing the bottle of wine they had started earlier over dinner.

He had cooked a meal for her, which was something he had never done for anyone before, not even his wife, and it had paid off. He had wanted her more than he had ever wanted anything in his life. Ever since the first time he saw her he'd known they were meant for each other. She had played the distant role she had been brought up to play, not getting too close too quickly especially with someone like him, but he'd hit the jackpot tonight. She had needed a little persuasion, but Pietr now felt like the world was his for the taking, as long as he had her by his side. And he intended to take it.

He put the cigarette out, drained the last of the ruby red wine from the glass and softly traced the outline of her body with his fingers. When he reached her throat he felt a moments regret over having bruised her fair skin and pulled the cover up to hide them.

Bea turned away from him and closed her eyes, pretending to sleep whilst fighting to keep her tears in.

'It is still quite early, lapushka. You sleep now and I will wake you later and we can continue our evening,' he whispered gently in her ear, and listened as her breathing became even. He closed his eyes with a smile. Life was good.

When the time came, she would see the world like he saw it, he was sure of that.

He was dozing with his arms around her when there was a loud knock on the door and he swore quietly to himself.

For a few seconds he remained where he was, eyes closed and with no intention of getting up. It would only be some bloody official who thought that he could just turn up, day or night, and he would solve all of their problems.

That was the problem, Stalin actually did think he owned you, and most of the party and its officials thought the same. This thought made Pietr change his mind, he quickly pulled on some clothes, and with a glance over to a sleeping Bea he smiled and pulled the door to.

He'd quickly get rid of whoever it was. The kitchen didn't look as clean and tidy as he would have like it, and he quickly scooped up Bea's clothes from the floor and threw them into the bedroom. Another loud set of knocks came through and he opened the door just in time to avoid another.

'Captain Alexandrow, you took your time.' General Carlos's hard lined face stared at Pietr who had expected to see one of his own men standing there.

He was surprised at the visit. Apart from a meeting here or there, they had nothing to do with one another.

Pietr looked down on the shorter man and wondered how he could avoid having to ask him to come inside.

'I'm sorry General Carlos, I was just trying to catch up on a little sleep. What can I help you with?'

'I'm hardly going to discuss it standing on the doorstep.'

Pietr sighed inwardly and stepped out of the way to let him in. General Carlos looked around the large dark room serving as kitchen and living room before removing his coat and settling his large body down into a worn green sofa which creaked under the strain.

'You do know that your rank entitles you to better accommodation than this,' The General said as he took his hat off and put it next to him. 'A drink would be nice.'

'Of course. Vodka?' Pietr went over to the cabinet and opened a new bottle. He wasn't a big drinker and he'd already had more than he normally would have.

The thought of Bea in his bed made him warm inside and he wondered how quickly he could get rid of the General. He couldn't for the life of him figure out what he wanted.

Pietr brought the drinks over and sat down in an armchair next to the sofa.

'So, what brings you over here General. It must be important.'

'It is, Captain, it is. Have you got company?' He nodded towards the bedroom door still ajar. Pietr shook his head slowly and hoped that Bea was asleep. He wasn't even sure why he was lying about it, he hadn't signed a contract of abstinence, but somehow he felt like he was protecting her by not admitting what had passed here only an hour or so ago.

He couldn't give a damn about reputations in general but he wanted to protect hers in public, because he knew that was what she wanted. He would have loved to show her off, especially to this high and mighty Spanish General whom he always felt looked down on the Russians.

'Good. What I have to say is for your ears only,' He paused for a moment. 'What's your first name?'

'Pietr. My first name is Pietr.' He couldn't figure out where this was leading, but he wished that the General would get to the point. His ears only - really. There were not a lot of secrets around, well there were secrets, almost everybody had some, but they weren't very secret in this town where gossip and very slack discipline ruled. That was why Pietr protected his own secrets like a hawk.

'Well, Pietr, do you mind if I call you Pietr?'

'No, General.'

'Good. I'm glad we're friends. It will make things easier' He drank some of his vodka. 'This is quite good. How did you come by it?'

'I can't remember. Probably from the barracks. If some more comes in I'll keep some aside for you'

He couldn't ask him what he wanted a third time. He would just have to wait for him to get past this social aspect of the visit, but a pause in the conversation lodged a feeling of unease in his stomach.

The General's eyes settled on and held his before sighing and taking another small sip.

'Well, let's get down to business. A couple of days ago we caught a spy, just outside Madrid. We'd had him under surveillance for a couple of days already to see where he might lead us, but he caught onto us and tried to run so we had to take him in. He was a clever old thing, had all the correct papers, but the soldiers that arrested him used to be in the regiment he claimed he was part of. His identity papers actually belonged to one of our soldiers who'd been killed further down south back in July. - He could have come up with a number of other identities, but maybe he was not so clever after all, eh?'

'Sounds stupid indeed. So, who was he?'

'That's the funny part you see. He kept on saying that he was on leave from his regiment and he stuck with this story through a lot of pain. In the end, when he finally realised he couldn't convince us of his story, he started claiming that he was indeed a spy - for us.'

'Well, maybe he is. That should be easy enough to check.'

'Oh, it is. He said he was your spy to be more precise.' The General kept his eyes on Pietr's face which he kept very still and neutral.

'What's his name?' Pietr asked, knowing that it was Enrique they had caught. He quickly tried to decide whether to say that he was indeed running him or denying all knowledge of him.

'His papers give his name as Alfredo Zabor, but he actually seems to answer to the name of Enrique Trejo. So, is he one of yours?'

Pietr looked thoughtful for a moment before answering.

'No. Not with those names, but I'll come and see him if you like. Maybe he is someone I recognise.' He needed to see him, to find out what he'd told them and slip him something final. He knew too much.

'That would be very kind of you, but also quite unnecessary.' The General slowly shook his head. 'I know he's not one of your spies... Pietr... because after a little more persuasion from the guards he changed his story yet again. I must tell you that this is quite common as they realise that they can't keep secrets in our little part of Madrid. But you must know this also in your line of work.'

Pietr kept his face calm even though his mind was buzzing from possible outcomes of this conversation.

On the other side of the wall, Bea leaned a little further forward towards the open door to hear the conversation clearer.

'What was his story changed to?'

'Quite the reverse actually - that you were his spy.'

Pietr forced a laugh and gulped down the rest of his drink. 'That's good. Who is this person who seems to have an obsession with me.' He shook his head unbelievingly. 'And who's side is he on?'

'He gave us dates you had met, and this will make you laugh, they correspond to dates that we have found you leaving Madrid on your own.'

Pietr narrowed his eyes to show his annoyance at being checked up on whilst wondering if this was it? He had his gun over in the corner of the room and his quick glance towards it was observed by the General. It spelt out his clear guilt more than anything else possibly could have and he cursed himself for it.

'I am not a spy, General. This man must just have been lucky with dates. Any time I have left Madrid without my driver has been to see my own men. The man is obviously mad. - I hope you are not taking this seriously.'

'We're taking it very seriously.' His smile was now all gone. 'My men are just outside and will collect you as soon as I give them the go ahead.'

Pietr got up from the chair and walked around the room trying to regain control.

'This is ridiculous, you can't arrest me for this.' He stopped a few feet away from the general 'I see what's going on here. This is all just political for you. Arrest me and score some points against the communist party.'

'I have a man accusing you of spying for the enemy, Captain. That is serious enough for anybody, and if you had not been the important man that you are, I would not have bothered coming here myself. You would already be in the Model Prison with all the other filth. Do you understand me?'

'You arrest me at your peril. Andriev will have your head for it.'

The name Andriev should at least make the General chose what he would do carefully. Andriev was in charge of all NKVD operations in Spain, quite unofficially of course, but it wouldn't hurt to let the General know that he had friends in high places.

The General let Pietr pace around for a few moments and then got up from the sofa. He slowly walked over to the cabinet where the vodka bottle stood and poured himself another large glass.

'Do you really want to contact Andriev? He might get you out of this trouble, but not because you're not guilty, just as a face saving exercise. I expect you'd be shipped back to Stalin fairly rapidly where you'd most likely be shot.' He stood in silence for a second or two. 'There might be another way out of this little hole for you. It is something that would benefit the both of us.'

The General remained by the bottle and Pietr stopped pacing the floor.

'The spy Enrique, mentioned that you had some gold.' He noted with satisfaction the effect this statement had on Pietr. 'Some gold stolen from the Republic.'

Pietr instantly knew where this was going and was glad he hadn't told Enrique where the gold was kept, it now gave him a bargaining nugget or two.

The General continued. 'He didn't know where it was though and believe me, he wanted to tell us, but in the end, we settled on asking you. So, where is the gold Pietr?'

'I don't know what you are talking about. I don't know anything about any gold or this blasted spy that you keep on...' Pietr almost spat out the words in feigned indignation.

'You shouldn't swear in front of a superior officer Captain, but I will forgive you as you are under stress.'

He walked towards the front door, and Bea, still out of sight, crept back into bed, pulled the blanket over her head and closed her eyes tight.

'I can see that you need a little time to digest the situation. I'll give you 48 hours to think about it, but don't leave Madrid and don't think for one moment that I won't arrest you.' He opened the front door. 'And Captain, don't double cross me, because you wouldn't want me as an enemy.' With this he left and Pietr shut the door behind him with a bang and leaned his head against it.

What was he going to do now? He didn't think his house was watched, not if the General wanted the gold for himself. He'd want to keep everyone else away from the whole thing until either he had the gold or until his guards were required to arrest him.

He walked back to the lounge and picked up the vodka bottle. He took a couple of swigs out of the bottle on his way to the bedroom. He shouldn't get back into bed, he only had 48 hours to sort this problem out, but as he saw her lying there asleep under the thin cover he decided that another hour or so wouldn't make much difference.

It was morning before he woke up and by then Bea was gone.

$$\sim 10 \sim$$

West of Madrid, October 1936

'No, no, no. That's not the way to do it. You take this piece here, hold it tight and firmly push it into place.'

Tom felt rather stupid as he'd had cadet training at school, but still seemed unable to put a rifle back together.

He'd been placed into the hands of a volunteer soldier called Adam Hart, whilst Captain Santos, who had brought him there, had gone to meet the commander of the troops they were visiting.

Sporadic fighting had been going on for days and there had not been a lot of movement. There was a small town, a mile or so in front of them, which the fascists had taken earlier in the week, and the Republic wanted it back. Trenches had been dug into the hillside where the pine tree coverings were not quite enough to hide them from the enemy that were based in the town on the hill opposite.

The sky threatened rain and there was an autumn chill in the air coming in from the north. It blew over the Sierra de Guadarrama mountain range and right through the trenches to where Tom was sitting with Adam, trying to keep his head down. Adam had tried to show him how to work his rifle, but it was so old that you needed to know it well to avoid it stalling, or worse, backfire and take your own head off instead.

'So, you've been here a while then?' Adam asked.

'No, not very long, although it seems like a lifetime ago now since I arrived. I just can't imagine being anywhere else.'

'Yeah, I know. We came here only a month or so ago, quick training and off we went. Me and Mikey came together and met Stuart,' he nodded towards one of the other guys. 'We came in over the Pyrenees. Have you ever done that?'

Tom shook his head.

'It was in the middle of the night and we had to do it quietly so that no border guards would catch us. My God, we were all knackered,' he grinned 'Oh, and at that point Frank was with us too, but he got shot the first day here. Didn't keep his head down stupid sod. Quite sad really.' He went quiet for a little while. 'He was a Cambridge history graduate. Such a shame to spend years learning and then just, bang, all gone, just like that in an instant. Could have been anyone of us.' He finished his tea. 'Come on. I'll show you around.' He got up and walked along the trench with Tom following, ensuring he kept his head down. 'Over there is the small town we're fighting for. We had it a couple of days ago, then the fascists took it and now we're trying to get it back again. Up there,' he pointed to up the hill. 'There, hidden amongst the bushes, is our pride and joy, our machine gun. Not a lot of regiments have one so we guard it with our lives.'

'How do you find the food? Are you getting enough of it out here?'

'I guess it's ok, but knowing that the food we get come from villagers or farmers who are on the breadline themselves makes you appreciate it more. However, when I get back home, I'll be glad never to see beans or garlic again.,' he grinned.

'Yeah, I swear I dream of a juicy steak and fried potatoes and a mountain of vegetables.' Tom's mouth salivated at the thought of it. 'So what did you do back in London?'

'We worked down the docks. Isle of Dogs generally, but it was never permanent. They just hired us for the hours they were required and that was ok for me, I have bigger plans, but for my dad who need the money to put food on the table and to pay the rent, it's not fair. With the black shirts marching through the East End, protected by the police, most decent people have had enough and realise that the black shirts and all fascism had to be stopped. So here we are.'

'Your parents didn't mind you coming out here?'

'Well, my dad was very supportive, but my mum not so much. Especially when my dad started getting ideas of coming over here himself. She came round in the end though, once my dad promised to stay put, that is. - Arriving in Spain was one of the best moments of my life. Finally, a country where it doesn't matter where you went to school or how rich you are. And you could smell the excitement in the air, with trade union flags on all the buildings and being greeted with "Compañero" by people you've never met before, and smiles everywhere, thanking us for coming to help. Makes it all worthwhile, you know.'

A faint motor sound could be heard over the general noise, and its dull drone was getting stronger.

'Shit, here we go again. You'd better get cover. This is what they do, they come over and bomb the trenches until we run and then they strafe us down. With no proper equipment we can't fight back. What can you do?'

Adam looked up to the grey patchy sky and moved along the trench towards a dugout cave cut out into the mud where a couple of people had already gathered. The dugout smelled of damp mud and inside there was total darkness. Tom gathered this was where food was prepared as to get into the cave you had to side step past a large area with a few cooking pots and a bits of wood prepared for lighting a fire.

'Couldn't it be one of ours?' Tom asked naively.

'Trust me, it won't be.' Adam replied. 'You stay here, I've got to go.'

'Hang on. I'm coming with you.' Tom ran after him and could see the planes coming nearer through the overhanging clouds and the noise was getting louder. He didn't think

Adam had noticed that he had tagged along and he ran towards the machine gun.

A machine gun strong enough to hit a plane? Tom was no expert, but it seemed unlikely.

And then the bombs fell.

Noise like thunder hit his eardrums with the force of a sledgehammer and he dived behind a large tree. The ground was shaking from the impact and Fabio, the guy on the machine gun, was shooting towards the planes, but didn't seem to hurt them much. Then another plane came lower. Looking out from behind the tree, Tom could see the battle between the machine gun operator and the pilot of the plane.

He couldn't stop watching even though he knew that he was close enough to get hit. The plane started its gun aiming for the machine gun and its operator and a row of bullets, tup tup tup tup got closer and closer, throwing up mud and stones as they hit the ground, but missed Fabio and his machine.

Having missed its target once, it returned and tried again, this time the strafing hit Fabio. It hit him so hard he flew away from the chair on his gun and landed by Tom's feet. The plane was still circling overhead and there was no point trying to see if Fabio was still alive. The bullets had nearly split him in half and his blood had splattered over Tom's trousers and was running over his shoes. He'd never had anyone literary ripped to shreds in front of him and he started breathing faster, his stomach turning and he thought he would be sick.

All of a sudden there were people coming running. The planes, having done what they came to do, had disappeared without Tom noticing. Adam was at the front, sweating and covered in mud he shouted at him.

'Shit, Tom. You were supposed to wait in the 'cave'. If anything had happened to you I would have got in trouble for it.'

'Well, nothing happened to me.' Tom looked down on the dead machine gun guy. 'I could see the bullet line coming straight at him and he must have seen it too but he didn't run. What makes you do that? Courage?'

'Yeah,' Mike agreed. 'No fucking use to him now though, eh?'

'You'll have to take him up Mike. Don't let her see him before you tell her.' Adam made him promise.

Mikey sighed and nodded.

'Come on, let's take him up to clearing.' He put the stretcher on the ground. 'What are you waiting for writing boy?' he indicated for Tom to help him get Fabio on to the stretcher.

'There are a lot more wounded and dead down there so hurry back with the stretcher.' Adam nodded towards the trench and left with some of the guys that had come running up as the planes left.

Only minutes earlier he had been intact with a life and dreams. Now they were trying to get his body onto the stretcher in one piece. The stretcher was basically a sheet tied between two long pieces of wood and it wobbled a lot more than one would think possible.

'Where are we taking him?' Tom asked as they walked up the hill side shielded from the enemy on the other side of the ridge by trees and bushes.

'Up to the clearing where you arrived. It's only a couple of minutes away. We have got to get him up there quickly as the stretcher is needed. The awful thing is that the nurse is his wife and ...,' his voice trailed off. 'I've got to tell her that her husband has been nearly cut in two. I'd rather be under gunfire than doing that.

'Do you think she'll stay on here or go back home?'

'She'll stay. The Spanish have a lot of courage and even more stubbornness. Especially the women. She'll stay.'

Tom was breathing heavily, loudly enough he thought, to be heard for miles and his arms felt like they were on fire from carrying the stretcher. However, the adrenaline was still pumping through his body and after what seemed like hours, but could not have been more than ten minutes, they reached the clearing.

Mikey went off to find Fabio's wife and Tom sat down on a rock not wanting to interfere. He could see them sitting on a bench around the corner talking. There must have been a deep well of strength in her as she did not break down or cry but listened to Mikey as he spoke.

Captain Santos came up to Tom and informed him that he was glad he'd made himself useful and that he would have to stay at least until the following day. The Captain had to go to another regiment further down the line to prepare them for a visit from President Azaña who was touring the battlefields to raise morale.

'When is Azaña coming?' Tom asked, smelling an opportunity for a scope but it was short lived as the Captain laughed and told him that there were enough journalists coming with the President already. With this the Captain started walking towards his car and Tom made a split second decision.

'Captain.'

'Yes.'

'Does the name 'Blackstone' mean anything to you?'

There was a moments silence and the Captain came back to where Tom stood. 'No. Should it?'

Tom shook his head. 'It's not important. Just a name that cropped up in an article I'm writing.'

There was a short silence before the Captain spoke.

'Take care Senior. Life in Spain is very cheap these days. Maybe your article is better not written.'

With this he walked back to his car. Tom stood for a moment staring after him, wondering what he meant. It was a strange reply and he had the impression that the Captain knew very well who Blackstone was. If the Captain's car had not already sped away from the camp, he would have asked him.

'Hey, Shakespeare. Don't just stand there. Get a move on.' Mike called out.

Tom looked back to where Fabio's wife was still sitting on the bench. Turned away from them her shoulders were shaking as she cried.

They ran purposefully down the hill, slipping and sliding as they went and then stopped as the trees thinned out. The heavens opened up and the rain soaked them to the bones.

They got another couple of injured soldiers up to the station and then there was only one more to go up, and he looked more dead than alive.

'Why didn't they take Mat first? He looks worse than the guy they carried up.'

Mikey ignored him or maybe he just hadn't heard the question as he led the way back up to the clearing again. Tom held the back end of the stretcher and found it much more difficult this time as the rain was running in little rivers along the hill side. There was no loud swearing from Mat as he lay there with his eyes closed and his face very pale whilst his blood soaked through his uniform where shelling had battered him.

They left him with Fabio's wife who had composed herself a little and was attending the wounded men already brought up. There would be an ambulance along during the afternoon and they would be sent off to hospital where hopefully they would be put back together again.

'They took the other guy because Mat is highly unlikely to live. Couldn't say that whilst he was listening could I, Shakespeare. We should really have left Fabio down there and taken the other two up first, but there is a certain amount of respect involved, you know. He had the worst job of all. Always the main target. - There was a guy who stood in for him yesterday and he was really good but the same thing as today happened and he ran. Still got shot, but he's in hospital now. It's a blessing to have the thing when you pull forward or to avert an attack, but also a reason for them to send over the planes to destroy it so that their ground troops can use their machine gun to aid their advance.'

The rain had slowed and was now just hanging in the air refusing them to get dry and evening was quickly falling.

There was food being prepared in the cave and Tom and Mikey headed over there. Some soldiers were shooting the odd bullet and insult over to the other side but apart from that it was quiet. The rain had stopped, but everything and everyone were still soggy and cold.

'They'll come tonight. Two days of aerial attacks it must be tonight. We should move forwards quickly, get the bloody town back before they have a chance to attack and drive us further back.' Mikey leaned back against the wall with a bowl of stew in front of him.

'You said that last night and nothing happened. Your predictions are useless man.'

'Tonight they will, I can feel it.' Mikey answered taking a large mouthful of stew. 'They'll try to drive us away before we have a chance to retake the town'

'Well, let's hope that doesn't happen before the bloody reinforcements get here. We'll need at least another five hundred men just to stop ourselves going backwards.'

'They'll be here before morning I'm sure. What could possibly take them this long, eh?' Mikey grinned.

There was certainly a lot of food and cigarettes around so at least the army was well fed, and in preparation for another stint in Madrid, Tom ate every scrap of food on his plate.

'Thanks for your help, Shakespeare. You did good. We had some word slinger with us a couple of weeks ago, and there wasn't even an attack when he had some kind of attack himself. I don't know what it was, but he couldn't breathe, so Mat, the guy we carried up the hill last, threw him over his shoulder and carried him back up to the station. We didn't see him again.'

'He had a panic attack. Easily done here,' a slim looking man with glasses said.

'We'd all have bloody panic attacks if we let ourselves. Especially with the lack of sleep. I swear I can't remember the last time I slept for more than an hour.'

'Yeah. If we ever get any leave I'm going to Madrid, having a good meal, watch a film and then sleep for the rest of the time.' The guy with the glasses said. 'And, it will be the best spent time of my life. Even if I get married and have children their arrivals will be second to my Madrid leave.'

'Lucky girl whoever she may be.'

It was nice and warm by the fire and Tom had mostly dried off when Adam came in.

'Fancy coming on a reccie?' he asked him. Thinking how cold it would be outside this little cave Tom really wanted to say no, but that was out of the question, so he tried to look excited and said yes.

'You don't have to look pleased about it. We'd all rather stay by the fire. Come on'

Tom got up and followed him out into the darkness, taking care not to trip over and make a total fool of himself. It was freezing, but the others must feel it too, and they were dressed far worse than him.

There were three of them there in the darkness, Tom, Adam and a Spanish guy called Mario moving along one of the trenches Tom had not yet been and all three of them being grateful for the cloudy sky hiding them from the reflections of the moon.

'Be careful when we move above ground,' Mario warned. 'They tend to sneak over and hang mines in the bushes. You brush it and you're gone.' He said it in Spanish and a few of the words in English.

Adam nodded.

They moved forward slowly, and every twig and leaf under their shoes seemed to make a loud noise when squashed down into the mud created by the earlier rain. In the distance was the enemy, their shadowy silhouettes moving almost like ghosts. Tom had spoken about them and written about them, but until now he'd never actually seen the enemy. This was the real thing. A year ago they might have had a drink together, a laugh, now they would shoot each other on sight. They took great care moving forwards slowly, knowing that there would be recce parties on the fascist side too.

'There's more activity than usual,' Mario whispered to Adam 'I'm sure they've had reinforcements.'

'Yeah, I agree. They're getting ready to push us back. I can't see any tanks, so I guess they are just relying on the planes chasing us out before they move forward,' Adam whispered. 'We'd better get back and hope that our reinforcements will arrive in the next couple of hours.'

They sneaked back the way they had come without any problems until they were nearly at the camp. The sentry on duty declared their password wrong by shooting a bullet at them.

'It's the fucking right password. He's obviously forgotten it.'

'It's Mario and Adam you stupid arse. We only went past you a couple of hours ago.'

They all kept their heads down until the sentry called out it was ok. He'd forgotten that the password had changed and was now very apologetic.

'You could have killed us there. And you probably had every person on this hill reaching for their guns expecting the Moors to come over.' Mario went up to the poor sentry who looked so young, and whereas the enemy didn't seem to scare him, Mario did.

'I'm sorry,' the youngster apologized. 'I'll make sure I remember in future.'

'You do that.' Mario now smiled at him 'and take care Compañero.'

'So young and constantly on edge. You have to let them off once.'

Adam and Mario went to see their commanding officer and returned shortly afterwards to Tom who had waited a little closer to the cave where he could see the fire still going.

'We are attacking just before dawn. You should get yourself back up to the station.' It wasn't said nastily, more like Adam didn't want Tom in the way.

'I'd like to stay down here if it's ok with you. I'll stay at the back.'

'OK fine, stay where you like.' He went over to the corner and picked up an old rifle and handed it to Tom. 'Here, you'd better take this. Do you know how to use it?' He'd obviously forgotten Tom's uselessness in putting one together earlier in the day.

'I have used rifles before but not this kind.' Tom had been in the Cadets at school but this one, like the one Adam had shown him earlier, was from the 19th century.

Adam turned to Mario. 'Could you show him how it works and make some use of him.'

Adam went back to the cave to get his men in order for the attack.

'You speak Spanish, yes?' he asked.

'I do, yes. Not the best Spanish but still ok. My friends say my Spanish is very old. I learned it from my mother who left Spain for England a long time ago.'

'Ah, so you have family here.'

'Maybe. I don't know,' he said vaguely thinking of the old man in the cellar. Some bloody family. 'My mother didn't want to talk about it. She hasn't been back since before I was born.'

Mario nodded. 'I'm glad you've come now. It is our hour of need and it warms my heart to see so many people coming to help.' He smiled. 'When we've won and Spain is free, you should find your family. Family and freedom is all that matters.'

'Where is your family?'

'Ah. My family is from down south in the rebel held territory. I don't know where they are. Like you, I will find them again after this war.'

He quickly showed Tom how to fire the rifle and reload again. That part was unnecessary as he had no more ammunition.

The soldiers had gathered and were getting ready to move forward. The night was passing, and soon the sun would rise and remove the darkness that made it impossible to see anything or anyone more than a couple of feet in front.

Tom did what he was asked and stayed in the back. As the first light came over the horizon they moved forwards, slowly and quietly, until the other side raised the alarm and the shooting started.

The machine gun, which had been fixed earlier on, was doing its job very well to start with, just like the other sides machine gun did, but after a short period of time it jammed. Several soldiers tried unsuccessfully to fix it whilst the fascist's gun still kept on going. It was a very short push forward and then they were almost back in their cosy little trench trying to fight off the enemy from home.

The 'back' where Tom stood was very quickly becoming the front and he moved back again, trying to keep out of reach of the bullets flying all around. There had been no re-inforcements, and they were fighting ten to one. The town would not be recaptured today. If they were lucky they'd hold on to this trench.

He could see casualties from both sides and crawled his way towards the closest one to see if he was alive. He wasn't, so Tom left him there and crawled back towards the cave.

In the background, over the gunfire, there was that dull droning sound again and it was getting closer and closer. Some who had survived had retreated back to the trenches and the gunfire slowed down as it became clear to all what was happening.

The machine gun was still jammed and the plane was now close enough to bomb the camp. It did so with the weak morning sun glinting off its silver wings. There were insults hurled at it as they all ran for cover further along the hillside. With the machine gun jammed they were no match for them, and as the plane turned majestically in the air and came back towards them, they ran in the opposite direction. There was nothing else they could do. Tom ran up the hill, towards the clearing at the top. His feet slipping on a carpet of muddy pine needles, his breath coming in short bursts as he tried to reach the protection of the trees. He was nearly there when he heard the now familiar tuc tuc tuc come closer. The bullets hit the ground in an almost straight line that was coming towards him. Tom threw himself behind a large rock and heard the bullets hit it just as he landed. Lying behind that stone he tried to calm his breathing. His stomach was tying itself in knots thinking that somehow he would have to move from there, out into the line of fire again. He wished he'd left things on a better note with Maria and he wished that he had written more often to his mother instead of taking it for granted that he would see her soon enough. He stayed behind the stone for a minute, catching his breath and briefly reflecting on what could have happened. The plane was further down the line now and Tom was close to the shelter of the trees. He crawled away from the rock and hid behind some bushes to catch his breath. The cold mud plastered itself onto his legs and arms as he continued crawling up to the now abandoned station.

Where were they all? Where the fuck were they all? At the corner of the old stone house he paused and looked around. There wasn't much time to decide where to go and he'd just decided to run south when something hit his head and sent him flying to the ground.

It was more the shock of the unexpected attack than the pain which left him on the ground for the second it took his attacker to stick a big boot on his back, making it impossible for Tom to move. His first thought was that he'd been captured and that the clearing was crawling with fascists, but he couldn't hear anybody else. Just the heavy breathing of the man holding him down.

'What do you want. I'm a journalist and unarmed.'

The foot was lifted and replaced with the barrel of a gun digging into his back. Tom stayed very still as a rapid storm of Spanish rattled out of the man. He could only catch a few words but he got the general idea. With a final kick to Tom's side, his attacker left. Tom got up on his knees quickly, hoping to catch sight of whoever it had been that had told him to leave Spain and stop asking questions.

There was no time to think about what's and why's. The fascists were too close. He started to run down the hill, away from the enemy's machine gun.

The only thing left for the bedraggled Republican battalion was to retreat towards the next line. Tom ran towards the south side of the hill, and down the road he could still hear the odd gunshot. With no time to loose he ran for all he was worth, until his breath came in gasps and he thought his lungs would explode, and then he saw some of the others. They were split up into little groups that grew as soldiers who'd escaped in different directions joined in. Injured and demoralised they walked on as the midday sun shone from a now cloudless, almost shimmering sky for mile upon mile.

There was no way of knowing who was killed, missing, injured, captured or just lost in the hills. Tom searched the faces of everybody he walked past, hoping that one of them would give something away, give Tom a clue as to who'd attacked him at the clearing.

He spotted Mikey easily enough and the guy in the glasses walking with him, but there was no sign of Mario or Adam. It was only when he thought of Adam that he realised that he'd left the rifle behind the stone that had saved his life.

He was just about to make his way up to Mikey to see if he knew where they were going when he spotted Gabriella, the wife of Fabio, walking alone and Tom slowed down to join her.

Her dress was splattered with blood and covered in mud, and her face determined as she carried a makeshift bag which he assumed contained her and Fabio's life possessions, or maybe it was just full of medical supplies. He offered to carry it for her, and after a few moments of considering the offer, she accepted. They walked along in silence for a while, keeping an eye on the others as he didn't like the prospect of getting lost.

'How long have you been with these guys?' he asked.

'Only for a month or so. We were in a band local to our village before then, but when the army reformed, Fabio was trained and sent here.'

She shrugged her shoulders as she marched on, faster now that she didn't have to carry the bag.

'They are all nice guys but..., it was different when we were fighting alongside people we grew up with and neighbours we knew had suffered in the same way our own families had suffered. This is all so big, like getting swept away on a wave and no way of stopping it. It's all gone too far to be stopped.'

'I'm sorry for what happened to your husband. It must be really difficult.'

'He was so proud of the Republic and I am so proud of him. I feel sorry for myself but now is not the time to think of that. Winning this war is more important than the life of any single person, including any of us. - I have a little sister at home who is only ten years old. I want her to grow up being able to choose her own life and knowing that if you work hard you will get properly rewarded, not kicked in the teeth and taxed to death, and to know that if she doesn't want to go to church every single day, she won't be seen as loose and dragged away to prison. Rights to a life worth living is what we want.' She was talking more to herself than to Tom, to make herself strong and to remind herself of the reasons why they had joined to start with. 'My uncle was killed when I was only little but I still remember it. He was killed near Barcelona by pistoleros for being an active union member in 1919, for wanting a fairer system. Is that right or fair?' She kicked a stone out of the way and continued. 'We have finally come this far and we can't let go now, if we do, we'll be back to living like dogs whilst the generals, the landowners and the church sit at their full tables telling us what we must do.' She looked at Tom and gave a sad smile.

'Sorry, Compañero, I didn't mean to talk so much.'

'You haven't. It's interesting.'

This seemed to embarrass her and they walked on in silence.

*****

'What a fucking mess.' Mikey was leaning against the trunk of an olive tree, his eyes closed as if that would shut out the world. They had come to a halt at another camp further on, and the wounded that could walk this far, got medical attention here. The rest of them got bean stew.

There had been a lot of casualties and neither Mario nor the young sentry were coming back and amongst the seriously wounded was Adam with shrapnel stuck in his back. They had not even had a chance to retrieve the bodies. It was grim.

The bean stew had been the final straw for Tom's stomach and he had been sick just behind the olive tree where Mikey had slumped. Taking deep gulps of earthy autumn air he sat down next to Mikey and gratefully drank the water somebody had fetched for him. The sun was shining, warming his face, and he too closed his eyes.

'I saw you talking to Gabriella on the way here. You know she's pregnant?' Mikey asked.

'No, I didn't know that.'

'She won't be coming with us when we leave. I really wish we could do something for her.'

'She mentioned a little sister so I guess she must have family to stay with?'

'Don't know about hers, but Fabio's family are from up north and I guess she'll have to go and stay with them. Must be a quiet life away from this for someone who believes in the Republic so strongly.'

'So, when are you off? Do you know where you're going?'

'You're not coming along then?' He looked up and smiled briefly

'Not this time.'

'You lucky bastard. Bath and a proper bed for you then. Never been to Madrid,.' he said as he closed his eyes again. 'Hopefully we'll make some progress and get a bit of leave, then I'll go.'

'When you do, make sure you come and see me.'

At that moment in time Tom had forgotten that soon maybe he would not have the option to go back to Madrid for food and sleep either, and would be in the same situation as Mikey and the others. If he joined up that was.

'You can show me the delights of Madrid,' Mikey said drowsily.

Tom couldn't remember if he replied or not as he drifted off to sleep.

Shortly afterwards he was offered a lift back to Madrid and wondered if he would ever see any of them again.

~ 11 ~

Madrid, October 1936

The priest felt conspicuous as he always did on the odd occasion when he had to venture outside in normal civilian clothes. He did not leave the house very often. When he did, it was always at lunchtime when there was less chance of being stopped and asked for papers as people milled around the streets.

There were no familiar faces from before the war, and even if there had been, they would not have recognised him. He had shaved off his beard and acquired a very bad posture which he thought made him look like one of the peasants who now ruled the place. He imagined the un-friendly eyes of his former flock burrowing into his back, following him down the old cobbled street. He was on edge, waiting for the shout of recognition and the gathering of a mob, tearing him to pieces.

The man on the corner, dressed in a dirty uniform and a rifle slung over his back, he could be the one to shout out. Leaning lazily against the wall, the soldier's eyes seemed to follow him as he walked past. The priest forced himself to calmly walk on down the street, but he couldn't help himself, he had to turn around to see if he was being followed. The soldier was still standing in the same place, but the second the priest turned around, their eyes met and for a moment everything around them stood still. Then the soldier pulled his rifle forward and shouted at the priest to put his hands up. They were still far enough away from each other for the priest to at least attempt an escape and he quickly jumped into a side alley and started running. The soldier's bullets echoed down the alleyway when they hit the corner of the building where the priest had just stood.

Not used to physical exercise, his breath came out in fast and wheezing gasps, and still he could hear the soldier behind him. He couldn't run any further, he needed somewhere to hide. The alleyways were empty of people and the priest took a couple of right turns, hoping that it would throw the soldier off. Then he came to a stop. He couldn't go any further, it was a dead end and for the first time in his life he was scared. He could either sneak back the way he'd come and hope that the soldier would be too far the other way to notice, or he could try to get back to the main street using one of the houses. The house in front of him looked deserted, but that didn't mean that nobody lived there. The door opened easily, and without making a sound, the priest walked past a dirty kitchen and up a set of stairs where, at the end of a short corridor, he could see the front door. In one of the rooms a baby was crying and he briefly considered taking the child and thus saving it from eternal damnation, but there was no time. Somebody was coming down the stairs and he hurried out of the front door and down the street.

There was no sign of any soldiers and he felt a little better. His legs were still shaking from the running and he felt the familiar anger on behalf of God for the way His people had turned away from Him and become instruments of the devil himself. They had turned their backs on Him, but the priest had no doubt that God would win this war, and he would then take great pleasure in punishing the population of Madrid and bringing them back to the bosom of the church.

He found the cafe he was looking for and ordered a coffee at the bar before sitting down at the only corner table there was. He kept his head low and his coat pulled up until the barman brought his drink over. The cafe was chosen because it was set aside from the main streets and the owner was not involved on an emotional level with the Republic. He had continued his pre wartime habit of turning a blind eye to most customers or transactions under his roof. As long as his customers paid for their drinks and didn't start a fight he didn't have a problem with them.

The priest had no doubt that if there was to be a raid or something similar, the owner would tell the militia what they wanted to hear, but as long as nothing happened he would not volunteer the information.

The table gave the priest a good view of the place and the lack of windows and lights made him sink into the shadows even more. There he sat feeling anxious, until the man he was meeting finally showed up.

Pietr had woken up to find the bed empty and Bea gone. He'd convinced himself that she had to get to the hospital early and that she hadn't wanted to wake him up. He was running late for his meeting because he had to go by the hospital to find out when he could see her next. It had, in the end, been a useless exercise as she had not been there. It irritated him that he would now have to go back later that afternoon. He did have more important things to do and he would inform her of this when he saw her next.

He walked briskly, business like, into the cafe and with a nod of his head towards the owner behind the bar he went to the priest's table and joined him in the shadows.

The priest's skin was sallow and yellowish white, signs of living in near darkness and no amount of civilian clothing could hide that. Maybe people would just think he was ill, but all the same, Pietr made a note of not meeting him outside again. Going to the house today had not been a possibility though. He hadn't spotted anybody following him, but he could be sure that his movements would from now on be monitored somehow. He couldn't even be sure that the General didn't have spies actually in his own office and he had to stop his thoughts going too far in that direction. It was one thing being aware and careful and quite another being paranoid.

'How are you?' he asked the priest.

'I'm fine. And you? It was short notice for a meeting. I assume something has happened.'

'It has.' Pietr paused whilst a coffee was put in front of him and then quietly he continued. 'I had a visitor last night. A General Carlos informed me that Enrique has been caught. And he's talked.' He drank some coffee and ensured he had the priest's full attention. 'The short version is that the General knows, or think he knows, everything. Including that we have the gold.'

'That's true though'

'I know it's bloody true... forgive me for swearing Father, but he wants the gold to keep quiet.'

'It was bound to happen at some point. I just didn't think it would happen so quickly. You will just have to leave Madrid and take the gold with you.' The priest said matter of factly.

'I can't leave yet. There is a way out of this somehow and I will find it. Anyway, the cases of gold that I've got would require a couple of trucks to move.'

'You did it before. Just use the same men and the same equipment.'

'They may be thieves, but they're still republicans. I can't tell them to drive it across the line. As it is, Andriev doesn't know that I have taken most of the stolen gold from him and left a pile of corpses guarding the rest.' Pietr was getting agitated. 'When he does find out, I can't have anybody associating that gold with me at all. I have seen him wreak revenge on others for crimes against Russia. This is personal and will be ten times worse.' He lit a cigarette and took a deep drag. Maybe it was time to leave, but he would not go without Bea and the gold, and he knew that Bea's heart was firmly with the Republic. If she found out what side he was on she would never see him again. After the war it would be different, he would be part of the victorious army and she would see the benefit of being with him. Until then though, he had to stay in Madrid, to make her change her mind.

'Let's deal with Carlos first.' Pietr stubbed his cigarette out.

'Is he bribable with only part of the gold maybe?' The priest shook his head in answer to his own question. 'No, the gold is still the property of Spain and not for us to use. Maybe you will have to kill him.'

'Who, the General or Enrique?'

'Maybe, both.'

'Only as a last resource. The General is too well guarded, but it may well have to come to that. My man over at the General's department tells me that Enrique is dead already. I guess the General didn't want anybody else to hear his confession. I don't expect that the guards that interrogated him will be alive for much longer either.'

'If the man is dead then surely they have nothing on you. Papers can be forged.'

'There will be a file with his written confession which I believe the General has hidden away somewhere out of sight. Somewhere nobody would think to look.'

'So you need to find that file and destroy it. Then all it will come down to is his word against yours, and you are not without influence. The Russians are the men behind the power here, no? They will back you up and probably take great pleasure in doing so too. Another chance for them to put the boot on the Spanish.'

'I can't allow anybody accusing me of stealing. Andriev would immediately go to Barcelona and find out what we've done. He's the chief of NKVD and I don't want to be here when he realises what's happened. I'm here, in Madrid, telling him that all is well and that his gold is safe, but if he went there himself, the finger of blame could only fall in my direction. I was hoping that you knew of someone closer to Carlos than I do. Someone who works for him or sleeps with him. Someone who would be able to look through his office and find the file for me.'

'Let me have a little think about it and let you know. If I can, I will of course help you.'

They both stopped talking for a moment when the door opened and an old man came in. He sat down at the bar facing them before the bar owner shooed him away to a table by the window over on the other side of the cafe.

'I had a strange visitor yesterday myself,' the priest mumbled quietly, and Pietr being too occupied with his own troubles, only partly listened.

'It was a young Englishman. Without going into too much detail it turns out he is my mother's grandson. It is a very shameful situation and I let him leave, which maybe I shouldn't have. I had the chance to shoot him and I didn't, but he only came here looking for his family and I don't think he will inform anybody of my presence in the house.' The priest saw the glazed over look in Pietr's eyes and coughed a little to get his attention back.

'I just thought I'd ask and see if you knew who he was.'

'Sorry, who is who?' Pietr tried to backtrack the conversation, but could not remember a word the priest had said about some visitor.

'The Englishman named Tom something. My nephew.' It hurt the priest to admit the kinship. 'I let him go but I think it will be ok. Called me *compañero!* Would you believe it.' He gave a brief description of his visitor.

'Tom Lancaster? It must be. Yes, I know him. He lives at the Pension on Calle Mayor and is desperate for some big story to catapult him into the spotlight. I'd say he's not very safe at all.'

'I don't think he will say anything,' the priest said again. 'He wouldn't do that to family, but if you could let me know if you hear anything to the contrary I would appreciate it. And I will try to find out for you, somebody who can help with the file issue.' The priest had decided not to mention what had happened earlier. There was nothing to be gained by it and he didn't want to add to his friend's troubles.

Pietr nodded and stood up.

'Take care of yourself Father, and maybe try to find somewhere else to live for a while. Until everything has settled down.'

'The Lord will look after me.'

'I hope he looks after all of us.'

The priest nodded and Pietr left the cafe as he had arrived, briskly and with purpose. He walked down the Calle del Carmen keeping his eyes ahead of him, hoping he was not followed.

~ 12 ~

When Tom finally got back to the Pension, nothing had mattered but sleep. He'd peeled off his muddy clothes and had a good long night's sleep. When he woke up he was ravenous, and all there was to eat was stale bread and a tomato that had lasted quite well. After his inadequate meal he sat down at his little table in front of the window and started writing.

The last few days had been so full of action that now he felt empty and missed the guys and the excitement. The experience had renewed his passion for the Republic and he no longer felt it necessary to delay his decision to join up. He did, however, still have to do the gold story. He should have started it days ago and he hoped José was still alright. Guiltily he promised himself that he would start making the preparations as soon as he'd written and sent off this article. Then he would also think about the strange incident up at the 'clearing' and Captain Santos' odd comment. He had to get his copy written and sent first.

The broken body of Fabio, the antiquated weapons, the stomach wrenching fear when the dull humming of a plane approached, it all poured out onto the sheet of paper in his typewriter.

Once finished, he took the article with him, and delivered it to the press office on-route to see Bea.

There wasn't a long queue at the Telefonica, and after a few discussions, his article was cleared by the censors and sent off.

The rain had stopped and started, on and off, ever since he left the Pension and it was getting colder too. Tom had heard from Auntie that Madrid weather was a law unto itself due to its location at a high altitude and between three mountain ranges, and the longer he spent there the more he agreed with her.

Soggily, he made his way to the hospital to see if Bea had a few moments to spare for a chat. He wanted to try to persuade her to go back home, whilst there was still time to do so. He didn't think she would listen, but he thought it important to try, because if Franco was to come marching in, he wouldn't take any notice of a British passport waved in front of him before shooting whoever held it up.

The hospital was a large building constructed in the beginning of the century by a religious order for the free care of workers. It was based on the Panoptyc model of Spanish prisons and traditional patterns of the 16th century and that would explain the foreboding feeling one got when one entered it. The stale smell of unwashed bodies and the petrol used for cleaning wounds filled Tom's airways as he walked down the linoleum corridors. With the front-line creeping closer all the time, there were many times the patients there now compared to even a month ago. The corridors were full of staff walking to or from wards, visitors looking lost and patients, both civilians and soldiers, waiting for someone to heal them. Finally, he managed to find someone who could tell him where to find Bea, and as luck would have it, she had a short break just as he found her.

They walked out to the cobbled courtyard, away from the noise and activity of the wards. There were other people out there too, some visitors and others hobbling along on crutches or in bandages, taking advantage of the brief break in the clouds. He wondered where they'd been when they had been injured or taken ill, where they were from, and where their friends and families were now. Every life here, and every death too he guessed, must have a story to tell. One day, when all this has calmed down, he would travel around Spain and write their experiences down, but that seemed to be a very long time away indeed. And would there be a Spain left worth writing about? He chided himself for these negative thoughts and brought his attention back to Bea.

'You look tired,' he said as they walked up to the now dry fountain.

'No surprise. I feel like a hundred years old. There has been nonstop work for days and you only manage to catch a fifteen minute nap here or there. It's coffee and the endless streams of injured that keep one going. I won't lie about it, I could really do with a couple of days away from here. 'We've had a few new doctors and nurses now so maybe we'll get on top of things. If only the incoming would slow down,' she sighed.

'This is new.' Tom pulled a little on the red scarf she had tied around her neck and quickly Bea slapped his hand away and gave him an angry look.

'I'm fine, just a little bit of a sore throat.'

'Well, something is sore that's for sure.' Tom shook his head at her as they sat down on a bench by the fountain and he lit a cigarette.

'You can't keep going like this forever.'

'It will all be alright.' She looked at him as if she had only just noticed that he was there. 'You look absolutely awful.' She ran a finger along the cut on his cheek. 'I thought you were going to report on what you saw, not get involved in it.'

'Well, sometimes things just happen.'

He gave her a brief version of the last couple of days and she laughed at little anecdotes he added for her benefit. It was lovely to see happiness sparkling from her eyes again, no matter how briefly it was for.

'Are you sure you're ok?' he asked, knowing she would have to go back in shortly

'Of course I am. Well, all is fine with me, but obviously not with the people around me. I think even the doctors may be ill here. Or just mad.'

'Maybe it helps being a little mad in times of war'

'Maybe,' she added as a loud painful scream came from one of the floors above. They both looked up towards it.

'That's the theatre. We're low on anesthetics, so only the most serious operations are performed with Chloroform, the rest just have to take their chances with alcohol. It makes your stomach turn doesn't it?'

'Oh my God. That's awful. Poor sods.'

'I know. That's Non-Intervention for you. I expect during the operation the majority of them would rather have been killed on the field than being on that table. Anyway, the ones that get better generally get sent back out in the fields rather quickly, which is where most of them want to be.' She lit a cigarette and looked back to him.

'Is Maria ok now. I haven't seen her since last Saturday night. A bit weird don't you find, just flying off the handle like that. She was really quite embarrassing.'

'Don't Bea. Don't talk about her that way. You'd be upset too if your family stood to get killed. Well, I'd hope you would be. If it gets too much for you here, you can always go running back to England. This is her country, she's got nowhere else to go.'

He stood up and Bea followed suit.

'Well, she's got you there to look after her, and on Saturday night it was plain to see that she'd got what she wanted.' Bea snapped back. 'She must have forgotten that you have a girlfriend in Paris, very convenient. Oh, that's right, she doesn't know.'

'What's up with you?' He had raised his voice. 'You have got to stop acting like this, or you will have no friends left. All you ever do these days is snap at people or talk ill of them.'

'I'm sorry. I work in this hellhole all day and usually all night too. Franco is on our doorstep and the government is really not very useful at all. Maybe I just see what is happening clearer than you do, and I see all the mistakes that are made because I have to listen to the heartbreaking screams and the silent weeping of the people who are paying the price for these mistakes. And they are the lucky ones. You'll just have to excuse me for not being "like I used to be". - I've changed Tom, this has changed me, and to be quite honest, I find it strange that it hasn't had more of an impact on you. What do you do all day? Apart from the last few days when you have actually helped the war effort, you run around Madrid, with no real purpose, or you go off to the embassy to tell them what I've been up to and who knows what else you tell them Tom. What secrets do you discuss on your weekly trip to Charles?'

Tom could feel his face getting red from anger, maybe it was because she hit a raw nerve, maybe it was because he'd never done or said anything to deliberately hurt her, like her comments now hurt him.

She looked up at his face and it must have shown that she'd gone too far.

'Tom, I'm sorry. I know you'd never do anything like that. I just get so mad sometimes about all of this. If only the government would be more decisive and pro-active we'd stand a chance of winning and I really do think we could win. Forgive me?' She bit her bottom lip and tried to take his hand, but he shook her off.

'You've gone too far. I didn't come here to quarrel. I came for a quick chat, to see that you were ok but quite frankly I don't really care at the moment,' he said as he turned his back to her and started walking away.

'Don't go. Let's start again. It's just been a rather bad day, that's all. I promise that once this war is over we'll all be back to normal, and there will be hunting parties and wild dinners at Laroux's again, and we'll all be happy. - You're my brother, you're all I have,' her voice trailed off. Her eyes welled up and she briefly wondered if indeed she was losing the plot. She needed to pull herself together as there was too much at stake now, but she didn't want to alienate Tom. He could never stay angry at her for more than a little while, no matter how much he wanted to. They had both had plenty of practice at that.

Tom walked back to her.

'Why do we always end up arguing? It's getting quite tiresome and to be honest, I've got bigger problems to think about. You should learn to control yourself a little. You're not a child anymore Bea and with growing up comes taking responsibility for your actions. And I have no doubt that what you do is stressful, but if you don't want to do it, then go home.'

'Tom, you do sound very grown up.'

'That's because I am. It doesn't stop me feeling like I'm still 20 years old most of the time though.'

'I know, I do too and of course we argue, that's what siblings do. We may not be blood related or even related in any other way, but we'll always have each other you and I, won't we?' She smiled as they sat down again. 'Now, what do you want to talk about? You'd better be quick, I should really be getting back inside,' she said and apologetically crinkled her nose.

'Well,' he paused for a moment. Trying to get her to go back home now would only result in another argument and he didn't have the energy for it. 'It was nothing in particular apart from me having to go away for a couple of days.'

'Oh, where are you going this time?'

'It's just the delayed Cartagena trip. I couldn't go last Sunday as the car wouldn't start. There is this rather odd story I'm looking into, and if I can get some more information about it my career might take a giant leap upwards. It'll either get very interesting, or it will turn into nothing. Judging from the interest generated from people not wanting me to do the story, I'd say it'll be a good one.'

'What is it about?'

'Oh, you'd be interested in it. I don't want to say too much right now, but it's to do with some stolen gold. All quite exciting, but I should have started it a couple of days ago really. - You know you can always go back to Maria and Auntie if you need to. If I'm not here,' he said carefully.

Bea was looking into a dream-world and he waved his hand in front of her to bring her back.

'I guess you'll be fine then.'

'I will be,' she smiled. 'I'm so sorry darling but I've got to go back to the ward now. Don't leave Madrid until I get a chance to talk to you properly. Maybe on Wednesday, at the Gran Via?' she said this as she was walking back towards her ward.

'Ok. I'll see you there,' Tom shouted after her before making his way towards the city centre and a late lunch.

Bea watched Tom leave the hospital from one of the lower the ward windows and sighed as she turned and went in search of head nurse Blackwell. She did not look forward to asking her for a couple of hours off but she had no choice and after begging for a few minutes Vivian Blackwell sighed and let her go. The girl had been acting oddly these last couple of days and Vivian hoped it wasn't the early signs of a breakdown.

She watched Bea disappear around the corner and shook her head. They were all under more stress than could be good for them, and it was likely to get worse. She popped a lemon sweet in her mouth and went back to her patients.

Bea quickly went up to the second floor and made sure that one of her patients was comfortable. After ensuring there was nobody else around, she stroked his dark face before running back downstairs and out of the hospital towards the town centre.

The Madrid Frontline

Possible Government Relocation

From Correspondent Thomas Lancaster on the Republican frontline

26 October 1936

The insurgents are now almost within sight of Madrid. Navalcarnero, 25 miles west of the city, has been taken and the government's attempt to retake Illesca has not been successful.

I have just come back from the front where I saw for myself the antiquated equipment used by the soldiers against the modern rifles and grenades that the insurgents have at their disposal. The troops were well fed and even though they were tired and not dressed for the cold weather, they were cheerful and confident. A large portion of the regiment I visited was made up of volunteers from other countries including Britain. Three of them, friends from an early age, came here together from the east end of London, all young men leaving their families to come to Spain to fight fascism. There are only two of them left now. One Spanish man was shot in front of me on my first day there by strafing and he left behind a young pregnant wife who worked as the camp nurse.

The courage of these men and women should never be far from our minds.

For an expanded version of the battlefield, please turn to page 11.

Also, today there are signs that the government is preparing for a possible re-location to either Barcelona or Valencia should Franco get much closer. Do not be fooled into thinking that this means that Madrid will not be fiercely defended. Every person living in the city is preparing to help the army to keep the insurgents out and to retake occupied territory.

$$\sim 13 \sim$$

'I was a little surprised receiving the request, but said I would have a word with you.' Alexander Andriev stood by Pietr's large tidy desk. He tapped his fingers on the edge and wondered if any piece of paper ever actually touched the dark polished wood, and where Captain Alexadrow kept all the reports that he himself had sent him over the last couple of months. 'It would seem that your reputation has reached even General Carlos' department Captain.'

'Why would he want me there?' Pietr asked even though he knew the answer. The 48 hour deadline had expired the previous evening and to give himself a little more time Pietr had not been back to the flat since. When he ventured out, he had his staff with him in the hope that the General would not want to contact him with the eyes and ears of the security staff on him.

He had planned to contact the General as soon as the file was in his hands but it would seem that he wasn't willing to wait any longer. And now he'd involved the big boss, Andriev, himself to ensure that Pietr played nicely. Pietr stood by the window looking out onto the street below, confident that Andriev would not send him away from his post here where he had worked wonders, making disciplined soldiers out of the riffraff that arrived weekly at his door. The other training camps showed them how to march and how to handle a weapon, very basically, before rushing them out to the frontline. When Pietr's soldiers left their training they were more than ready to take on anyone of Franco's soldiers. Whatever else Pietr was up to, he had a lot of professional pride.

'He brought me the request report himself and he thinks that his department would benefit from your training expertise. It would only be for a few weeks and it's a good chance for us to see what they get up to over there. Make some friends.'

'Is it an order?' Pietr turned from the window and walked back to his desk wishing he could chop of Andriev's fingers which were still tapping at the desk as if he didn't even realise he was doing it.

'No, it is simply a request which I hope you will agree to. It would be beneficial to both of us as the government has plans to ship out of Madrid together with all the senior army personnel if the fascists get much closer. Only civilian training will remain in the city which would leave your department in a pickle. You would probably have to move to Madrigueras or Albacete, and I know you want to remain here in Madrid. - Maybe in a few weeks everything will have changed and we can convince them that this department should stay here. - There is something else too. I need a favour and if you do it quickly there will be a promotion for you.' Andriev let that hang in the air, thinking that a promotion was what everybody wanted, after all, was that not why they were doing this. For the power and the glory of knowing that their Russian know how and discipline had won the war for the Spanish government. And that would of course create a Russian friendly country on the Mediterranean, which would be very handy if the Germans didn't pull back their growing war machine and stopped making trouble for Europe and Russia.

'Well, you give me little choice so I will just have to accept the General's kind offer. I need to get certain things in order here so it will have to wait a few days.' Pietr said resignedly thinking that maybe the General would actually have an accident before then. Something would have to happen.

'He specifically requested that you join them as soon as possible. I think he actually mentioned tomorrow.'

'There are people, our people, that I have to inform of this and I can't do it by tomorrow. It has to be next week.'

'If you can't do it sooner Captain that will have to be fine for the General.' He paused for a moment with an amused look on his face. 'By the way Captain, this girl you have been seen out with, you do know who her father is?'

'Of course General.'

'I'm not sure you do. If you did, you would have reported it I'm sure.'

'I don't know what you mean.'

'No, I don't think you do. Whatever you do, don't let her go and don't mention anything that goes on in here to her.'

'Of course, but who is he.'

General Andriev picked up his hat from one of the leather chairs that were lined up against one of the walls.

'Come with me for a drink. Your office disturbs me and I haven't yet told you what it is I want you to do.'

~ 14 ~

By the time Tom had eaten his lunch and made his way over to Silke's hotel it was getting dark outside. He gratefully sat down in the hotel bar and ordered a large drink. There was no point in specifying what you wanted. It tasted awful of course, the first glass of whatever they served you nowadays always did, but after that they weren't too bad. Compared to the priest's drinks, this one was like nectar of the Gods.

The bar was small, dark and empty. The bar man had disappeared to do some other chore, leaving Tom alone with his thoughts and the muffled tunes of the barman singing his own version of the International in a far off room somewhere.

All day he had hoped not to bump into Maria, and now he wanted to go back to the café to see her, and felt like a coward for not doing so. There was some truth in what Bea had said; he did have a girlfriend in Paris that he hadn't mentioned to Maria, but that was not something he'd done on purpose. He hadn't mentioned Emilie to anyone in Madrid, because when he got back from his travels around

Andalucía, he had sort of forgotten about her. He'd assumed that she'd forgotten about him too, and then it didn't seem important anymore. He'd seen other girls when he shouldn't have, he'd ignored her for long periods of time and now spent the last year in Spain.

Poor Emilie, he felt guilty thinking about her. He was sure that she had moved on by now and found herself someone who deserved her. This was a comforting thought and he pondered on it imagining what kind of undeserving chap that would be until Silke arrived.

'Ahh, Tom, excellent, you're here already. Where's that bloody barman gone?' Silke looked around the room before going behind the bar to help himself and continued in his Texan drawl. 'Call this a hotel. It's a joke. What's the point of making your opinions known if there is nobody here to hear them.' He shouted towards the reception area. There was no reply. 'If I'm going to get another heart attack it'll be from the lack of service at this hotel.' He sat down next to Tom at the bar.

'Apart from that, all is going well?' Tom asked with raised eyebrows.

'Yeah, well. You know what I mean. I have some good news for you though. I've just come from a meeting with a young fella called Lobo. You've got to feel a bit sorry for him, he's got a birthmark right over his left eye. I reckon he's had it quite tough. Anyway, turns out that he's heard of this Blackstone. It's a cover name for one of their officers down in Cartagena and he's willing to introduce you to

him. I didn't mention why you wanted to see him or anything like that.'

'That's a bit of a breakthrough. How do you know him?'

'Turns out he's a friend of Louise's, my nurse, and we
bumped into him in a bar last night.'

'It's quite a coincidence though. I'm going down there
later this week.'

'Not a coincidence really if you think about it. That is
where the gold is kept and if he was to be found anywhere,
that's a very probable place to find him. Don't you think?
Also, he's meeting you there on Wednesday so you're going
to have to re-organise your trip.'

'I guess that won't be a problem. I'll find a car that
works somewhere.'

'One more thing. He's a communist at heart, but he has
a very capitalist brain so you owe me some Jack.'

'Alright, how much are we talking here? Would I have it
in my pocket, or do I need to go to the bank?'

'Don't worry about that now, we'll talk about it later.
Anyway, he could have asked for a lot more and maybe he
will when you meet him down Cartagena.'

Silke looked rather pleased with himself and Tom felt
almost speechless. This was turning out to be easier than
he thought. What he would ask this person when he got
there or how he would do it without getting into trouble
was something he'd figure out later on. He was quite good
at inventing stories.

'Didn't he want to know why I wanted to go there?'

'He asked and I just said you were a journalist. A trust-worthy one at that.' He chuckled to himself. 'I don't know one single journalist who wouldn't cut of his own arm for a good story. For THE story he'd probably cut off his... you know.' He looked downwards and laughed.

'This will be a good story Silke. If you want to come along I'll let you in on it. A day away from the town. Come along, bring your camera.'

'No, thank you. I'm not leaving Madrid just yet, because as soon as I leave, Franco will come marching in and I'll have missed the biggest scope of the war. Too much riding on this one.'

'I'll have to see if Eduardo wants to come along then. I do need someone with a camera, but I'm not sure how an anarchist will be received in the camp. Should be alright if he can keep quiet for the time we're there. Anyway, if there is ever anything I can do for you...' Tom put his glass down with a big smile on his face and lit a cigarette.

'Well, I quite like the idea of getting tight tonight, and you're one of the best to get tight with kid.' He tapped on his empty glass and Tom went up to the bar and got both their glasses refilled.

In the end they didn't get very tight, a telegram came through for Silke and he had to rush off so Tom went home. It was evening when he got back to the pension, and knowing that he wouldn't be able to sleep, he started writing up his next piece for the paper. The words flowed, but it was too easy to make heroes out of the militia, putting their stories forward together with his own experience, and when he re-read the story, it could have come out of the propaganda office.

Putting it to one side, ready to be edited with a fresh head in the morning, he could hear Maria and Auntie pottering about on the stairs outside his room. Normally he would have gone out there and had a chat, but now he just lay on his bed, staring at the ceiling, wishing he still could. It went quiet for a few moments, and then there were footsteps on the creaky stairs and other voices, and child was crying. Deciding that he couldn't hide forever he got up, opened the door and peeked out onto the landing.

There were new guests arriving, although by the look of them they were refugees rather than customers. He could see Maria standing in the room across the landing from his with the new family, chatting with them whilst comforting the small child who had now stopped crying and grabbed hold of her hair instead.

Feeling that someone was watching, she turned around and her smile stayed as she waved him over.

'Tom, come and meet our new lodgers. - This is Señor & Señora Vaidez and this is their little one, Justino.'

They all looked tired and drawn as they stood there awkwardly, no doubt wanting to be left alone.

'Buenas tardes,' he said.

'Tardes,' the singular reply came back

'Tom is English, he's a writer.' Maria said, somehow explaining his lack of conversation and the Vaidez nodded to show they understood this.

'Anyway Tom, I'm glad you're here, Señor Vaidez has a leg injury and needs to rest, so I was hoping you wouldn't mind helping me to carry their belongings up here. Auntie is downstairs in the cafe still.' Maria successfully negotiated the return of her hair and handed the child over to his mother.

'Of course, yes, glad to help,' he smiled and nodded awkwardly at the new guests and to Maria, certain that this would get things back to normal between them.

The new guests gratefully sat down on the bed and Tom and Maria made their way downstairs.

'Is that a chicken running around down there?' he asked Maria halfway down the stairs.

'It is. They brought all they could and chickens are valuable. There is also a donkey tied up outside, how long he'll stay there is anybody's guess.' Her laugh sparkled across the hall as they walked down the same steps they'd sat on a few nights earlier.

'Eduardo's wife, Prada, asked auntie this afternoon if we had room to spare for a family of refugees, and of course auntie said yes. It is very sad, they have been walking for days to get to Madrid leaving their home and most of their things behind. There are lots more like them coming I think. I hope it won't happen to us.'

Tom felt relieved that there was no awkwardness between them, and slightly worried that he wanted to repeat that night's mistake, but he would control himself this time. Seeing her smile was just what he needed, it lit up the room and was infectious.

After having carried the Vaidez's belongings upstairs, they concentrated on running around trying to catch the three chickens that had managed to escape. They laughed quietly as the chickens continued to trick them. When they were finally caught, and put outside in the courtyard to run around the broken old cafe tables and chairs left there from previous years, Tom and Maria went back upstairs. The Vaidez's door was shut and the room was quiet; they must have fallen asleep.

'Goodnight, Tom. Don't stay away again,' she started walking upstairs to her rooms.

'Goodnight Maria.'

Tom watched her disappear up the stairs and went back into his room.

There were still gunshots from all over town at night, and the noise carried for miles in the stillness of the curfew. He was suddenly glad that he'd known Madrid before the war when the only noise disturbing the peace had been music and laughter. If he closed his eyes he could hear the guns tenfold, and he could see the broken body of Fabio in front of him, spraying him with blood and he could still feel the terror of the strafing coming towards him as he jumped behind the rock.

Before getting into bed, he went over to the window and looked down, and there, tied to a stick outside the pension front door, in the middle of the city, was the donkey, and somewhere past the rooftops of Madrid, was the ever advancing fascist army.

$$\sim 15 \sim$$

The following morning the sun was out and the sky was pale blue and beautiful. The night had been filled with the crying of the little child next door, and at some point, Señora Vaidez had decided to get up and take the little one outside to allow her husband a little more sleep. There was no smell of fried eggs so Tom guessed the chickens hadn't settled in yet, but not having seen, never mind eaten, an egg for many weeks now, the thought of eggs for breakfast at some point in the future excited him more than words could say.

The donkey was still tied outside and drew looks and giggles from passersby, and even though the possessions they had brought were meagre, it was still more than a lot of others in the same position had.

His last bit of his stale bread had finally acquired a white fluffy mold and there were no tomatoes left. With a sigh he descended the empty stairs to the cafe, hoping that there would be something edible there.

The café was bustling with neighbours and militia alike and Tom was sitting at his usual table when Eduardo stuck his head in the door and looked around. Once he noticed Tom was there, he came over and sat down opposite him.

'Auntie, un café a qui, por favour,' he waved his arms to get her attention.

'Sí.sí..' The brief reply came back from the busy bar

'I have found a car we can borrow, but I have to work in the morning so we can't leave until the afternoon.'

'I'll be ready. It'll be good to get away for a couple of days and even if nothing comes of it I can make something to write home about from the trip itself.'

Tom knew why Eduardo wanted to go, he wanted to find some secret communist base sitting on a few pots of gold belonging to the Republic, so that he could publish it and deeply discredit the communist party. If all the political parties could aim their mistrust and ill will towards Franco, this war would have been won already.

'How is Pabla and that sweet little son of yours?' Auntie asked as she brought Eduardo's coffee over.

'They are well enough. She wants to do something to help the war, but I told her that it's all very well young girls doing what they like these days, but if you have children, your place must be in the home. I'm not sure she agreed, but she adores the little one so at the moment all is well and calm in our house.'

'It was the way it always used to be. Now things are changing with the younger generation. Just take Maria, working and running around. In my days she would have been married with a couple of little ones running around by now.' She shook her head and smiled mischievously. 'I'm just envious.'

Auntie went back to the bar to serve another neighbour who'd come in for a coffee and a chat about the donkey. Maria was clearing the tables and smiled at him when she caught him looking over. Tom nodded back at her and turned his attention to Eduardo who finished his coffee and grinned at Tom.

'You should get yourself a wife my friend. All very well running around footloose and fancy free, but you will want children yes? Someone to come home to.'

'You sounded just like my mother then. It's not really the time to think about that now, besides, there will be plenty of time for all that later,' Tom replied awkwardly

Eduardo shook his head and got up

'Don't let this war get in the way of love.' He nodded over to where Maria was standing. 'It's written all over your face my friend. You should grab it while you can, it might not be here tomorrow.' He turned to the bar and shouted, 'Gracias, Auntie,' and disappeared out the door.

Tom was left at the table feeling rather confused, and with Eduardo's coffee to pay for.

The trip to the coast was set for the following afternoon. Tom was due to meet up with Bea in the evening so he'd asked Maria to let her know that he'd be away for a couple of days. He then sat down in his room to quickly re-write his article which had to be sent off within the next couple of hours and managed to get it somewhat more impartial.

He finished it and trudged along the cobbled streets up to Plaza Mayor and across the old square towards the Gran Via and the Telefonica building.

It was the 27th of October and the propaganda was still pouring out all over town through the loudspeakers urging everyone to do their bit. ¡NO PASARAN!.

At the Office of Foreign Press at the Telefonica there was much excitement as the first Russian tanks were just arriving by train, straight from the ship that brought them over from Russia. Heavy armored, modern, T26 Tanks straight from Moscow and out to the battlefields of Madrid where they would be more than welcome by soldiers who would now be able to fight back, and the words on everybody's lips was that, maybe now, the situation was finally changing.

Tom should have been at the press office either the previous night or first thing that morning, but he didn't have a night pass like most other journalists so he couldn't get there before 6.30. Anyway he'd only just finished it. Due to this very annoying fact, he had to wait for hours before one of the censors would look at his copy and then wait again for the telephone to become available to send the story through whilst another operator was listening in to ensure that there were no alterations to the censored piece. There were beds piled on top of each other along one of the walls where journalists that needed to get their daily reports through before morning slept whilst waiting for the censors to approve their articles and for the telephone to become free. It seemed to Tom, that if he were to continue reporting, he should really put in more hours and dedication to his job like everybody else. Finally he saw someone pick up his dog eared copy and started hoping that at some point he could leave the building.

It was well into the afternoon before his two short pieces had been given the go ahead and sent off to Paris. He knew that some of the other journalists got stories through by using slang that the censors didn't understand and so got information to their respective papers which would otherwise have been stopped. Tom never did, he stuck by the rules and he had already decided that if anything came of the gold story, he'd make an emergency dash back to Paris and hope that they would let him back in. The censoring on the Republican side was a lot better than what the reporters on the Nationalists side had to put up with. If you tried to send an unapproved article, you'd get a slap on the wrist and a telling off, but in the Nationalist press office you were likely to be thrown out of the country if you were lucky, but it was more likely that you'd get to spend a while in one of Franco's prisons before that.

Tom turned down an offer of drinks with some of the other journalists and started walking back to the Pension. The main streets were still busy, and for a moment he thought he saw Bea coming out of the War Administration building with a stern look on her face. She had disappeared into the busy street outside in seconds, and he'd paid no further attention to it as he slowly strolled towards the

Pension, deep in thought about the following day's journey.

He was just about to turn the corner into Calle Mayor when a hunched up man in a hurry pushed past him and sent him tumbling into the old walls of the Plaza Mayor. The rough stones on the walls scratched his already tired looking suit and he swore as he picked up his hat. He brushed it off and angrily shouted after the man to look where he was going before quickly checking his pockets to make sure he still had his wallet and lighter which he did. There was also a piece of paper which Tom was just about to throw away and continue his walk home through the grand portal towards the Pension when he noticed some writing on it.

He was sure that the wrinkled piece of paper hadn't been there before as he'd used his lighter only minutes earlier and would have noticed the note then. He could only assume that it was the person who had just bumped into him who had put it there and it was with some excitement he made his way further down the road and into a small square opposite the Casa Ciriaco where an anarchist bomb, disguised as a bouquet of flowers, had been thrown out of the first floor window back in 1906 towards the then Royal couple. They had escaped unhurt but twenty three well-wishers were killed by the bomb.

Tom took the note back out of his pocket and opened it. It was very neatly written in blue ink and Tom read the short message twice and by the end of it, he was quite disappointed. It was from his uncle, urging him to leave Spain quickly because it was no longer safe for him to stay. He rambled on about his grandmother wanting him to keep safe. What a lot of rubbish.

It was not signed but there was the name of a road and a capital S at the end of the note. Tom assumed that this was the old Priest's way of letting him know where in Seville his grandmother was. He also assumed that this was the priests way of making sure that Tom did not go to the authorities and tell them of his hiding place.

Putting the note back in his pocket he sighed disappointedly, he wasn't going to leave Madrid any time soon.

~ 16 ~

Tom had been trying to delay his next task all day and whilst preparing for it, he forgot all about the priest's note. He had, earlier in the day, promised Auntie that he'd build some kind of cover for the chickens out of the old tables that were just laying around in the courtyard at the back of the house.

He wasn't sure why he'd thought he'd be able to do it. He'd never built anything in his life before, but at the time he'd said yes, thinking how hard can it be? The answer was, very. His first attempt fell flat, and he thanked his lucky star that there were no chickens under it at the time, as very wisely, they were staying well clear of Tom and his hammer. Once he had decided that it was best to build it in the corner where it would have more support, it went better and even if it looked a bit home-made, it stood up on its own and seemed safe enough.

He was standing there admiring his work as the chickens picked around his feet when he could hear laughter coming from behind. It was Maria and the child, Justino, both standing in the doorway watching him whilst quietly giggling to themselves.

'It's a good little house for the chickens, yes?' she said laughingly as the child picked up some straw to put in the chickens new home.

'Listen, I never said I was any good at it.'

'It's wonderful. It'll keep them dry when it rains and we can all have some eggs.'

Señora Vaidez came out to collect the boy and thanked Tom quietly for making the chicken shed.

The chickens still didn't go anywhere near their new home, but they all agreed that it would grow on them.

'If there's anything else I can do to help, just ask.' Tom said cheerfully.

'We are going to take the donkey for a walk in the park now so he can eat something.' She picked up her son and took him back inside, leaving Tom and Maria alone in the yard.

'See, the chickens are moving closer. I think they like it,' she said

'Yeah. I just hope they don't get crushed if it falls down on them. I'd have to run far away from here.'

'Thank you for helping. I know they are finding it hard at the moment. I would, if I was in their shoes.' She walked over to the chicken house and looked inside. 'When are you off?'

'I'm going to Cartagena tomorrow, but I'll be back in a couple of days.'

'I know that. When are you going to join?'

'I don't know.' He didn't want to go anywhere, but couldn't bring himself to say so. He could feel the blood rushing in his ears and started moving towards the door, leaving her there. Staying would be asking for trouble. 'I'll see you when I get back.'

'Yeah. I'll see you then,' she said still standing there as he reluctantly walked into the house.

What was he so worried about. He was pretty sure she liked him, but he'd had been known to be wrong about these kind of things in the past.

Oh, God. There was only one way to find out.

She was still standing there, and looked up from having inspected the chicken house as he strode back outside.

'I'm sorry for the way I have behaved Maria. I'm sorry for the way I handled things the other night, I'm even sorry about the stupid war. But I'm not sorry I kissed you. - I'd do it again.'

She was standing still and quiet looking at Tom with the last of the sunshine in her hair looking lovely.

'The truth is that I can't stop thinking about you. I've tried but even with bullets flying past my head you were there. All I could think was that I might not see you again and leaving things like that....' He stopped talking and walked closer.

'I've felt that way since you first came to stay, but you are a difficult man.' She smiled

'Difficult, eh? So, what do we do now?' he asked as he pulled her closer and felt her heartbeat just below his own. He was totally sober when he kissed her this time, and it was different from the other night, this was all that mattered now, and he could have stayed there forever. After a moment or two, Maria glanced up towards the windows to see if anyone was watching them, and then put her chin on his chest and looked up at him with a mischievous smile. Standing there with a big grin on his face and chickens running around his feet, he felt happy like never before and he could once again feel her breath on his neck. That was how it had started.

'What do we do now?' Maria asked. 'I don't want auntie to see us here.'

'Well, it's still light. Do you want to go for a walk?' he asked in a voice he didn't recognise as his own.

'Yes, let's. I just have to tell her that I'm going out for a little while though. Don't leave without me.' She gave him a quick kiss on the cheek and ran indoors.

Tom slowly walked back in to the house and out through the front door to wait for her outside. The donkey was still out for his dinner and the street was quiet. He lit up a cigarette and he found himself unable to stop smiling. He had actually done the right thing and must remember to thank Eduardo. Maria came running down the stairs and they walked hand in hand down the cobbled Calle Mayor and towards what used to be the royal park.

The conversation that had so easily come to them in the past now changed into a slightly awkward silence as they strolled along past the old royal palace. The king, Alfonso XIII had left Spain in April 1931 and gone into exile in Rome as the second Republic came into being. His great 3,000 room Palace, loosely modelled on the palace of Versailles, and his hunting ground, Casa del Campo, both became public property. The throne and the altar had had its final day in Spain.

There was a lot of military activity along the Casa del Campo and northwards, but not quite as much as one might have expected for the defense of a capital city. They diverted their walk back into town.

'Did you see the tanks come in this morning?' she asked

'No, I was at the press office, but I did hear about them.'

'I didn't see them either, I was working.'

'The army will be very pleased as now they can actually fight back. Maybe things are turning around.'

'It feels a bit strange.'

'You'll get used to better news.'

'I meant us silly.' She laughed and lightly jabbed his arm.

'I know,' he said and turned to look at her. He knew her already. He knew that she liked to sing old songs that she'd learnt growing up and he knew she did it well, he knew what she liked and what annoyed her and how beautiful her laugh had been when Bea tried to teach her the Charleston on the landing. So much he'd like to ask but what was the etiquette here, the right way to go about it all. He'd been out with a lot of women but he'd never done it 'the right way'.

He lit another cigarette and smiled. To finish with Emilie was probably the first thing to do.

They walked along for a while and just as they were about to turn back home, the faint slow drone of Junkers could be heard. The planes had approached almost silently but as they quickly grew louder, people came out onto the street to have a look. There had not yet been a bombing raid on the centre of Madrid so nobody was in a hurry to get to a shelter, thinking that they would settle for the outskirts like they had done before.

There they stood in silence looking up to the sky where the large silvery green planes could be seen overhead, flying south east with the evening sun glinting off their wings. Remembering his last experience with these planes, every cell in his body screamed at him to run for cover and he grabbed Maria and ran back up the road, past the Palace and towards Calle Mayor and the Pension, as the first fascist bombs fell over the city of Madrid.

One after the other they fell, shaking buildings and sending people scattering in search of shelter, fearing that the next one to fall would be on them.

By the time they got back to the Pension, the planes had done their work and headed back home. They found Auntie out on the street together with Señor Vaidez who was trying to calm down the donkey who was wildly pulling his rope and Señora Vaidez squeezing their little boy in her arms. His large dark eyes looked at the madness surrounding him on the street, and no doubt wondering why his mother was crying so. She had kept herself under control when they had to leave their home and through the long journey to Madrid but the thought that they might have to leave again, that there was nowhere to keep her family safe, had been the last straw.

'Maria, Tom I didn't know where you'd gone. Thank God you went in that direction.' Auntie rushed up and hugged her niece, happy they were all safe.

'When it happens again, you have to run to the shelter.' Tom insisted. 'All of you.'

Nobody paid any attention to him. Maria tried to comfort Señora Vaidez and offered to hold the boy, but she wouldn't let go, and Señor Vaidez led her back inside.

All the neighbours on the street had congregated for an exchange of views and a general discussion outside Eduardo's house where Prada was making her views known, and Auntie, now secure in the knowledge that they were safe, went over and joined in.

'I'm going to head over to where the bombs fell and see if I can help,' Tom said looking at Maria

'I'll come with you.'

'No, Maria, you stay here.' Auntie turned around from her conversation with Pabla's old neighbour.

'Auntie, I'm a nurse. They might need my help,' she shouted over her shoulder as she tried to catch up with Tom.

'You look after her Tom,' Auntie shouted after him

'I will,' he shouted back and turned around to take Maria's hand and noticed Aunties knowing look as he did so.

They walked quickly in the direction of the smoke rising up above the buildings. When they asked a man coming from that direction, he told them that it was the Plaza Colon that had been hit. They rushed forward, following a stream of people moving towards the square.

The dust and smoke from the fires rising above the collapsed houses showing only shadows of the walking wounded trying to find their friends and family under the rubble in an eerie, dreamlike, state of shock.

People came running from all directions to help, and the militia was arriving together with makeshift ambulances to take the injured to hospital. Somebody had found buckets which were being filled up with water and carried over to put the fires out, and Tom joined them. Maria had gone over to where an ambulance had parked and she was seeing to the wounded there.

The shocked silence that had engulfed the place when they arrived had very quickly been replaced with wailing sirens and shouting as instructions and cries for help came from all directions. The dust clung to his face, and mixed with sweat as he carried the heavy water from the emergency tap to the fires. Then the call came to stop as the remaining fires would be tended to by the fire brigade and all attention to be concentrated on finding survivors. Tom left his bucket by the tap and stood there rather awkwardly, wondering where to help.

'Compañero, we need help over here.' The call came from a man a few meters away from where Tom was standing.

There were three of them, two older men and one, Tom guessed, about his own age, all in their shirtsleeves and with their caps pulled down low to avoid the dust going into their eyes.

They were trying to lift a large piece of heavy masonry which had landed on the legs of a small boy. The boy himself was not conscious but Tom assumed he was still alive.

'We can't drop this, so make sure you have a good grip,' the younger man instructed them. They all nodded solemnly and took a deep breath.

'Ono, dos, tres.'

And they lifted it up, slowly and carefully and Tom tried not to look down on what was below as he felt the concrete cutting into his fingers and held onto it for dear life. He could feel his grip slipping, and whilst still holding his breath, they slowly moved the masonry away before it crashed down on the ground, safely away from the boy.

The man who had called him over stroked the little boys face, and cried when he saw his crushed legs before once again shouting out for the medical staff to come and attend him.

'Gracias, Compañeros. What kind of people does this to little children?' He looked up to the sky. 'The bomb hit a queue of women, waiting to buy milk for their children for God's sake.'

A man came over, Tom guessed he was a doctor and he quickly called over a stretcher onto which the little boy was carefully moved. He was still unconscious and blissfully unaware of what had happened.

'Are you his father?' the doctor asked the younger man

'No, I am a friend of his family. His father is fighting in the north and I saw his mother being carried away from here earlier. His name is Bernardo Quevedo, doctor. Can I come with him'

The doctor nodded and they walked off towards the ambulances. As they left, the man turned around and raised his clenched fist in a red salut.

The other two men had moved out of the way and were standing chatting over a cigarette. Tom didn't join them.

Most of the injured and the dead had now been dealt with, and groups of men had started clearing the rubble away from the square. Tom joined them until he saw Maria coming towards him.

'They have no need for me now and they said the best thing I could do was to get a good night's sleep before my shift tomorrow.'

'Yeah, I think they have got all the living out now. Do you know what happened to the little boy with the crushed legs? He was brought over to your side about an hour ago.' Tom asked, hoping that she would have some good news.

'I'm sorry, his heart stopped as he was moved into the ambulance. Maybe it was for the best. It sounds horrible to say, but for a little boy with no family here and no legs, what future would there be for him?'

'That's a very callous thing to say.'

'Maybe, but I think it is a sensible thing to say.' She took his dusty arm as they made their way back to the street they had come from and away from the crowd of people still clearing up the Plaza. They all feared that this was just the beginning of what was to come.

'I was so happy less than an hour ago. I'd almost forgotten about... everything else.' She looked up at him

They stopped there on the corner of Calle Hortaleza and the Gran Via and they could still hear the sirens and shouts from Plaza Colon in the background.

'Maria listen to me, there is nothing we can do to stop this. It's like a wave hovering over us, just waiting to crash down, and this is where we have to be strong like so many others have had to be. - I met one of them when I was out on the front, there was this woman, Gabriella, who was the nurse, and her husband was in the regiment too. On my first day there he was killed and we had to tell her what happened. She cried like her heart was breaking for a little while, and then she pulled herself together, put her grief to one side, and got on with tending the wounded, because there was no other option. You have to think like her. When all this gets to you, which it will, you have stay strong and just keep on going. Keep going until we've won.'

'It's difficult sometimes when there is no escape. What happened to this Gabriella?'

'I don't know. She was pregnant and they wouldn't allow her to continue doing what she was doing, which is understandable. I expect she went home to her village, if it was still there. If not, someone in the regiment would have made sure she had somewhere to go. I think you also have to grab moments of happiness when and where you can because you don't know what will happen tomorrow.'

With her face so close, he lightly brushed her cheek with his hand, and put it under her chin, before softly kissing her. He was grabbing all he could.

They got back to the house just after curfew, but with all that was happening, they would not be the only ones back home late. The house was dark but they could hear pacing on the top floor where Auntie was obviously awaiting Maria's homecoming.

'I'm working early tomorrow morning at the hospital, but I'll be back in time to say goodbye'

'I'll only be gone a day or two but I'll still miss you. When I get back I'll take you out somewhere nice.' He said before he had a chance to think. There weren't that many nice places to go and for a moment he wished he could take her to Paris for a stroll along the Seine and a lovely romantic meal.

'We can go for a picnic in the park or to the cinema,' she suggested.

The door upstairs opened and Auntie's voice called down.

'Maria, is that you?

'Yes, auntie. I'm just coming up.' She turned and started walking up the stairs.

'Goodnight Tom.' She blew him a kiss.

'Goodnight. Sweet dreams.'

Tom went into his little room and got into bed.

Knowing she was only a few floorboards away, he found it difficult to sleep.

~ 17 ~

Just before the planes came over and bombed Madrid, Pietr was meeting up with Manuela, one of the maids working in General Carlos' house. She was a dreary woman; middle aged and dressed in a standard black dress she could have been anyone of a thousand maids. She knocked quietly on the door to his office whilst her eyes darted nervously around.

She had been working for the General for a month only, but knew him from before the war. Then they had lived in the same street and he had greeted her as an equal whenever they met. A true socialist, Senior Carlos as she used to know him, had been crucial to the Republican army in the early days with his knowledge of wars and battles, and as a lifelong Union member he flew up the ranks. How he'd got quite this far she did not understand. He'd hired her because he thought he could trust an old friend to keep his secrets, an old friend who should have been his equal, but was not, an old friend who should not be meeting disguised priests in order to save her soul, but still did.

Like Maria, she was torn between what she should do and what she felt she had to do, but whereas Maria stayed true to the Republic, Manuela became a fifth columnist who wished she could have her cake and eat it too.

Pietr opened the door and let her in. He offered her a drink, which she declined and a selection of olives which she finished before the conversation even started. Pietr who had not left his office for a couple of days smiled at her to keep her sweet. He treated her as a friend fighting for the same cause as he did not know if he would need her services again. If nothing else, she would hear things that he might want to know, and that in itself was worth a little effort on his part.

He pulled a chair over and sat down next her and he could tell that she was still very tense.

'Have you got the file Señora?'

She nodded and pulled a very thin brown file from her bag and handed it over to him with slightly shaky hands. He smiled nicely back and put the file on his desk.

'Thank you. This will really make a lot of difference to our cause and I promise that you will be rewarded properly when we win.' He leaned back in his chair. 'In the meantime, you should let me know anything you hear at the General's house or if you notice anything different.'

'He will know that somebody has stolen the file and he will know it was me,' she said whilst wringing her hands in her lap. For a moment Pietr regretted having invited her to come here to deliver the file. She could have given it to the priest and Pietr would have stayed anonymous, but he had wanted a direct line to the General's household. He trained people in these things every day, he could certainly calm this old woman and make sure that she stayed loyal. To him.

'Just act as if you don't know what he is talking about. You took all the precautions you were told to?'

'Sí.'

'He'll know it was me, but you will be fine. As long as you don't ever tell anybody about this, because if you do, you and your family will be arrested.' Pietr spoke to her slowly in his pigeon Spanish.

Having got the file and brought her attention as to how she could help further, he stood up to indicate the end of their meeting. He handed her a couple of extra food ration coupons which she accepted and slipped into a pocket in her skirt before leaving.

Once he had closed the door behind her, Pietr opened the thin file and smiled to himself. It had just been too easy to get it. He almost wanted to hand it back to the General and tell him to try harder, but instead, after reading it through, he tore it to minute little pieces and set fire to them one by one in the ashtray.

He felt a little sorry for Enrique, but this quickly passed and once there was nothing left of the contents, he put the file cover in his drawer to make sure that there would not be another failure like this. Pietr closed the drawer and looked forward to the next part of this wrapping up exercise. It would be so much easier to take care of it here in Madrid, but that would be to disobey orders. He was in an exceedingly good mood and he decided to go to the hospital to see Bea. Just as he was putting his coat on, the office shook and the muffled sound of bombs hitting ground found their way in through the walls.

~ 18 ~

The awareness that Madrid's civil population was now a target for the nationalist bombers sat uneasily with everyone. They went about their normal tasks with the knowledge that it would happen again. For the families that had not sent their children away from the city earlier in the autumn, the attack was enough for them to make that decision now.

Eduardo arrived with the car at midday and Auntie had packed them some lunch to see them through until they got to Cartagena.

'There are no tomatoes I'm afraid,' she looked at Tom and smiled. 'I thought maybe you would like something else for a change and I managed to get hold of some cheese, so you have cheese, bread and some lucky oranges. We're lucky that I found them.'

'Thank you very much,' Tom grinned and kissed her cheek. 'I am a little fed up with tomatoes.'

They got in the car, and as it started up, Maria came running down the street with Bea trailing behind.

'Hold on Eduardo.' He'd hoped that Maria would be back in time. It was only a little trip, but he had missed her since the previous night.

'Tom. I'm so glad we got here before you left. I wanted to say goodbye.' Unsaid things hung heavily in the air for all to see and Tom coughed.

'We'll be back soon,' Tom said not knowing what else to say under Auntie's gaze.

The silence was broken by Bea jumping in to the back of the car and slamming the door shut behind her.

'You're in luck chaps. I'm coming with you,' she said cheerfully.

Tom angrily turned round to face her. 'No, you're not'

'I got some time off. Doctor Zahen said I should get some fresh air, and I hear you're off to the countryside. You wouldn't deny me that would you darling.' She arranged her pale green dress over her knees, adjusted her awful blue stone necklace and straightened her back.

'It's not a pleasure trip Bea, we're working. Isn't that so Eduardo?'

'We are, but Bea can come along if she wants.' He shrugged his shoulders. 'It's not dangerous and it will be nice to have someone else to talk to.' Eduardo grinned at Tom knowing that he had counted on his support.

Resignedly, Tom looked back to Maria and could see in her eyes that she wanted to come too, but knew that her auntie would never agree to it.

'I promise I'll come back as soon as I can,' he said.

'Go. I will see you when you get back,' she replied waving them off.

And off towards Cartagena and a possible scoop they went.

'If we could just get out of Madrid quickly the journey shouldn't take more than a couple of hours maximum,' Eduardo said.

But it did take quite a while to get out of the city. The roads in and out had become fewer and fewer as Franco cut them off, and now there was only one way out and it was packed. There were rumours of anarchists in the villages along this road who wanted people to stay in the capital to fight, and if you were unlucky to encounter them, you were likely to be turned back. They had their own anarchist in the car, and he should be able to see them through any such trouble.

The road was filled with army vehicles going to and from the city and refugees with bags containing their worldly belongings and the odd donkey pulling a cart along with empty looking families in. That was the real face of war, the one that the politicians and the Generals didn't see. The sad leftovers of life clung onto with exhausted determination.

Finally they got out of the city and on to another road. Still moving slowly, but at least they were moving. After a while they left the Valencia Road and turned off to another smaller road with less traffic leading them south east towards the sea. Bea had started the journey by talking a lot, but had quietened down. Tom and Eduardo couldn't hear her very well in the front anyway and she'd gotten fed up with repeating herself. Assuming it was the same the other way, Eduardo congratulated him on finally getting together with Maria. Strange to think that he'd had only known Eduardo a short time, relatively speaking, but he had become a very good friend and the only one he could talk to about anything.

That's anything apart from his hidden uncle. Strangely enough, he was feeling sorry for the old priest now, even though he had considered himself no relative of Tom's and was generally a narrow minded sod. That was another thing to do when he got back to Madrid, he would go and have a quick word with him about that note. Tom had no doubt that it was just to get him out of the way, even the address in Seville was probably not right. And in the afternoon he'd take Maria for a pick-nick. How could he ask Auntie for some food without telling her what he needed it for. If Auntie found out about them she would probably not let them see each other in private again.

'You look very thoughtful there.'

'I was just thinking that I'll be very busy when we get back home.'

'That's good. Have you thought any more on joining up?'

'I don't know. I feel I should and if I joined the communists I'd more than likely be on the Madrid front which would mean still being close to Maria and Bea. I just can't imagine not being near them.'

'You can't just join a party on the basis of where they are going to send you. You're mad, and more than that, mad with no principles. Anyway, you know what I think on the subject, if you'd only come and work with me you could stay at the pension and keep seeing Maria. Maybe even marry the girl.'

'Will you look after her when I'm not here. Her and Auntie. I'd worry less about them if I knew you were keeping an eye on them. Because I will go at some point, I'm just not sure when.'

'That goes without saying. I will call in for a coffee every morning and check up on them.' Eduardo smiled as he slowed down for a road check.

Speaking in rapid Spanish there seemed to be some kind of issue with their paperwork. The burly soldier who had been speaking to Eduardo moved away from the car and pointed his rifle at them whilst ordering them to get out.

Carefully and slowly Eduardo, Tom and Bea got out and stood still next to the open car doors. The two soldiers were now just standing a few meters away from them looking towards the road where they had come from, as if they were waiting for something to appear. None of them could figure out what was wrong,. They were entitled to travel, their papers were real, and Eduardo was getting agitated by the soldiers lack of respect.

'What is the problem.' Eduardo waved his arms around and let of a stream of insults which rewarded him with a rough hit with a rifle butt and Bea screamed. Tom bent down to help Eduardo up, but got a kick under his chin which knocked him backwards and he could taste blood. He shook his head and tried to get back up but was again kicked to the ground and he could hear Bea scream for them to stop as the kicks continued to rain down on him.

Tom managed to get his arms up to protect his head from the myriad of kicks, but the pain was so severe he was already falling into a deep darkness.

He woke up with a jolt as a shock of cold water was thrown at him and gaspingly he tried to shake it off. Trying to move his hands he found they were tied to the back of whatever he was sitting on. His body was in agony and he couldn't remember where he was straight away. For a moment he thought he'd been captured by fascists, then he heard someone move behind him.

'Tom, Tom. What are you doing here? You should have stayed at home.'

He tried to look around to see who was speaking. The voice was familiar but his muddled mind couldn't place it. Turning his head to try to see who it was only rewarded him with a punch from the huge soldier who had appeared next to him. It took the wind from him and he fell forward over his knees, gasping for breath.

Right then, Tom knew who it was standing behind him. It was Pietr, and a sense of relief came over him. If he could only explain to him what had happened he'd let him go. Why wouldn't he? He'd done nothing wrong.

'Pietr. Thank God, it's you Comrade. I can explain...' Tom then realised he couldn't tell him where they were going without jeopardising Jose and Maria. '...we were just having a day away from Madrid.' The relief that he had felt a moment ago vanished as quickly as it had arrived.

This must be about the gold, because if it had been about his uncle they would just have arrested him and Tom couldn't think of any other reason this would happen to any one of them. Pietr must be involved in the gold theft and Alex's warning in the restaurant came back to him. What was happening here, where was Eduardo.

Oh God, what about Bea. Please don't let them hurt her. Pietr wouldn't do that. He adored her.

'See, it's not just your life you're playing with now. See your poor friend over there and what you have done to him. Dragging others into your fascist fantasies.' The fat soldier next to Tom grabbed his chair and turned it around to show him what the Russian meant.

A deep raw gasp was all that came out when Tom saw what they meant. He struggled not to throw up. Eduardo's beaten body was laying in the corner, his eyes wide open, staring into space. There was something unreal about it all. The pain was real enough, but it must be a dream, because it was too awful to be true. Tom could hear them laughing behind him.

'You fucking bastards. You fucking fascist bastards.' He screamed at them, trying to get of the chair and kill them. Still laughing, the fat one kicked the chair and Tom toppled over.

'You did this to him Tom. Not us. He could have been at home with his anarchist wife and screaming brat if it wasn't for you. Really, you have a nerve calling us fascists when the most likely fascist here is you.'

Tom could hear Pietr walking up behind him but he didn't turn his head. He pulled the chair and Tom with it back up straight again. 'Why are you here, Tom? You can still walk away from this if you tell us. If you tell me now. Otherwise, there will be no more Tom.'

Tom took a gulp of air, but kept his silence. He didn't know much about anything, but what he did know, he couldn't tell them whatever they did. He wouldn't tell them. It all led back to Maria and her family. So he didn't say anything and the silence hung led like in the air.

'You'll wish you had.' Pietr sighed and nodded to the person next to Tom and the beating began, ended and began again. The pain was so bad he would have told them anything but what they wanted to know. His mind was all fuzzled and his body so broken, and then they stopped. He had no idea how long he'd been there, but then there was another bucket of cold water to catch his attention and that's when they brought her in.

She had a red mark across her cheek, but that was the only mark on her face. Her blue eyes wide as she saw Tom and noticed Eduardo in the corner. Tom couldn't look at her, he was supposed to protect her but he couldn't move.

The soldier that brought her in was smiling.

Surprise and anger registered on Pietr's face and his eyes darted between the two of them even though she was taken at the same time as him and he must have known she was there.

'You brought her with you? Why would you do that.' Pietr didn't even look at her now and he put his head in his hands.

'Please, just let her go, she only came here for a day out. She knows nothing.' Tom's mouth was so swelled up that he was surprised he could speak. Pietr wouldn't hurt her.

'She knows nothing about what? You tell me what that is Tom, and I will let her go. You are in too much of a state now, but I will let her go. I'll even give her a lift back to Madrid. You have to tell me though, why you were going on your little outing.'

'I told you already. It was just a drive in the country.' He couldn't think straight, did they know where they were going? Had he said anything earlier. He didn't know. Pietr loved her, Tom had seen it at the restaurant and knew he wouldn't hurt her.

'You keep saying that, but nobody goes for drives in the country now. Do they? There is a fucking war on.'

He bent down and came within an inch of Tom's face. His blue eyes and red face were blurry through Tom's swelled up eyes but they held his stare.

'Let. Her. Go.'

'Unbelievable.' He stood back up. 'You bring her with you and then try to act like it's my fault. This is all down to you.'

He turned to the soldier holding Bea, who hadn't said a word since she was brought in, and he nodded at him.

There was an unexpected bang, the loud noise hit Tom's eardrums and reverberated around the room before it all went quiet. The only thing cutting through the silence was Tom's sobbing. He didn't know how long they kept him there for, all he knew was that she too was dead.

Someone cut the rope that held his hands tied to the back of the chair.

'Come on. It's your turn, but we'll do it outside. The boss has gone and it'll be quick and painless.' Tom barely registered that he had a birthmark around the left eye as he lifted him off the chair.

He wanted to die. Truly he did, he didn't deserve to live because Pietr had been right. This was all his fault. He had brought them to this place. He'd had plenty of warnings to leave.

As he was pulled out of the room, he saw Bea lying there on the floor, not far from Eduardo's dead staring eyes in a pool of blood. There was only the man dragging him along the floor left, everyone else had gone.

Outside the small hut Tom was pushed down onto the gravel and there he sat, shaking, with his head bent down waiting for the trigger to be pulled.

There was already only darkness inside him and when the bang came he welcomed it.

~ 19 ~

Perpignan, May 1937

Tom awoke with a jolt, and for a second or two he couldn't remember where he was. The train had stopped at its final station, and Aaron, who was collecting his things together, ready to alight, asked if he was alright.

Outside, the platform was full of travelers, but still he spotted his old friend Marcel's tall shape quite easily. Tom collected his small suitcase from the shelf and joined Aaron on the platform. Aaron was smiling, happy to be off the train whilst Tom felt detached, as if the scene in front of him was a play, or a dream. This was it. It was actually happening. Spain was only just across the mountains. He didn't know if it was fear or excitement or a mixture of both that made him feel as if it was all happening to someone else.

'Tom, my old friend,' Marcel came rushing towards them with a big grin. 'How are you? How was your journey. How is the lovely Paris?'

There was a short pause in Marcel's questioning, which allowed Tom enough time to introduce Aaron to his friend before they left the station. It was only a short walk to Marcel's house where they were spending the night before crossing the border the following morning.

Tom had started his career with Marcel, two lowly journalists covering cake competitions and other stories that nobody else wanted to do. Marcel was Parisian through and through, and he had shown Tom the delights of a Paris usually reserved for locals only. He'd easily adapted to Marcel's lifestyle and so a great friendship had begun. Then Marcel met Madeleine, got married and moved south. Tom had missed him when he left.

Marcel led them down the cobbled streets at speed. Past small shops selling pottery and wine, and past cafes where people braved the Tramontane to have their aperitif outside.

The wind was chilly now that the sun had almost disappeared over the horizon, and Tom was pleased when they stepped through Marcel's front door.

It was in this house he had recuperated on his return from Spain back in November. He'd had a broken jaw, broken ribs, concussion and a bullet wound in his shoulder, and that was on top of the bruises and cuts which had almost covered his entire body, but the most damaged part was his soul and that still hadn't healed. Once he was allowed to leave hospital, Marcel and Madeleine had insisted he stay with them until he was well enough to travel back to Paris.

Those long winter days he had spent talking to Madeleine in front of the kitchen fire whilst Marcel worked. She was the only one who knew the full story of what happened in Spain, and she was the only one who saw him cry remembering it. Now she greeted them with a wide smile and genuine affection, and he envied Marcel.

It was late by the time they finally sat down to eat and Tom started relaxing. Aaron awkwardly explained to their hosts that being Jewish he would just stick to the potatoes and vegetables, but what he didn't have in pork he made up for in wine, and Tom had more than he should too.

They had a very early start the next morning and needed to keep their heads clear for the border crossing and indeed for the rest of the journey to Valencia.

'We have helped a few of the guys get across to Spain, but some of them still get caught. British, French, anti fascist Germans and Italians.' Marcel leaned back in his chair 'It's just not right. These volunteers, most of them never having been abroad before, going to fight for something they believe so strongly in and risking arrest and a prison sentence for their efforts.' He shook his head 'Your country has a lot to answer for,' he looked challenging at Tom.

'Well, don't look at me. I don't agree with the Non-Intervention, and one day, when fascists are walking down Whitehall, Eden and Baldwin will realise what they have done. Besides, I seem to remember that the initial idea came from France.'

'Only because Britain threatened to rescind the Locarno agreement if we helped the Spanish Government. This country is very quickly becoming surrounded by fascist states, but instead of standing idly by, hoping they will be peaceful neighbours, France, and Britain too, should take action. Germany, Italy and Franco will just go on and on otherwise, taking what they want.'

Tom nodded. 'There are plenty of right wing people in the rest of Europe too. Last year's riots in the east end of London were only the beginning and I guess it will all come to a head soon. There's too much tension in the air. You can almost feel it. And the poor bloody Spanish still thinks that England will change their minds and help them.'

The atmosphere in the room had changed from jolly to glum and Aaron would have none of it.

'Enough politics for one evening.' Aaron insisted and so the conversation turned to Paris and her many distractions. The evening went on, good wine, good food and good friends. They lulled Tom into a false sense of security thinking that all would go well.

How wrong he was.

Once again they were on a train, but this time it was taking them into a country at war with itself. Brother against brother, sister against sister.

Earlier that morning Marcel had walked them back to the train station and waved them off in a jolly manner. There had been problems with the trains for the last few days and as a result theirs was full to the brim with reporters, writers, nurses and all other humans involved in war.

Luckily they had managed to find two hard wooden seats opposite an elderly gentleman and a young looking lad. None of them were very talkative, but the rest of the carriage was buzzing with excitement and various versions of The International, repeated again and again. At first it had made him smile, but by the tenth time he'd wanted to stick cotton wool in his ears.

The headache he'd woken up with was not improved by the bumping of the train jerking to and fro whilst making its way along the coast line track. The train was old and spitting out large quantities of grey steam which tumbled overhead and towards the back before dissolving into the horizon. The uncomfortable hard red covered seats had seen better days, but they were preferable to standing up.

Aaron didn't seem to mind them though as he slumbered in his seat. His head moved down towards Tom's shoulder and then back up again, continuously. If he started snoring again Tom would have to jab him. Really, the man did not seem able to keep his eyes open on any kind of transport. Tom put his hand in the inside pocket of his jacket and felt the outlines of the folded papers that would get him through the border controls. What if they weren't right? Things changed in Spain from one day to another. He tried to relax. Arthur wouldn't have given him anything but the best. What if they were too good? He was just being silly now. And nobody would recognise him either, why would they? Why would they indeed.

They approached Cerbere with the sea glittering blue in the fresh morning sunshine matched only by the amazingly sapphire sky. It set a stunning backdrop to the seabirds hunting for breakfast along the coast. It all seemed so normal. Shortly afterwards the sea disappeared behind the mountains and they went through the Tunnel des Balitres to Portbou and Spain.

The French train shuddered to a halt at the station in Portbou where they had to clear the Spanish border control and change trains. Armed militia men paraded up and down the platform, their guns held at the ready searching for unwanted visitors and Tom's nerves tensed. Slowly he got off the train and walked towards the border officials at the end of the platform. He tried to hide in the crowd of passengers exiting the train and somewhere he lost Aaron. He looked around but couldn't see him anywhere. The sun was picking up heat rapidly and Tom was glad of it. It would hide the nervous drops of sweat he felt trickling down his back and forehead whilst the crowd of people formed into a line. Suddenly he heard his name shouted out and his heart jumped. Looking around he saw Aaron jumping up and down further down the line trying to get his attention and moving towards him. Tom felt sick already and extra attention from the militia didn't help. Aaron re-joined him and the queue progressed slowly. When they finally got to the front, he produced his visa and other papers, all the while convincing himself that the official was about to call his bluff. The guards slumping on the corner of the desks would stand up and point their guns at him, his cover blown and Pietr informed.

The official checked his papers against a list and his photo against the original. Then with a bored look on his face he waved him through. Tom swore he heard him mutter something about 'another bloody journalist'. Once past the controls, they were allowed onto the other platform where the Spanish train was yet to arrive.

There were sun-faded red, and red and black banners hanging around the platform, and they ignited a spark of excitement in him. Just like the Republic always had done. Just like coming home. Only it was no longer his home, was it? How could it be, after everything that had happened.

Like Cerbere, the station at Portbou was raised up above the level of the small town below. Both the station and the town had been bombed back in February, and the train line to Barcelona had been cut. The fascists had dropped thirty bombs which had wounded fifteen civilians. One of the victims was a woman who died shortly after. She would have had a family, people who loved and depended on her, and they must be mourning the loss. And what would she have died for? Some cut railway tracks which were easily fixed by a few railway workers.

The platform was just big enough to accommodate all the passengers, but there were not enough places to sit down. The few benches that were there had already been taken so Tom and Aaron stood up at the end of the platform, waiting for the train to arrive. The excitement he'd felt when they first got through the border controls was slowly fading and the sun was getting hotter by every passing minute.

The train arrived just short of three hours late, and it was with relief that they sat down on the hard wooden seats in the front carriage. After ensuring all the windows in the carriage were open to relieve the heat, they finally started to relax.

The father and son who had been sitting opposite them on the French side, were now sitting at the far end of their carriage looking much happier and chatting away to the people next to them. Maybe it was just their company they hadn't liked. The train snaked its way along the track so slowly that one could quite easily have jumped on and off at any point.

Their first stop in Spain was Figueras. Some of the volunteers that had come to join the International Brigades got off the train and made their way towards the large 18th century Figueras Fort for a short initial training and subsequent dispatch to wherever they were needed. Then the train chugged slowly along towards the next stop, Barcelona.

Now, the Catalan capital of Barcelona was having troubles of its own. Not with fascists, but with internal political issues. There had been distrust between the Anarchist CNT organisation and the Communists for a long time and only a couple of weeks earlier a large number of Assault Guards, under the influence of the Stalinist Communist Party of Spain, went to the Telephone Exchange on Plaza Catalunya and tried to take it by force from the CNT, who had been in charge of it since the beginning of the war. The CNT members in the Exchange had fought back and the news of this attempted take-over spread throughout the city like wildfire and had resulted in five days of street fighting between the Assault Guards and the CNT together with their ally, the Marxist Party POUM. The cobbles from the streets had been dug up and used to build barricades, and the whole city had been on edge, keeping off the streets. A war in the middle of a war. The anarchists were in the end forced to accept a truce when the government sent 10,000 assault guards to the city to take control.

Through no fault of their own, the CNT and the POUM had been left defeated, and by fighting the government troops they had played straight into the Communists hands who increased their own influence in the government whilst discrediting the two organisations they hated.

That was less than three weeks ago and now there was a new prime minister of the Republic, the former Minister of Finance, Juan Negrin, who had formed a government with no CNT ministers involved at all. It would seem the coup at the telephone exchange had done its job. Juan Negrin was also the man behind the decision to move the majority of the Spanish gold to Russia.

It was late evening by the time they reached Barcelona and darkness had settled in for the night. Most of the passengers got off the train and those ones still on board were informed that they wouldn't be going anywhere until the morning. Curfew was only a short hour away and the remaining passengers were given permission to stay onboard. Tom's body ached from the long hours spent on a hard wooden seat and cursed Sir Arthur for not organising a flight for them instead of this long drawn out hell. He found himself getting in a worse and worse mood but finally managed to fall asleep. As the morning sunlight filtered in through the dirty windows, they awoke to the sound of new passengers boarding. There was a wide mix of soldiers and civilians, workers and suit wearers. Nobody was singing. The revolution in Barcelona seemed to have cooled down.

~ 20 ~

Valencia, Spain, May 1937

The hotel room was small and still warm from the day's sunshine. Its nicotine stained walls had cracks in places and the plaster still resting on the wide floorboards. Tom had stayed there before and finally having a little time on his own, he opened up the bottle of brandy he'd brought and took a swig. It burnt his throat and relaxed his nerves whilst he threw his suitcase on the bed and hung up his shirts. Taking another swig, he then opened the secret compartment in the case and checked that the spare ID and gun were still there. He toyed with the idea of bringing it along downstairs, but decided against it and closed the case. He hoped that the staff wouldn't think him interesting enough to go through it.

There was dust on the small table, holes in the blanket on the bed and a large crack in the window glass from bombings, but he guessed there were more important things to do and worry about than those details. His body still ached from the long train journey and more than anything he wanted to lie down in a comfortable bed and sleep until morning. But, he'd promised to join Aaron for a drink in the bar and hoped that it would lift his mood which hadn't improved from their night on the train. He quickly splashed some water on his face and after checking that his door locked, he went down to the bar.

The dark stained stairs with its faded and frayed red carpet running down the middle, curved steeply down towards the busy reception area. You could still see the faded elegance of a hotel that before the war had entertained people such as Panama Al Brown and other celebrities. Now they had to make do with a bunch of journalists and the odd government official. The reception desk was manned by the same somber looking man that had checked him and Aaron in earlier on whilst a couple of casual looking men were hanging around waiting for their turn to come. He could spot a journalist a mile off and they both had that look in their eyes, as if the next big story was just around the corner and they'd be damned if they'd let anybody else get it.

The calming benefit of the brandy was waning; his nerves were on edge and he needed another drink. The bar area was just around the corner from the reception by the revolving front doors. It was a run-down bar in a faded hotel. What had he expected? This was Spain now, suspended in time, holding its breath, and hoping for the best. He noticed Aaron in there already, sitting at the end of the long bar chatting to a redheaded woman. There was another handful of people at a couple of tables further away, but not a single person that he recognised, or anyone looking suspicious. He was just about to walk up to the bar and order a drink when someone tapped him on the shoulder and his heart stopped for a short second. He turned around, and there was Anthony Silke, the American journalist whom he had last seen in Madrid back in October when he'd done Tom a favour, or at least thought he did. He wasn't to know that he had sent him to a trap, or least Tom didn't think he knew. He had been the villain in a couple of Tom's theories on what had happened back in November, but then again, he'd had these theories about most people that were around at the time.

'Bloody hell, you scared the living daylight out of me.' His heart still beating faster than it should.

'I'm sorry, but I saw you just standing there and thought to myself 'Too much to drink again old man, you're seeing ghosts.'' He sounded out of breath and was thinner than when Tom saw him last in the bar of the hotel in Sol.

'Really good to see you. Not a lot of the old gang left here. Come, have a nightcap with me and tell me what you've been up to. I'm a bit tight already,' he laughed with a wheeze, 'but I promised I'd meet a friend and she hasn't showed up yet.' They walked into the bar, past Aaron and the redhead and sat down at a table by the window.

The shutters were closed with the slats down tight to avoid the low light from the bar escaping out and alerting a potential fascist bomber to where they were.

'So tell me, what happened to you? When you disappeared from Madrid, there were rumours that you'd hit a bullet, and then some new guys arrived and mentioned that you were back in France in a bad way, but no one had any details of why you left. The last thing I knew you were going to join up and fight for love and glory or some such like. It was just as you left that all hell broke loose and Mola came within an inch, almost literally, to have his coffee on the Via.' He took his Har-Bro cigarette case out and placed it on the table whilst looking through his pockets for the lighter to go with it. 'Once the front had come to a standstill, they even put a sarcastic "Reserved" note on one of the tables at Café Molinero for him. Good to know the Spanish haven't lost their sense of humour, eh?'

This was a reference to a comment made by General Mola in early October last year when he had planned to march in to Madrid on the 12th of October, the day of the Feast of the Spanish Race, and he had said that on that day he would have his coffee on the Gran Via. Luckily for Madrid, he didn't make it.

'Yeah, I remember you saying that you couldn't come with us because you didn't want to miss the big push. Think of yourself as a very lucky man Silke. I am the only one still alive from that trip.' Tom took a deep breath. 'How is Eduardo's family?'

Silke looked at him and bit his lip. 'Did he go with you?'

Tom nodded.

'All I know is that his body was found outside the CNT headquarters one morning. It sucks, the whole thing sucks. It was assumed that he'd been the victim of a fifth columnist attack. I knocked on their door a couple of weeks afterwards, but there was no answer. A neighbour said his wife had left and gone to Casa del Campo to fight.'

Tom rubbed his eyes and shook his head slightly.

'Poor Pabla. I have to see her, tell her what really happened.'

Tom remembered the laughter in the kitchen on his last visit to their house and his heart felt heavy with grief for all three of them.

Silke's eyes narrowed. 'Go on then. What the devil happened on that trip. What did you find?' He leaned forward with a hand under his chin ready to listen, but Tom wasn't too keen to talk about it. He'd rather find out about the soldier with the birthmark. The one that Silke had set him up to meet in Cartagena, the one that had been part of Pietr's gang. It was a link to find Pietr, as well as the girl impersonating Bea.

'We never got to Cartagena. Some soldiers stopped us on our way there and ... well, you know how it ended. Eduardo and Bea both got killed and I got rather badly beaten and shot. I don't know how I got back to France, can't remember a thing about it.'

'Shit. Bea too? I'm so sorry.'

'You weren't to know. Anyway, I'd be grateful if you'd keep all of this to yourself , including that I'm back. At least for now, give me a chance to sort out some personal stuff before I find Captain Pietr Alexandrow.'

'Yeah of course I will, but people come and go all the time and I'm really sorry to say this, but you were forgotten about within a couple of days. Bigger things are happening now, a whole lot of new journalists are coming and going, well established and well paid ones. Not to mention the celebrities that are doing their tours, especially now that Hemingway is holding court in his tower at the Florida.'

'Yeah, I know.'

'Hang on a minute. Did you say Captain Alexandrow?'

Tom confirmed that he had.

'You'll have some trouble finding him. Unless you cross over the line to the other side.'

'What, he's dead?'

'No, he's a fascist. Don't mention that you got this from me because it's not common knowledge. He'd been spying for Franco ever since he arrived here and just as he was about to be arrested, he made a run for it. He was with some priest at the time I think.'

'Are you sure about this Silke. It's not just some rumour doing the rounds?'

'No, I'm quite sure. I know someone who was there at the time and needed my help to get out of Madrid. Afterwards the security service went after anybody who'd had any dealings with Alexandrow and didn't deal with them too kindly. Anyway, I got this guy out of Madrid and up to Barcelona where he had some friends to stay with for a while.'

'Who was the priest?' Tom asked even though he was pretty sure he knew the answer.

'I don't know.' He shrugged his shoulders. 'He's unlikely to be alive now.'

The news saddened Tom. The lines between family and enemy were blurred. He'd tried to help Tom, to warn him and he wished the priest was still in his little cellar waiting for his time to come. He couldn't think about it now though. And Pietr a fascist all along. Well, well, well. That was unexpected.

'I did not expect that. Alexandrow an enemy spy?'

'So, is that why you're back? To find Alexandrow?'

Silke picked up his drink that had just arrived.

'No, not really,' Tom lied. 'Do you remember a girl in Madrid called Maria. Her aunt has the Café Rosa and she works at the hospital. She used to come out with us sometimes.'

'Yeah, I remember her. Spanish girl, quite proper? I haven't been in Madrid for a few weeks now though. Took my leave of her in April, after having spent what must surely be the coldest winter in my life there, but when the rationing actually started to affect me I knew it was time to go. So, you're stuck on a girl?' He scratched his head. 'The women here, especially the nurses, have changed Tom. They've all become quite hard, to cope with all the misery, you see. I'm not saying that's what's happened to your girl, just that you shouldn't expect things to be the way they were.'

'I'll remember that. I don't even know if she's still there.'

Glancing over his shoulder, Tom saw Aaron chatting away to the redhead still and turned his attention back to Silke.

'So where are you off to next?' Tom changed the conversation.

'I'm going up to Barcelona later in the week. I know it's a bit late in the day, but I want to meet up with someone rather important, somebody who doesn't normally give interviews.'

'Who?'

'Sorry, can't say. All rather hush, hush I'm afraid, but he is in the POUM. After all that's happened there, it wouldn't be good for my health, never mind his, to let it get out.'

'Oh, I see.' Tom said, but he didn't and quite frankly didn't care that much. His head was buzzing around Pietr's defection and the death of his uncle.

'I only managed to get in touch with him because I know his son and he put a word in for me. The guy I helped get out of Madrid. See it's never what you know, always who you know.' Silke smiled.

'That's very true.'

'Actually, that reminds me. You owe me some cash for the information I got for you before you left. I only remembered it because the guy whose father I'm seeing next week is the one that gave me that information. The one with a birthmark around one eye. Come on Tom, it's not my fault it all went pear shaped.'

'I want to meet him.'

'Fine, come with me to Barcelona. I'm here for another couple of days and then I'll give you a lift up there. Just let me get the interview with his father first.'

'I tell you what, I'll give you the money and in return you can clear that conscious of yours by letting me borrow your car for a couple of days. Then you take me with you to Barcelona.'

'I already have a clear conscious, thank you.'

'I think it's slightly tainted with the blood of a good friend, and possibly the lives of his wife and little boy too.'

'Bloody hell, you're painting it on thick. Fine have the car.' He threw his hands in the air. 'But don't lose it, or get it blown up will you, it's worth its weight in gold. And so is the petrol that's in it.' He shook his head and then smiled. 'Forget about the cash too. You don't think that I had any-thing to do with the whole set up do you?'

'No, of course I don't.' Tom shook his head although the thought that he might have been involved had sneaked into his mind occasionally. He knew that Silke was, deep down, a genuinely nice person. Well, for a journalist any-way. 'You're one of the good ones.' Tom said as he scooped up the car keys from the table.

'Where are you taking it?'

'Just to Madrid and back. I'll get it back to you in one piece though. I promise.'

'Is that supposed to reassure me? The last trip you went on didn't end all that well.'

'This is different. I'm just going to see some old friends.'

He could see Aaron's new friend saying goodnight at the bar.

'Who's your friend' Tom asked innocently as Aaron joined him and Silke. Aaron's face went red as he sat down.

'Would you believe she was a prostitute. She took offence that I wasn't going upstairs with her.' He laughed. 'How was I to know.'

'I could have told you that.' Silke said.

'She should have told me at the start. I would still have bought her a drink.'

'You'll learn,' Silke said as he got up. 'Thrash that car Tom, and I'll kill you. With a clear conscience. Night all.'

~ 21 ~

The following morning Tom and Aaron tried to get their press credentials stamped and registered, but this was Spain and everything was done mañana. They only had the car for a couple of days and didn't have time to hang around the press office to wait for someone to deal with their request. Instead they decided to go off to Madrid without registering, and for now, just rely on their visas.

Silke's car was an old black Talbot which he'd brought with him from France when he first came over. He must have had the luck of the devil as it had not been stolen, and a lot of valuable connections, as it was full of petrol. It was dented and filthy with dust, but it still worked. Tom felt a little dented and dusty himself that morning after too many drinks the night before and no water available at the hotel to wash in. Something to do with timings, and he should have been awake earlier if he'd wanted to get clean. The manager was sure he'd told them this when they checked in the previous evening.

Tom didn't care. He had a new lease of life and felt full of the joys of being back without having to worry about Pietr finding out. He would find him one day, on his own terms.

Smiling to himself, Tom navigated the old Talbot with Aaron in the passenger seat, out of the old and narrow streets of Valencia towards Madrid.

His good mood dwindled as he started to worry about Maria and Aaron's incessant whining didn't help matters. They had already decided to stop off at Maria's village on the way to Madrid and this was no doubt what made him feel edgy and nervous. What if she didn't want to see him. What if she had found someone else. The possibility of her having died by one of the thousands of bombs thrown on Madrid was something he didn't allow himself to think of.

What if his visa was found to be a forgery. All these things were going around his head together with the thought of driving back into Madrid, the same way he had left it that last afternoon together with Eduardo and Bea, and it made him a little tetchy.

The sky was a hazy blue and dust clouds from the vehicles in front made their throats dry. Aaron was taking in the scenery whilst on and off complaining about all the traffic slowing them down and still grumbling about the lack of food.

'The hotel doesn't look too bad, but no dinner last night and only bread and coffee for breakfast today? I'm absolutely bloody starving. And the bed was so uncomfortable that I hardly got any sleep.' He paused for a moment and then continued. 'I'm sorry. I know there's shortages and stuff but my stomach has always ruled my head. Jacqueline's cooking is, according to herself, rather awful and I think she expects us to eat out every night when we get married or get a cook or something. Better make sure I get some good snapps out here, eh, to fund it all. – I am so hungry, there must be somewhere we can stop.'

'You're giving me a headache,' Tom snapped. 'There are some Petit-Beurre biscuits in the boot you can have when we stop.'

The Valencia Road was now the only route into and out of Madrid. Back in February Franco's army had tried to cross the Jarama river and cut the road off, but the Republican Army and the International Brigades pushed them back. The battle of Jarama had cost thousands and thousands of lives but if the fascists had won it, Madrid would have starved, and the war would probably be over. As these thoughts filtered through Tom's head he remembered Mikey and Adam and wondered if they'd been there, if they were still alive.

The road was full of lorries carrying food and equipment to the capital and carrying refugees with them back out. He started to worry that they wouldn't make it to the village by nightfall. It was difficult enough to navigate here in the day time, in the dark it would be almost impossible.

A few kilometers further on they were stopped and asked for papers by a couple of Spanish soldiers. They looked at the documents for a few moments and asked them where they were going. Tom told them and the younger one smiled and offered a few words of advice.

'The village is a base for the XI regiment at the moment. You'll have to report to the officer in charge because you're not going to make it all the way to Madrid today.'

'Thanks. Do you know if the road from there to Madrid is still open?'

'It is, but I'd avoid it like the plague. It gets more congested as you get closer, full of lorries and it still gets bombed from time to time.'

They thanked him for his help and drove on.

The drive and the checkpoint had taken longer than expected and darkness was falling as they approached the village. There was a lot of activity and Tom would have preferred to avoid going into the actual village if he could have, but as it was, they had to go and report their presence to the officer in charge. It really wouldn't do to be caught roaming around in the dark and ending up shot as spies. It was also too late in the day to go to the farm to find Maria. He wasn't even sure she'd be there.

They drove into the village and parked the car in what would once have been the main street. They hoped it would be safe there. Soldiers were standing around the old church, chatting or cleaning their weapons. Their arrival didn't seem to stir anyone's attention. It could have been Tom standing there cleaning his rifle, having a laugh with his comrades, glad to be out of the trenches and safe from the shelling for a short while. Another couple of days in

Madrid and he might have joined up. And if he hadn't procrastinated for weeks. his two friends would still be alive too.

Not knowing where to go, they asked a ginger haired soldier where to find the officer in charge.

'That would be Captain Rutowski, he's over there, in the corner house. Ugly Polish fellow with a big mop of blond hair. His Spanish is fairly decent so you should be able to make yourselves understood.' He said in an American southern drawl. They thanked him and walked over to the corner house.

'You're sure they are going to be OK with us just showing up wanting a bed for the night?' Aaron asked.

'I have no idea, but there are not a lot of other options, are there?'

The Captain was standing with another couple of officers, talking whilst looking at a creased map on the table.

'Captain Rutkowski?' Tom asked.

'Yo soy él,' he replied in broken Spanish. 'Who wants to know?'

'I'm Tom Reid from the London Times and this is Aaron Prutzhanski, my photographer.'

Captain Rutkowski was very tall, and he did indeed have a great big mop of blond hair over which, his beret hardly fitted and there was an aura of authority about him, more so than a lot of the officers Tom had met earlier in the war. The other officers lit up cigarettes and continued talking amongst themselves, whilst glancing curiously over their way occasionally.

'So, what are you doing here? We have enough journalists sticking their noses into everything, delaying and distracting us.' He said in his broken Spanish with one eye still on the map.

'We are just doing a story on the civilian population and got delayed on route to Madrid. We won't get in your way. In fact we'll be gone by tomorrow morning, but we need somewhere to sleep tonight.'

'Sorry, I didn't mean to sound harsh, Compañero.' He turned his attention to them and rubbed his eyes. 'You'll need to stay here for the night no matter what so find somewhere to kip and the lads will show you where to get some food.' He blinked a couple of times and continued. 'Any questions? No. Good.' With that he turned back to the other officers and Tom and Aaron were left to hunt for some kind of sleeping arrangement.

They wandered back down the dusty street and Tom explained the conversation to Aaron.

'Food, eh? Always knew that armies marched on their stomachs and I can feel the bones sticking out of mine.'

Highly unlikely, Tom thought to himself. They spotted the ginger chap from earlier and walked up to him.

'Did you find the Captain?' he asked cheerfully.

'We did,' Aaron replied, 'and we were to ask you to show us where to sleep and where to grab some grub'

He thought for a moment. 'Come, I'll show you. There should still be some going but I warn you, it's very basic. I don't think any one of us has got used to it.' He walked back down the main street. 'Plenty of oranges though,' he added, 'and they are in season, so they aren't dried up as usual. Tell you what, I've never had so many bloody oranges in my life. I'm Johnny by the way.'

They followed him into a typically white washed village house where the heavy smell of garlic hit them as soon as they stepped inside. Not the kind you smell when you enter a plush restaurant in Paris either, but stewed and pungent. The room was small with only one table and a few chairs left by the family who used to live there. It was gloomy inside as the darkness outside got heavier, and there was only a small oil light in the corner to make it possible to see at all.

'Don't let him rattle your bones.' Johnny nodded towards the cook who looked rather menacingly at them arriving just as he was about to pack up for the night. 'Miserable sod. He has managed to keep us fed since we got here though and that's an achievement in itself.'

Johnny was right about the food. Oily beans and garlic stewed for quite some time by the look of them, was slapped in to a tin container and they took it outside together with some bread and a couple of oranges. They hadn't eaten since that morning and were starving, hence it didn't taste too bad. Mopping up the last bit of gravy with a bit of dry bread they finished their meal, and Johnny showed them two camp beds in the corner of a barn, slightly out of the centre, whose occupants were away for a few days.

They looked very well used and none too clean, but they were proper beds. Tom had expected they'd be thrown into a barn and told to make do.

The food had made him tired, but he was persuaded by Aaron to come for a couple of drinks with him and Johnny. He could tell Aaron was full of excitement and itching to get involved. This was after all what he had come here for.

Never having seen war before, and not having encountered his own mortality, Tom couldn't blame him. He had been the same not that long ago.

Having spent a lot of his time in Paris where even cheap wine is good, Tom found the alcoholic liquid presented to them in a porrón not deserving of the name. He wasn't a snob in any way, but this stuff actually scratched his throat as it made its way down to his unsuspecting stomach. Never having drunk from one before, the result was inevitable, but he did manage to catch a small amount of the red liquid flowing from the stem in to his mouth. The idea is obviously that you can share the drink without touching it with your mouth. Aaron seemed to have a natural talent for it and even Tom improved as the evening went on.

'Why don't you come with us tomorrow. We're going via Madrid on our way to Guadalajara, but you've got to be ready to leave at lunch time. It's only me and Harry here going and it'll be good to have someone else in the truck to talk to. What do you say?'

'Yeah. That would be great thanks.' Tom turned to Aaron 'Do you mind taking the car back to Valencia? My life won't be worth living if it doesn't get back there, intact and by tomorrow evening.'

Aaron was quiet for a moment or two before answering. 'No, of course not.' He didn't look happy about it and Tom felt a little guilty for sending him back. It would be easier and quicker to get to Madrid in an army van rather than a private motor car. Also, if Maria was still in the city, he didn't want Aaron tagging along. He'd be fine, he could make his way there easy enough in a few days' time.

'Are there still a lot of local people left here?' He changed the subject.

'There's still a few old people around, their sons and husbands off fighting somewhere. That's the way of most villages along this route now, all old people who don't want to move, because why should they have to, have stayed, and all the young people are either out fighting or have escaped further into the Republican area.'

'I used to know a family who had a small farm just a five minute drive north of here.'

'Sorry, I've no idea. There are a few houses further on, and I'm sure I've seen some people there, but I don't know any locals at all.'

'Don't worry about it. I'll have a look tomorrow before we go.'

'How do you know them?'

'I stayed at a pension in Madrid for most of last year and the lady that owned it came from this village. It would be good to know that she's ok.'

'Ah, so you knew Madrid before it was bombed? It's almost shelled to pieces now, and the bombs are still dropping. We were there back in November, when Mola's lot were about to come marching in, and I'll tell you, it was hard going, but the reception we got from the Madrileños was overwhelming. They lined the streets as we marched through, all cheering thinking we were Russians, which was amusing,' he laughed to himself, 'and then straight onto the battlefields. Talk about a baptism of fire, but by God we kept them out. Well, obviously not just us, most of the population was helping in one way or another.'

He looked up and across the square where someone was waving for him to come over.

'Johnny, the Captain wants you.'

'Sorry, guys, duty calls. I'll catch you later.' With a mock salute he got up and left Tom and Aaron on their own.

They had a few more drinks, and Tom managed to get Aaron out of his bad mood. Aaron still wasn't too keen on the idea of Tom going to Madrid on his own and asked questions about where he would stay so that he could reach him if he needed to. Tom told him where he could be reached in an emergency but he'd be back in Valencia in a few days' time. He hadn't taken Aaron for quite such an old worrying woman. Even if Aaron had come with him to

Madrid, Tom would have checked him into a hotel and left him to his own devices. They had only travelled down together because Tom felt that even Aaron's company was better than nobody's and Aaron was supposed to find his friend Cloudy. Tomorrow he'd find Maria, wherever she was. Part of him hoped she was well away from this whole area and another part, the selfish one, hoped that she was here with her family or still in Madrid. It would be awful to find her at the farm and have to leave her again to go to Madrid. He had to find this woman posing as Bea and to do that, he had to see Charlie. This time though, he'd come back for her.

Tom finally fell asleep well after midnight. Thoughts of Maria, Bea and Blackstone worked his mind and prevented sleep. The girl pretending to be Bea was obviously involved with the stolen gold and so was Blackstone. He'd find her and he'd make her talk. That woman and the soldier with the birthmark were his only leads to what had happened now that Pietr wasn't available for his revenge. Finally, he fell asleep and wasn't happy when, at sunrise, he was woken up by a dog barking madly at him. The mongrel sat itself between his and Aaron's beds and looked hungrily at Tom who was still recovering from his abrupt awakening. It also woke up a bleary eyed Aaron, who was in no mood for being friendly.

'Get the fuck out of here,' he growled in a hoarse voice at the dog. The dog went quiet and lay down between their beds whilst still looking at Aaron, but now with admiration in its eyes. It was most likely hoping for some scraps of food and Tom, knowing he'd not be able to go to sleep, sat himself up in bed and hoped the dog would go away. Aaron had put his head straight back on the pillow looking like he was going back to sleep. The dog, realising that they were not his best bet for breakfast, slunk away through the large gap in the door to try his luck somewhere else. Tom decided it was a good time to get up.

'Aaron' he said quietly, but he had either gone back to sleep or he was ignoring him.

'Aaron, wake up.' This time louder whilst throwing some orange peel from last night on his head.

'What?' Came the grumpy reply. 'My head is killing me. Have we got any water?'

'All self-inflicted I'm afraid.' Tom said with hint of smugness whilst handing a bottle of water to him.

'What do they put in their drink. My head would have felt better if it had been trampled by herd of cows'

Outside there were trucks coming and going and voices, laughter and shouting.

Time to move on.

The farm was not difficult to find, as in the daylight, you could see it from the village. There was no answer when they knocked on the old worn front door. Unwilling to give up they walked around the back, but there was nothing there, no people, no animals and the silence accompanying this emptiness dampened Tom's spirit. They went back to the front and knocked again, calling out if there was anybody there. He knew it was the right place, he remembered the partly collapsed roof on the corner of the L shaped house in which Maria, and Auntie too, had grown up.

'I'm sorry Tom. It seems you've had a wasted journey.' Aaron said as they knocked one last time.

'Shit.' He stepped back and looked up at the house. He felt frustrated and disappointed and he considering going in anyway. If nobody was there, what did it matter? The door didn't look very strong and he was surprised it had stayed on its hinges when they knocked. It wouldn't be a problem getting in, but what would be the point in that?

Still standing looking at the house, considering his new idea, Tom heard the click of a rifle being aimed at them from a window above.

'*Vete o disparo.*' A woman's stern and hostile voice came from an upstairs window, but even the rifle didn't stop Tom's spirit rising a little. At least, whoever this woman was, she would probably know where the others were. That was if she didn't shoot them first.

'Señora, my name is Tom Lancaster,' he said looking up towards where the gun was showing out of the window. 'I'm a friend of,' he struggled to remember auntie's last name and decided it didn't matter. 'Auntie and Maria's, from Madrid.' He assumed that even if they had left the farm, this mad woman would know them.

'I don't know you, just go away or I'll shoot.'

'Compañero, I've just come to see if they are ok. Are they here?'

'Oh, mio Dio, the idiot talks like he's one of us.' The woman spoke to somebody indoors.

This somebody's response in rapid Spanish reached Tom's ears and even though it was spoken too quickly for him to fully understand, he recognised the voice. Only a moment later, the front door opened and a smiling Auntie came rushing out. Arms wide open she hugged him like a long lost friend.

'Tomás. I can't believe it's you. Where have you been. Come in, come in.' She ushered them inside whilst shouting up to her sister to put the gun down and be quiet. This resulted in another outburst of Spanish Tom couldn't understand and a door slamming upstairs.

If Auntie was here, then maybe Maria was too.

She led them out to the back of the house where there were a couple of chairs to sit on. Aaron went for a walk, staying well clear of the house with Maria's mother in.

'You have to excuse my sister. It's only the two of us here and she's a bit jumpy, expecting fascists or criminals at the door always. I'm not sure what she thinks they'll do if they do come, we have nothing to steal and I'm sure they wouldn't kill us just for the sake of it. We're only two old women'

'You're not old, Auntie, you're in the prime of your life and looking beautiful as always.'

'You were always one with words,' she smiled. 'We were told you were dead Tom. Just like poor Eduardo. Oh, it was awful, his body was left outside the CNT building, and poor Prada, having to bury him. Nobody knew how it happened.'

'I know. He was a good friend, probably my best friend.' Tom still found it difficult to talk about it. He knew what had happened, he could think about it without getting emotional but he still found it difficult to speak of the details out loud. Therefore it was easier to just speak of it as if it happened to someone else. No details, just in general terms.

'So what did happened. We got a message to say that you had been caught up in crossfire and died from a gunshot wound.'

'It's a long story Auntie. Suffice to say that we were ambushed just a few miles outside Madrid.' Tom took a deep breath and continued. 'They didn't just kill Eduardo, they also killed Bea.'

'Ah, mi Dios.' Auntie threw her arms in the air in a gesture of despair. 'Maria tried to find out what had happened but could find no trace of Bea at the hospital and no answers were given to her anywhere else. She had just vanished. Then the fascists came so close to home, and the bombs were falling every day, and she was warned off asking more questions about you at the ministry.' Auntie shook her head. 'Oh, Tom. She was so upset.'

'Where is she now'

'She's still in Madrid and we haven't heard from her for months. It would be very difficult to get a message to or from Madrid, but I hope she is still ok. We're not happy about her still being there, but what can we do. We can't drag her here against her will. She's staying at the pension still, with some of the refugees and others whose houses have been demolished by bombs. The Calle Mayor is a mess with houses in pieces on the street and it used to be such a happy street.' She looked up at Tom and smiled. 'It is good news that you are here, a bit of our lives disappeared when we were told you'd died.'

'I'm going to Madrid in a couple of hours, and I will find her, and make sure she's ok. How is Juan?'

Auntie, looked briefly at the ground and took a deep breath.

'Ah, my poor, poor boy, he died in November, shortly after you left.' She left it at that.

'Auntie, I'm so sorry to hear that.' He was her only son, and all that was left of her own family in Madrid, and Tom didn't ask how, or where it happened.

Despite the smile she had put back on her face, she had an aura of sadness about her, like her life force had drained away with the loss of Juan and the café. He wanted to tell her that it would all work out, that all would be well, but that was impossible, lives destroyed could never go back to being the way they were, and he took her hand instead as she continued.

'I was made to leave Madrid. I don't remember how it happened, but the death of Juan, the constant bombing, the worry about Maria and what would happen if the fascists took the city got too much for me, and then the café got hit, only a small hit thankfully, but all of a sudden I was back here.'

'It is a beautiful spot.' He looked around at the small dry back garden with a good view of the Júcar river and the Moorish castle on top of the hillside opposite. 'A good place to recover in.'

Auntie squeezed his hand before letting go, 'I wish I could go back now, get the café back up and running. It will be done, but not until Madrid is safe, and I wish that Maria would come back here until it is.'

Tom nodded.

'I have missed her, Auntie. And I've missed you too. Once the war is over, we'll get your café back again, and it will be like old times. Maria learning English from some customer whilst serving and you up to your neck in paperwork.' He said, remembering all the times he'd seen her at one of the café tables cursing over prices and regulations whilst still keeping her good humour.

This brought a glint to her eye.

'I know we will. It will be like the old times again. Now, I'm getting too sentimental,' she continued 'if you are going to Madrid, I'd suggest getting a lift with the army boys in the village. There are many road checks and it will take you a long long time to get there otherwise, or you might just get stopped and asked to turn around.' She stood up.

'That is just what I'm doing. In fact I've got to go, or they'll go without me. You take care of yourself Auntie.'

'I will, and give my love to Maria, and her crazy mother's too. Tell her to come home. And you come back here too, until it all calms down.'

She stood by the front door waving them goodbye. Walking back to the car, Tom felt himself choking up.

~ 22 ~

Madrid, Spain, May 1937

Travelling with Johnny and Harry didn't avoid checkpoints, but they got through fairly quickly and reached Madrid without problems. The three of them were sitting in the front of an old army truck bouncing up and down every time they hit a bump on the road, and smoked some of the cigarettes Tom had brought along.

The destruction of Madrid was visible from a distance as they drove up the road he'd driven so many times before, Even though he knew that the capital had taken quite a beating, it was difficult to see just how bad it actually was. Smoke rose from various places that had recently been hit by the shelling that came in from the front line that was only a short tram journey from the city centre.

Johnny and Harry dropped him off on Paseo Del Prado and set off for the centre of the city to deliver their post. After that they'd be on their way to the regiment's new base.

Paseao Del Prado was halfway between where the British embassy used to be and the house where his uncle had been hiding. As he knew he would, he walked purposefully towards that house. His time there before the war, a distant memory only a few hours ago, now came back as though he'd never been away, but the city seemed more hostile, as if it had been swapped for another place where he no longer belonged. The houses and roads were in the same places they'd always been, and he could even see the Retiro Park across the road, but he no longer felt part of it. It frightened him to think that maybe that would be what Maria would think too.

They had many happy times there before, and actually during the first part of the war, when Madrid seemed to be the centre of the world. They had felt part of something big that would change the world for the better and that had made them feel so alive.

That was before Bea had changed and before he had fallen head over heels for Maria, and before someone stole some Spanish gold destined for Russia and killed his friends. Now it all just seemed drained and frail. Madrid had been buzzing in the early days with enthusiasm and surety that the Republic would win and a fairer Spain would emerge. It wasn't buzzing anymore.

It had only been six little months since he was last there but they had been six months of Madrid fighting for her life. The bombing of the Plaza which had seemed so bad at the time had now happened to most streets and squares but besieged and bombed she still held out. People in the street looked tired, weary and thin, but some shops were still open, what they found to sell was anyone's guess.

He turned the corner from the busy main street towards his grandmother's house. A queue of people spilled out from a grocery shop and down the pavement. Their bored eyes followed him down the street. To avoid anybody noticing his interest in the house, he walked along the pavement on the opposite side of the road and stopped to light a cigarette. He had no intention of going in, he just wanted to see it, to see if it was still standing. Whilst pretending to search his pockets for a lighter he noticed that it was indeed still standing although the windows had been blown out by the shelling, and the now battered front door hung on to only one of its hinges. He had no doubt that it was his uncle that had been caught with Pietr and arrested. They would have executed him somewhere public to make sure that people knew what happened to a fifth columnists, priest or not.

Two young women in uniform were coming down the street towards him and he quickly lit his cigarette and started walking.

'¡oiga.'

Tom's heart almost stopped when he heard the shout. It would be a bad idea to ignore them so with a deep breath, and what he hoped came across as confidence, he met their eyes. Their uniforms were dirty and the taller of the two had one hand in bandages.

'Give us a cigarette,' the taller of the two said harshly.

Not wanting to give them any cause for further action he obliged.

'Sure.' He held out the packet for them to take one or a couple each but clearly they wanted them all and took the whole pack. They were French cigarettes and she looked at the packet before putting them in her pocket.

'Where are you from?'

'England, Compañero. I'm a journalist.' He just wanted to walk on, away from these two militias that could, if they wanted, get him into trouble.

'I know some journalists here. Famous ones,' she said, 'from America'.

Tom just nodded in response.

'Are you a famous journalist? Like Senior Hemingway.'

'No. I'm not famous at all.'

Then she smiled, showing a glint of what she used to be before all this.

'Here. Have your packet of cigarettes back. We don't smoke.'

With that she walked down the street with her friend in tow and Tom started walking in the opposite direction towards the Gran Via.

Glad to be away from them he walked on towards the city centre; past the restaurant they'd been to that last Saturday night, still open, still looking like it was doing good business. Layers of sandbags piled on top of each other in front of doors and crossed tape on most of the windows set the back drop to the customers sitting drinking at the few tables outside.

After that last night in there, he'd not seen Alex again and he wondered what had happened to him. When he got back to France he'd find out. There was debris from bombed houses and mangled roads everywhere, and the tallest building in Madrid, the Telefonica, had been particularly badly hit. One could only assume that the censoring office had moved somewhere else for the time being. There were a lot of people trying to clear the roads to allow cars and trams back on it again.

He crossed over the road, nearly tripping over on the rubble several times, and then down to Sol which only the previous year had been crammed with people celebrating the victory of the Republic in the elections. Now that beautiful square was, like the Gran Via, bombed to pieces and lot of the houses around it only had their façades left. Large holes in the cobbled ground where direct hits had been taken from the shelling completed the picture of utter destruction. From the Puerta del Sol it was only a short stroll to the Pension Rosa and he walked towards it slowly, worried what he would find.

The scenery along the way stayed the same and as the Rosa came into view he saw the large gaping hole in the front, showing its broken interiors to the world.

It was certainly not a small hit and he was glad that Auntie wasn't there to see it. Next to it was the Pension which still stood. The glass panes in the windows were mostly missing or broken and they had been replaced with a variety of other materials and small bits of wall had disappeared, but it was still standing and he hoped that meant that Maria would be alright too.

He had left it thinking he would be back in a few days. That was last year. All his bits and pieces he'd had sent over from Paris had been left behind, together with all the little things one collects in life; the cheap typewriter he'd bought when he'd first decided to stay in Madrid indefinitely and some old books he'd found in a little shop in Valencia. He had not missed any of them, the only thing that had penetrated his guilt and grief for Bea and Eduardo, had been his longing for Maria and his hatred for Pietr.

He stood back and saw that Eduardo's house slightly further down on the corner was no longer there. Again, the outside walls and the floors had collapsed but you could still see the wall paper on the walls and the staircase going up to the bedroom where Pabla had put Alejandro to sleep the last time he saw her.

He had to look away before he made a fool of himself. Maybe Maria would know a little more about what had happened to them.

He knocked loudly on the door to the pension and heard someone coming slowly down the stairs. The door opened and he recognised Señora Vaidez. She however needed a reminder of who he was.

'I used to stay in the room opposite you when you first arrived.' She still didn't recognise him. 'And I built the chicken hutch for you,' he tried. How could she not remember, it wasn't that long ago.

'Ah, sí. I remember now.' She nodded to herself. 'The chicken house fell down, but all the chickens were stolen already.'

'Oh, I'm sorry about that.' What else could he say. Looking over her shoulder into the familiar hallway he asked if Maria was home.

'No. She is at the hospital almost all the time now and I am not sure when she will be back. The girl comes and goes as she pleases now her auntie isn't here to look after her.'

'Thank you, I will go up to the hospital and see her.'

He turned to go away when he remembered something.

'What happened to the donkey. Did someone steal him too?'

'No. He died of heart attack when the bombs fell,' she said and closed the door.

The hospital hadn't been hit as badly as the rest of the city. Due to its location in the richer parts of Madrid, where Franco didn't want to ruin the houses of his supporters, the hospital hadn't been as badly hit as the rest of the city. It wasn't ideal to see Maria here, he'd thought about meeting her again so many times and in his dreams they were always alone, not surrounded by the masses of patients that now took up every space available. He learnt from a grumpy nurse that over four hundred shells had fallen on Madrid the day before and the hospital, normally very busy due to the front line being within walking distance, was at breaking point.

Tom wandered along the corridors full of broken men and women wondering what they had done to deserve this. A nurse, looking curiously at him, pointed him in the direction of the theatre, where he'd find Maria and he made his way there. He obviously couldn't go in, so he settled down on the stairs nearby, keeping out of the way as staff and patients walked past. He sat there for quite a while, smoking quite a few cigarettes, as every creak or sound from behind the door made his heart jump thinking it might be her.

This is what he was doing when, from the opposite direction, she came walking up the stairs. Feeling her presence he turned his head from the theatre door towards the lower stairs and saw her standing there. She had stopped halfway up the stairs, hand over her mouth and a shocked expression on her face.

'Maria,' he said breathlessly as he stood up.

'Is it really you?' She looked disbelievingly at him.

Tom nodded, for a moment unable to do anything but stand there and look at her. Everything about her looked different to what he remembered, she was thinner and paler but she was still his beautiful Maria. Maria that he'd thought he'd never see again.

'Oh mi Dio.' She walked up the stairs slowly, her eyes not leaving his as if he might disappear if she glanced away for even a moment.

Tom, finally able to move, smiled as he pulled her to him and buried his face in her hair.

'I've missed you so much.' He mumbled and didn't care who saw or heard them as he held her shaking shoulders close. His lips rested on her soft skin tasting of home and he'd never let her go again.

A couple of partly patched up soldiers jeered loudly from a bench nearby and they pulled slightly apart.

'I can't believe you're here.' Maria dried her eyes and looked disbelievingly at him. 'I thought you were dead. Where have you been?'

'It's a long story. I didn't leave voluntarily, I would never have done that. I'll tell you everything as soon as we can leave here.'

Maria nodded. 'I will try to leave early, but it's difficult. Will you wait for me here?' she asked, her large dark eyes worried that he would leave.

'I'm not going anywhere without you.' He couldn't stop looking at her and grinned. He felt like it was the first time he'd smiled since he left.

'When I tell them you are here they will let me go straight away I'm sure. I have so many questions. Is it really you?'

Her hand touched his cheek as if she still didn't quite believe it was true.

They both heard her name called out from the theatre room. She let go of his hand and reluctantly started moving down the corridor.

'Don't leave.' She turned around and started running towards whoever it was that had called.

Still smiling, Tom sat down on the same step as earlier. His world had changed and he was no longer a stranger here, but a returning son of Madrid. Now that he'd found her again he wouldn't let her go. He wouldn't think of the fact that he couldn't stay in the city for long, that he was there on false papers and that there were other things he had to do within the next couple of days. He'd think about all that later; for now all he wanted to do was to take Maria home.

Her escape from work took longer than she thought and it was getting dark outside when they finally made their way from the hospital towards the town.

'What do you want do. Go for something to eat or a coffee? I owe you a proper date, remember?'

'Anywhere we can talk, and I don't like being in town, it's full of military and not very nice ones either, it's not like it used to be. I don't mean to be mean about them, they have kept Franco out of Madrid against all odds, but it's not full of Madrilenos any longer. We can go back to the Pension but it's very close to the front and it is difficult to sleep there because you always hear the sound of the guns. Also, Señora Vaidez is rather judgmental, but I have found it is best to just ignore her. Since auntie left she has taken it upon herself to be in charge of the Pension, and also, she thinks she is in charge of me. It's ok. I take no notice of her.'

She shrugged her shoulders, smiled and took his hand as they walked back towards Calle Mayor.

'I have so many questions for you Tomás Lancaster. I don't know where to start.'

'I'll tell you what happened when we get back to the pension,' he said softly, squeezing her hand, not wanting anybody else to hear what he had to say.

She nodded understandingly and he continued.

'I went to your village on my way here thinking that you would have had the sense to leave Madrid last year. I almost ended up being shot by your mother.' Tom smiled at the memory.

'Really. How was she? How was auntie?'

'I only saw your mother through the window where she stood with the gun, but Auntie was fine. She was worrying about you though.'

'I miss her so much, but I'm also glad she is not here to see what has become of the café and the whole road. How her Madrid has changed, but I will go and see her soon. My mother, I think, has gone a little crazy,' she laughed.

They walked along in silence for a moment.

'Someone stole the chickens you know.'

'Yes, Señora Vaidez said. Did you get any eggs from them?'

'No. None. And we could have done with them over the winter when there was no food.'

Tom guiltily kept the lovely meals that first Madeleine and then Emilie had prepared for him in Perpignan and

Paris over the winter to make him better. There had been no lack of food there.

'So do you know who stole them?'

'I have my suspicions, and told auntie we should demand to see the courtyard of Señora Martinez across the street. Auntie said we couldn't just accuse people and left it at that. Only later I'm sure I heard chickens in their gardens and for some weeks, they did not look quite as hungry as the rest of us.'

She pointed out the house of the alleged chicken thieves as they reached the pension and then opened the door to let them in. Señora Vaidez was luckily enough nowhere to be seen and Maria led the way up the stairs to his old room.

'I'm sorry but there is nowhere else we can go here.' She shrugged her shoulders. 'I took your room when auntie left as it made more sense for a family to be upstairs. As long as they don't get too comfortable because once the war is over auntie will want it back.' She almost whispered as they went in.

There it was. His room was almost the same as when he left. Apart from a pretty quilt on the bed and a couple of photographs of her family on the wide wooden windowsill she had kept most of his things where they were. His old desk had moved towards a corner but with his prized typewriter still there.

'I kept your things for you. People kept telling me you were dead and wouldn't come back but I never believed them.' She went over to the wardrobe and pulled out a bag.

'Maybe there are things in there missing. We had a break in the day you left, but they didn't steal much so probably everything is still there.'

He sat down on the edge of the bed and wished that she would sit next to him but she busied herself around the room and even managed to make a cup of something hot from the heat of an old oil lamp.

He needed some food but there wasn't any so he lit a cigarette instead. There were some biscuits and tins in the car but that would be back in Valencia by now and probably finished off by Aaron already.

Finally Maria had run out of things to do and sat down on the little chair that Tom had used for the desk. Darkness had fallen outside and even with the curtains drawn they only dared to have one small light on and their faces flickered yellow against the otherwise complete darkness. They tried to block out the sound of gunfire and shelling that came from the front line only a short stroll away from where they were sitting.

'So you can tell me now why you left. We were so worried about you and when ...'

Tom took her hand. 'I can't talk to you all the way over there.' He grinned and pulled her closer to him. There'd be plenty of time for talking later.

$$\sim 23 \sim$$

Tom turned over and watched her sleep peacefully next to him. He felt happy and content until he thought about the next day and the day after that. What would they do after tonight? He thought about this for a little while whilst trying not to listen to the sound of the never ending machine guns down the road in University City.

He had to see Charlie and get some clues as to who this woman claiming to be Bea was. If he could find her he might be able to find out the reason why it all happened, what had been the purpose of the murder of his two friends and why he had been spared. He had to find her because he also needed to find out where Bea's body was. Maybe she was just another pawn in some larger game but she was the only clue he had, there was no other way for him to move forward. He had dreamt of meeting Pietr again, for the roles to be reversed and revenge to be his, but with Pietr on the other side of the front line that would have to wait. At least he didn't need to worry about bumping in to him on the streets of Madrid. He had no idea how long it would take Charlie to get exit visas for both himself and

Maria. That was if he could persuade her to come to Paris with him.

Suddenly he felt tired and within minutes of putting his head back on the shared pillow, he was asleep.

'Maria, wake up.' Tom briefly sat down on the bed and gently shook her shoulder.

She opened her eyes slowly and sleepily and remembering the previous day before she sat herself up and smiled.

'Good morning. I slept so well I could.... What's wrong?' Her smile disappeared when she noticed Tom's serious expression.

'I think we are being watched.' He nodded towards the window whilst putting his jacket on. 'Come on, you'd better get up.'

He gave her a kiss before having another cautious look out of the window. The bright early morning sunshine streamed in through the gaps in the curtains and had woken him up ten minutes earlier. The two watchers in civilian clothes on the corner opposite the Pension had been easy enough to spot. The main entrance to the Pension was about ten meters down the street from Tom's window and therefore he could see the two watchers hiding around the corner opposite his room. They were quite blatantly watching their front door and Tom was pretty sure it wasn't Señora Vaidez they were after. Why they were there he didn't know but he wasn't going to take any chances. Not when he knew from experience what they were capable of. How they knew where he was and why they cared that he was there he didn't know. Pietr was gone and probably the gold too so what did it matter?

Last night he hadn't wanted to talk about what had happened to him, Bea and Eduardo the previous October. According to Auntie, Maria didn't know that Bea was dead and he hadn't wanted to tell her. He hadn't told her why or how he'd left Madrid back in the autumn and why, apart from finding her, he was back. She must have guessed he'd got into some kind of trouble because she didn't need asking twice to get ready to leave.

A few moments later they were both ready and Tom took her hand in his and went out onto the landing where only moments later they heard the door downstairs open.

'Señora Vaidez must have left it unlocked when she left this morning.' Maria whispered. 'What do we do.' She had not finished the sentence before she dragged him up the stairs towards the part of the house where he'd never been, where she had shared her life with Auntie. The two men downstairs opened creaky door after creaky door and quietly moved up the stairs towards the first floor.

This was not something Tom had planned for and he desperately tried to keep his head clear as the 'watchers' moved upwards.

Quietly Tom and Maria moved up the stairs slowly, slowly. The two men below gave up the quiet game and started kicking in doors to speed up their advance. Maria nodded towards one of the small balconies that lined the top floor windows, the glass now shattered by shelling and a variety of old blankets hung up to keep out the weather. These balconies had always had an abundance of flowers before the war, now they were empty and partly hanging off the wall where a bomb or a shell blast had ripped them off. They slipped behind one of the blankets with only one way of escape; the roof.

The men below swore loudly as they realised that nobody was on that floor and quickly moved on up the stairs to the next floor. Tom and Maria didn't have more than a few seconds to get up onto the roof from the balcony before the two men would reach their floor.

Tom helped Maria up onto the roof and the iron railings of the balcony creaked. The roof was intact for a few houses along and Maria got hold of a secure tile and pulled herself up. The early morning noise from the Pension had attracted the attention of some passers by who, not knowing what was happening, took the safe option of hurrying past quicker than they normally would have with their faces turned away.

Maria was now safely on the roof and Tom, worried that what was left of the balcony would not carry his weight much longer, managed to pull himself up and join her.

The roof felt much steeper than it looked from the ground and the ceramic tiles cut into their hands as they struggled to get to the other side of the roof bend in time to be hidden from view. A trail of blood from a cut on his hand marked their progress towards the roof bend. It could only be a matter of seconds before their escape route was discovered. Just as they got to the other side of the roof, loud footsteps running towards the window they had just climbed out made them stop and dip their heads to make sure they weren't seen. The 'watchers' must know where they'd gone and it wouldn't take them very long to get down to the street where Tom and Maria would have to find a way down. They scrambled over the roof tiles as fast as they could, trying not to look down, trying not to make a sound and trying not to fall down onto the hard courtyards below.

Pulling himself onto the roof had aggravated Tom's old bullet wound and his shoulder was now sending shards of pain through his arm and down his back, but the pain was somewhat softened by adrenaline flooding his body. The 'watchers' were yelling at someone, probably Señora Vaidez who must have returned from her errands and Maria's pace slowed. Would the Señora be in trouble for their escape? Before Tom had to convince Maria to stay on the roof and not to go back two shots rang out and instantly, as if time had frozen, they stopped and held their breaths. The silence echoed over the roof tops for some moments before a long tirade of swearwords from Señora Vaidez confirmed that she was fine. Too many bad things had happened to the señora the last few years for her to be intimidated by some whippersnappers with guns. Tom hoped that she would hold them off for a minute or two to allow them just a little more time to get back down.

At the end of the street there was a bombed out house with rubble piled high up the sides, which allowed them to get off the roof fairly easily and out onto a side street. There was still shouting to be heard from the Pension in the otherwise quiet street. It would seem that Señora Vaidez was not a woman to be on the wrong side of, and Tom was relieved, because for a moment there he thought she'd been shot and that Maria would turn around and go back.

Once down on the ground they dusted themselves off as best they could and walked fast down the cobbled street towards the poorer part of town. They avoided the temptation of looking back to see if there were any signs of the armed men and hurried along the street. They no doubt looked like the two escapees they were but they could do nothing about that.

Walking along in silence they finally found a small empty bar that was open and they went in. The sun had not yet reached the windows and the bar was still dark and smelled of sweat and cigarettes. The old barman looked totally uninterested in their disheveled appearance, he probably had a lot of guests like them these days.

Tom took a gulp of the drink he'd ordered and squeezed Maria's hand reassuringly under the table. Happy just sitting near her, knowing that she felt the same way and an intense fear that once again someone else's life was in danger because of him. What did they want? He'd never been a threat to anyone apart from the gold story but that was all over now. Wasn't it? Nobody would care anymore, and more importantly, nobody would listen to anything he had to say on the matter.

He should have stayed away from Madrid and Maria until the war was over, that would have been a true, unselfish thing to do. He should have stayed in Paris, allowing himself to drown in self-pity instead of thinking that if he could only get back to Madrid, back to her, it would all be ok. Even after a morning such as this, she still looked beautiful. Dust clung to her dress and wisps of hair had found its way out of the ribbon that she had quickly tied around it only half an hour earlier.

Now the Pension was no longer safe so she'd have to go back to her family. Whatever it took, Tom would make sure she was safe and right now, that meant staying away from him. At least for the time being.

'Were they after you?' Maria asked matter of factly, breaking the silence that had been wedged between them since they sat down and he nodded in response.

Last night had been so perfect that he hadn't wanted to spoil it by bringing up what had happened, because he thought there would be more time.

'You should tell me why they were looking for you. I assume that this has something to do with your disappearance last year, yes.'

'I promise I will tell you later. You have to leave Madrid, Maria. I'll make sure you get back home to your family. Auntie will be happy to see you.' Tom said whilst cleaning some blood from his hand where a sharp tile from the roof had cut it. It stung.

'You have only been back here five minutes and think you know what is best for me. Think you can tell me what to do? I'm not going back home. Also, how could I go back to who I used to be before I came to Madrid, before the war? The things I've seen and done, the freedom I've had. No' Her eyes showed her determination not to go back and Tom didn't feel up to arguing with her. As she said, he'd only been back five minutes, why would she listen to him. Back for five minutes after months of longing for her and now they were arguing.

'What's the alternative?' He wanted to add something sweet to the end of that sentence but the look on her face told him not to.

'If I cannot stay here, I am coming with you. You can take me to England with you. I'm fed up with death and despair,' she sighed. The anger had slipped away. 'I know I should fight on, people from all over the world are coming here, leaving their families and jobs to come and help us fight for a better world - and I just want to run away.' She swallowed hard. 'I just don't care anymore. Everyone I ever cared for have left and until you came back I had no one. No one. All I cared about was that we kept Franco out of the city. - We have kept him out.'

Her eyes were welling up as she continued. 'You know that when Jose died, my auntie cried for three day straight. Not moving or eating just lying on her bed there crying quietly and I could see her will to live drain away. She didn't care then about anything, she was in a world of her own where the only thing that mattered was that her son, her only son, had been killed. That God had taken both her husband and her son leaving her with nothing. I tried to help her, but I couldn't and I knew that if I did nothing, she would die from a broken heart in front of me. That's when I arranged for her to go back to the farm and I don't think she quite realised what was happening, because I know that she would never have allowed me to stay here on my own if she had.'

'I'm so sorry Maria.'

'In the winter there was no food and no heat, but at least the Pension still stood and we kept Franco out of here even though they were pounding us with bombs and shells and leaflets telling us what would happen if we didn't surrender. Like we needed to be told. I used to go to bed whenever I wasn't working just so I wouldn't freeze, and then the shelling, almost constantly and daily air raids by those bastardos.' She looked up and wiped her cheeks with her sleeve. 'I try to remember that there are a lot of people a lot worse off than me, like that nurse you told me about, but it's been so hard here. You are the only good thing that have happened to me, and I thought I'd lost you too. So you see, I can't let you go now.' She lit up one of Tom's cigarettes and shrugged her shoulders. 'Besides, even Bea left a couple of weeks ago.'

It took Tom a moment or two to realise what she just said.

'Did you just say that Bea left a couple of weeks ago? Our Bea?'

'Who else is called Bea here? Please.' She blew out a large puff of smoke, drained her coffee cup and made a face when she was sure the owner wasn't looking over. 'This is not coffee. We would never have served this.'

'It can't possibly have been Bea.' Tom took one of her hands in his.

'What do you mean?'

Tom took a deep breath. 'She died that same day as Eduardo, when we went to Cartagena...' He trailed off and Maria interrupted.

'What? Look, Tom. I know her, I have known her for quite some time and the last few weeks before she left she stayed with me at the Pension. Trust me, she's not dead.' She raised her eyebrows as if he'd gone slightly mad.

For the first time since Paris and the conversation with Sir Arthur, he started to doubt himself. He had not for one moment thought that Arthur had been right, and he had decided to grab the chance to go to Madrid for purely selfish reasons, but it was different with Maria. It could not just be someone who looked a lot like Bea because the two of them had been friends since Bea arrived and she knew Bea well. Yet Tom knew she was dead.

'When did you see her last?'

'I think it was about ten days ago. It was in the middle of the Barcelona troubles and I was hoping she was not heading in that direction.'

'Did she say where she was going or what had happened to her after Cartagena?'

'She said you'd made her get out of the car a few minutes after leaving the cafe and she'd gone away with another friend for a few days. Is that not true?'

Tom was starting to wonder himself what the truth actually was. He stared into space for a few moments whilst trying to make sense of what she was telling him. It was no use, everything was tied up in knots that wouldn't undo and he brought his attention back to Maria.

'Where is she now?'

'She made me promise not to tell anyone.'

'Look, this isn't a game.' His voice was low and intense as he tried to explain the seriousness of the situation to her. 'I need to know what happened to her and where she's gone because she did go with us that day, the same day and to the same place where Eduardo was killed and I saw her get shot. I need to find out if somehow she survived, and if so, why all the secrecy. I have been in hell for the last six months thinking that she died because of me, because of my stupidity. There is a memorial stone in the village at home with her name on it which her father put there because he thought his only child was dead.' He looked into her eyes. 'Do you understand now that you have to tell me?'

Maria looked confused and he briefly explained what had happened that afternoon in October and his meeting with Sir Arthur in Paris.

'Oh Tom.' Maria brushed a strand of hair from his forehead. 'I have no idea what you are talking about. Bea said she was asking around to find out where you'd gone but she got no answers from anyone. I did the same with the same results and in the end there was no one left to ask. One night she did say that I shouldn't give up hope and that you'd come back here one day when we least expected it. Looks like she was right eh?' She stubbed out her cigarette.

'Mmm...' What was happening here? Had he imagined the whole thing? He had been in a bad state at the time, but he was sure that he saw, on the floor of that house, her dead body. He could still see it when he closed his eyes. Her's and Eduardo's. His body had obviously been recovered, or rather delivered by someone back to Madrid, but there was no body for Bea.

Maybe it was all true. He didn't want to think that she was alive until he actually saw her with his own eyes.

'Right, if she's still alive we have to find her. I don't know what she's up to, but she might be in trouble. Also, her father is at home, worrying himself to death over her.' That was a slight exaggeration but still, he was worried. 'How come she stayed with you and not at her own flat?'

'She came to see me a couple of months ago, asking a favour. Once I found out what it was I wished I'd said no.'

'What was the favour?'

Maria hesitated. 'I wasn't at the hospital for a few weeks as Señora Vaidez was ill and I needed to care for her. There was no one else since Senior Vaidez was up the Casa de Campo fighting and the little boy had been evacuated to a family in the country somewhere so I was at the house most of the time. Anyway, Bea asked if I would look after a friend of hers who needed to recuperate somewhere for a couple of months whilst she was away. She was in love. Yes, again. I said yes as there was the room across the hall which was empty now that the family had moved upstairs. The Vaidez' old room, you remember?'

Tom nodded.

'I should have asked her why he could not go to the hospital, but when he was delivered to the Pension, in the dead of night by a couple of soldiers, I saw why. He was one of them. One of the Moroccans who have sold their souls to Franco. What could I do, but hope that nobody had seen his dark face on the way here and wait for Bea to return.' She shrugged her shoulders

'If she had not reassured me that it was for our side I would have handed him over to the authorities, but I didn't, and besides, he was delivered by our soldiers so I figured he must be ok. Then Bea came back and as soon as he was well enough, they left. She wanted me to go with her, but I said no.'

'So where were they going?'

'Morocco'

'Morocco? Nationalist held Spanish Morocco?' Tom repeated quietly and unbelievingly

'Yes.'

He leaned back in the chair.

'Did she say anything else? Like how she'd get there, why she was going?'

'Not really. I tried to ask her, but she always avoided the question and laughed it off when I tried to talk her out of leaving. She did say that she loved him and the Republic in equal measures and that she would come back soon. He's a descendant of some warrior family and comes from a small village just south of some town apparently painted blue. I think it was called Chefchaouen or something like that and I assumed that that's where they were going.'

'I don't think that you pretend to be dead to your friends and family, to go and see possible future in-laws. Let's ignore the love issue, she's been in love more times than I've had hot dinners. Why would she go to Morocco, where the uprising started, and is totally in Franco's hands?'

His face fell as he realised that he'd have to go to bloody Morocco. Tom was on one side so confused because he knew that he had seen her dead, and on the other side there was an enormous relief that she might be alive.

There was also a third side, showing itself more than the other two and it was extremely angry. How dare she let them think she was dead, the Bea that he used to know would never do anything like that. She'd be selfish to the end but she was kind hearted and behind her devil may care attitude she really cared about people. Or at least she used to.

She did change whilst he was still there and he remembered the sweet, but headstrong and spoilt girl, who had made her way out to Spain at the end of the summer after an argument with her father. Her laughter and incessant talking never changed, but there was a weariness in her eyes and her chatter turned more political and moody as the weeks went past, and towards the end of Tom's time in Madrid they had argued almost as much as they had talked. He knew that if there was the slightest chance that she was still alive, he would have to find her.

Right, the only way forward was to take Maria either back home to her family and go to find Bea by himself, or to take Maria with him. He knew she didn't like the former option so he guessed she'd have to come along. The next issue was more difficult, how would one get over to Morocco? Normally it wouldn't be a problem, but as the Nationalists has taken most of southern Spain and all kinds of vessels, all of them unfriendly, patrolling the waters in between the two countries, he could see more than a few obstacles in the way.

He'd have to go and see Charlie.

~ 24 ~

Charles had hardly changed at all in the months since Tom saw him last. He'd perhaps lost a little weight as his suit now fitted better and even though the park he used to take a walk in at lunch time every day did not really resemble a park anymore, due to piles of debris having been dumped there from the nearby bombed buildings, he was still there keeping his old routine going. Tom was not sure how good it was to have routines in his line of work, but then again he was no expert.

He watched him walking around the rubble in the sunshine like he was taking a stroll in Hyde Park. He had not wanted to go to the building where Charlie was now based, assuming that it was kept under the watchful eyes of several spies, all with different paymasters. This was Madrid, and it had been filling up with spies from everywhere since the outbreak of war the previous summer and Tom saw no reason why they should have left just because it was under siege. He expected that was an added bonus for a spy, to stop work getting too boring.

Charles himself looked after a few spies here in the city, Tom knew that as he used to be one of them. Well sort of, in fact Tom hadn't been a spy at all, more of a gossip catcher and even the gossip he had conveyed to him had been watered down to mean next to nothing. Charles must have known that and only been interested in what he had to say about Bea so that he could forward it to her father. What Tom hadn't known though, strangely enough was that Charles had been engaged to Bea. There could surely not be two more different people and he could see why it hadn't lasted, but he'd love to know how had it come about in the first place? He'd also like to know why neither of them had mentioned it to him. Bea was probably just embarrassed and Charles too stuffy and English to bring it up.

There were hardly any people around and after watching him for a while Tom decided it was all safe and walked up alongside him. Charles looked up and gave a brief smile.

'Hello Tom,' he said in his normal, uneventful voice. 'I thought you might pop by. I must say I thought you'd be here earlier.' He looked at his watch. 'Anyway, how are you old chap?'

'Not too bad thank you. How is Spain treating you these days?'

'It's not been boring, I'll tell you that. I think I'm ready for a few weeks back home now. The food is playing havoc with my stomach and we eat quite well compared to the civilians, how they keep going I don't know. The sooner they hand Madrid over the better for everyone.' He looked around to make sure nobody had heard him.

'I think defeatism is punishable by death.' Tom added smilingly. There was no point getting annoyed with him for not being on the Republican side. He was, like most of the British Government employees out here, sitting nicely on the fence drinking gin and tonics, knowing they could not be seen to take sides. More importantly, Tom needed his help.

'I need a favour from you,' he said

'Ah, this is after telling Sir Arthur I'm a liar, is it?' He looked at Tom with his intensely blue eyes. It didn't really bother him at all that Sir Arthur had mentioned their conversation to Charles, but he thought maybe an explanation was in order.

'You must be able to see it from my point of view. The last time I saw her, she had just been shot and was lying on the floor drenched in blood. What was I supposed to say. Oh jolly good, I'm glad she's well, send my regards? Anyway, I apologise if I offended you in any way.'

They walked along the path and Tom continued. 'However, there may well be a chance that she is alive' He said and told him about the events that had taken place that morning and what Maria had told him in the bar only an hour earlier.

'I expect you have someone over in Morocco already who can do a bit of investigating?' He asked hopefully and Charles laughed.

'I spoke to Sir Arthur only yesterday and he told me there would be no involvement of government staff on this one. Not in Spain anyway, and I assume that includes Spanish held Morocco.' His smile went a little wider when he saw the disappointment on Tom's face.

Well, that was it then. He had to get over there himself, and when he found her, he would kill her himself.

'Right. Well, if I'm going over there, I'll need transport. In fact, I have no idea how to get there, the water is obviously a no no. Due to our troubles this morning I'll also need new papers, Republican and Nationalist ones for me and for Maria.' He nodded towards a bench further down the street where Maria was sitting watching them. She smiled when she saw them looking towards her. 'She can't go back home now and we owe her at least a chance to get out of here. Besides I won't go without her.'

'It's a tall order Tom. I can't just magically get these things out of thin air.' Biting his lower lip he continued.

'I have to talk to Sir Arthur. And the bloody phone lines are down again. Well they were down before I went for my walk and I expect they'll be down for a while yet as mañana rules dictate. - Let me see what I can do Tom. Meet me here tomorrow morning, around 10ish. Just keep an eye out before you approach me as they do follow me around from time to time, again that'll be the mañana rule.'

He looked over towards Maria.

'She's too pretty for you, you know.' He smiled a little. 'There is a flat on Genova which is free for a night or two if you need somewhere to stay. There should be a few bits to eat and drink too. Nothing very exciting, but it'll keep you alive.'

He looked at his watch once again.

'I'm a little surprised that Sir Arthur sent you.'

Assuming that Charles' comment referred to Tom's family's relationship with Sir Arthur, he shrugged his shoulders.

'That makes two of us.'

Charles nodded and looked at him for a moment.

'Well, I'll see you tomorrow. Go straight to the flat and keep a low profile until the morning eh.'

With this he left and Tom walked back to Maria.

The flat on Genova was neither comfortable, well stocked or clean for that matter, but it was intact and better than spending the night out on the street.

Maria didn't like it because the only way out was the front door and the mornings events had stayed with her. Gathering up a couple of tins of food they left the flat and walked up to the hospital where Maria talked to one of the nurses who agreed to let them stay in her room over-night.

It was a small room in the basement of the house where Bea used to live and they heated up their food over the small cooker and settled down to their picnic. The evening fell quickly and they sat down on the floor with the contents of the tins in front of them. Hardly stunning surroundings, but she was sitting next to him, and he wouldn't be anywhere else.

Early the next morning, they were woken up by the nurse whose room it was, needing a cup of tea and her bed. After a weak cup of tea they left her fast asleep on the arm-chair and walked towards the park. The birds were singing in the trees, the sky a perfect blue and it promised to be a lovely day. The only two things missing were a proper cup of coffee to wake him up and some water to have a wash in, but it could be a lot worse.

Maria was telling him about one of her old friends from the school here in Madrid and how she had got a job as a secretary somewhere in the government, and she was still chatting away when there was a distant whining noise, turning into a roar as it got closer. Tom looked quickly to Maria just as there was an explosion nearby. She looked back at him and shrugged her shoulders.

'Shall we go to a shelter?' she asked calmly.

That distant whining could be faintly heard again as military motorcyclists with the sirens blaring raced through the streets and people mostly taking cover where they could, not having the time or the inclination maybe to go to the shelters.

'It seems like a good idea.' Tom said more sarcastically than he meant to.

'Let's go down to the underground station there.' She pulled him along and they ran down the street towards an underground station when the next blast came. Smoke and dust from the streets and buildings that had been hit drifted towards them from nearby side streets. There was only a trickle of people running down the stairs to the station, but it was crowded once you reached the central area.

The smell of hundreds of humans, all crammed into the small space available was unpleasant, and the two of them stopped very close to the exit.

'Charles won't be there during the shelling anyway,' Maria said quietly whilst looking around the station. 'The underground stations have been known to collapse with a direct hit but we should be better off here than on the streets.'

That made Tom wonder if maybe they would actually have been better off out on the open streets rather than down there, where, if there was a direct hit, and they survived it, they would probably not make it out. Anyway, they were there now and the shelling was still going on above, making the ground shake both above and underneath them and in between there was the whining and squeaking of the shells as they flew closer and closer before hitting their targets.

They stood quietly in the semi darkness whilst people around were catching up on local gossip and news and wincing when another shell hit. Silently they waited until it seemed certain that it had stopped for the time being and people, eager to get on with their daily lives, poured out of the station, happy that once again luck had been on their side.

They walked back up the stairs onto the streets where a fine mist of dust and Lyddite from the shells hung heavily in the air and they walked quickly towards the park, hoping to leave the smell of explosives behind. The streets were back to normal even though everybody knew that there could be more shells on the way and you would not know it until seconds before they hit, and they could hit anywhere and at any time. One of the houses on their route had taken a direct hit, throwing walls, plaster and meagre belongings onto the street and Tom hoped that there had been nobody inside when it had been hit.

Charles was at the park already, as arranged.

'Good morning Tom. Maria.' He nodded his head to Maria.

Tom apologised for being late as Charles led them to a more secluded part of the park.

'It's like this every day. How one is supposed to get anything done is beyond me.' He looked at both of them. 'Right, I haven't got a lot of time I'm afraid so I'll be brief. I have papers here for the two of you but they are however far from perfect so use them only if you have to. The same goes for the Nationalist ones which you have to be even more careful with. If you are caught with them here, you will be shot and there is nothing we can do about it. Do you understand?' They both nodded.

'On a good note, I'm coming with you.'

Tom was surprised. 'You are? Why?' He didn't relish the thought of having Charles along, bossing them about and generally slowing them down.

'Because Sir Arthur asked me to and that is all there is to it.'

'He must have given a reason. It's not that I don't want you to come along of course but who would look after your job here?'

'All he said was that if I got you and Bea back to England in one piece, he'd get me a transfer back to London. I would do a lot more than go to Morocco for that.'

Defeated Tom nodded, unable to come up with any other reasons for him to stay in Madrid.

'I haven't managed to get a car. Ridiculous as it seems, they are harder to come by than the plane I have organised to take us over to Morocco. The pilot will be waiting for us at this location here.' He pointed on a small well folded map.

'We'll have to be careful as this is rather close to the southern front-line and I'd hate for us to get caught by the other side. The car that delivers the post to us here from Valencia will take us back with him. He should be here by now, but the roads are so congested that it's anybody's guess when he will actually arrive. We'll need to find a car in Valencia but that shouldn't be a problem.' He looked at Tom. 'Any questions?'

'If we do find her in Morocco, how are we going to get out of there?'

'We'll worry about that when it happens.'

That response didn't fill Tom with confidence and Charles continued.

'Jolly good then. Normally the plane is reserved for politicians and such like. It should be exciting.'

Oh good, Charles saw this as some kind of an adventure.

He thanked him anyway for taking the trouble to organise it all.

'That's ok. We'll get her back home safe and sound. Now, off you go back to the flat. A car of some description will pick you up in less than an hour. I have to tell my housekeeper I am going away for a few days. I don't like her to worry.' He shooed them away.

~ 25 ~

Valencia, Spain, May 1937

'Good God, I only saw you a couple of days ago. How did you manage to piss people off this quickly?' Aaron asked whilst looking over Tom's slightly disheveled state. He'd had a wash in the house where they were staying the night with one of Charles' friends, but there had been no spare clothes and he was still wearing the crumpled shirt he'd changed into at the camp and his trousers had dust smears and a couple of tears from their roof top escape. The car Charles thought they'd be able to borrow had been requisitioned by the government and Tom had foolishly said he might be able to get hold of one.

He quickly put away the gun Aaron had brought from the hotel and managed a tired smile.

'Didn't you ever wonder why I was here with false papers?' he asked Aaron with a weary smile .

'Well, yes and I did ask, but you were never that forthcoming with any kind of information. If I remember correctly, one night at the club you told me to piss off and mind my own business. I think that was the last time I asked.'

'Ah, yes, I think I remember something like that now. Sorry.'

'Look, don't worry about it. You went in and out of your moods like a bloody yoyo.'

'Talk about the pot calling the kettle black.'

'So go on then, tell me why you are using someone else's name.'

'I haven't really got the time to tell you the full story right now, but suffice to say that I found something out last year that I wasn't supposed to and that there are people here, on the Republican side, that would rather I was still in Paris or dead,' he said whilst scanning the empty streets around them. 'Look, Aaron, don't mention to anyone you've seen me here. I'm heading south and that's all I can tell you. - By the way, is that Silke's car I see over there?' He said looking over Aaron's shoulder where the old Talbot stood, just waiting for them to use it. He knew Silke wouldn't have gone off to Barcelona yet.

'Yeah. You were right, he caught another cold and is laid up in bed still. I've borrowed it from him these last couple of days to take his rather gorgeous nurse out and about. Got my papers stamped properly now so I can go...' His voice trailed off as he realised the reason Tom had asked.

'No. He entrusted it to me to look after and I like the old guy. You'll just have to find another way to get wherever it is you're going, just steal one somewhere, I'm sure you'd know how.'

He said with his arms crossed in front of him whilst moving so that Tom's view of the car would be blocked. Aaron made him laugh.

'Oh, come on. I'll let you know where I leave it and you can take some pictures of the country side when you pick it up. It'll work a treat, you'll see. Trust me. Besides, his last cold lasted several weeks so he'll never know.'

'No. It's not going to happen.' Aaron insisted looking back towards the hotel for an escape.

'You know you'll give in in the end so you might as well give me the keys now.' Tom smiled encouragingly and held out his hand.

'Oh my God. Fine, but I'm coming with you so I can drive it back, ok. Where are you going anyway?'

'Probably best I don't tell you, but it's not far.' Tom lied, settling for Aaron coming along. He was harmless enough and he could chat away to Charles. That's two problems sorted with one car.

'I'll pick you up from the narrow end of Plaza Emilio Castelar at, let's say 7am tomorrow morning. That way I should be back by nightfall.' He looked around to see if anyone else was about. Tom's paranoia must be rubbing off on him, that was not a bad thing. 'I'll bring some clean clothes for you too. You look such mess we'll never get through a checkpoint without questions. By the cloak and dagger way you got my attention earlier I assume you'll not be staying at the hotel tonight?'

Tom shook his head.

'Well, I'd better get back to the hotel, I'm meeting Louise in the bar shortly. And no, I won't mention anything to her. See you tomorrow Tom.'

'Thanks Aaron.'

Tom went back down the narrow street to where Maria was waiting for him. He'd tried to get her to stay in the house with Charles and his friend but she'd insisted on coming with him to meet Aaron. The town was full with refugees from further south and nobody took any notice of them as they made their way back to the house. It was a mild night and the sound of a solitary duck quacking made him smile to himself as they walked along the slow flow-ing brown river in silence. It must have been a very lonely and indeed lucky duck as anything that could be eaten had been killed already.

The journey from Madrid had gone smoothly and there had been no more attacks of any kind as they waited at the flat for the embassy car to pick them up. The young driver had looked at them curiously but had asked no questions of Tom's rather shabby appearance or the reason why he had been lumbered with them and Charles.

The hours spent in the car with him had however been hard work as he had complained about his posting to Spain, the weather and the fact that he had a degree from Oxford and was still made to do post runs. He obviously didn't know who Charles was or he'd not been so vocal with the disapproval of his duties. Suffice to say that everyone were happy when they finally got to Valencia.

When he and Maria got back to the house he told Charles of the car he'd managed to get for them and with a 'Well done old chap' Charles went back to the study where his friend was waiting and shut the door behind him. Tom and Maria took the opportunity to have a quick bite to eat and an early night.

In the middle of the night, after they had finally nodded off, they were woken up by bombs being dropped on the city and the port. Staying where they were they tried to get another couple of hours sleep. Sirens were heard screeching through the city streets and the vague smell of lyddite and smoke from buildings on fire drifted in through the broken window on a soft spring breeze.

The following morning the three of them made their way to the car. From the city centre came wisps of smoke from some of the houses that had been hit and as they got closer they saw that the fires had not yet been completely put out. There were people outside some of them, neighbours and friends trying to find out if there had been any casualties or helping to move collapsed floors and roofs to drag out any survivors, or bodies, from the rubble.

The car was parked at the narrow end of the triangular square just as Aaron had said it would be. Aaron himself was standing on the pavement tapping his fingers on the roof as he waited. Tom, Maria and Charles walked confidently past the middle of the square locally referred to as La Tortada due to it being very recently elevated by four meters to allow flower sellers to set up their stalls underneath. These days it was more used as a shelter from enemy bombs and shelling. It didn't seem deep or sturdy enough to offer much protection from neither.

They got into the car and after a brief introduction they were on their way. It didn't take them long to exit the city and onto a small white road going south where the car kicked up a cloud of dust behind them. The birds were singing in the morning sunshine and the smell of wild rosemary, which grew along the roadside, perfumed the air.

Once out of the city, Aaron stopped the car so that they could get changed. Also, Tom wanted to show him on the map where they were going. It was a beautiful spot to stop, next to some very old and gnarly olive trees with the distant sea to one side and overhanging imposing mountains on the other. Tom took a deep breath and prepared himself for the wrath of Aaron as he showed him where they wanted to be by the end of the day.

'I'm sorry? I must be going mad because I could have sworn that yesterday, when I agreed to take you, you said it was a very short trip and that I would be back by the evening.' Aaron did not look happy and Maria sat back down in the car waiting for an argument to start. Charles had disappeared behind a tree for some personal business.

'You still could be, if you drive fast.' Tom grinned carefully.

'I could be bloody Louis Chiron and I wouldn't be back in Valencia before tomorrow evening at least. That's it, I'm going back now. Come on, get back in the car.' He tried to shoo Tom back in the car and Maria quickly pulled her feet into it as he came up and shut her door.

'I have no intention of going back to Valencia.' Tom said laughingly moving quickly away from his friend. 'You'll just have to leave me here.'

'Yeah, you laugh because I may well do that.' He turned around and got behind the wheel and started the engine as Tom opened Maria's door and helped her out in an over dramatic way and shut the door behind her.

'Why is he leaving?' she asked whilst throwing a confused look at Aaron who was trying to turn the car around and get it back on the road.

'He won't, he won't leave us here.' Tom said more confident than he felt as Aaron got the car back on the road and started driving back down the road they'd come from.

'I think he is,' Maria said as she went to sit down by the olive tree. 'So, what do we do now?'

'Funny, I was sure he wouldn't leave. We'll be fine though, we'll find someone who'll give us a lift.'

He felt slightly less confident of that as they looked around and the only sign of life on the road was the dust cloud kicked up by Aaron as he sped along the road back towards Valencia.

'What is going on?' Charles came back from behind the tree. 'Where's the car?'

'It would seem that Aaron had urgent business else-where.'

He didn't want to mention to Charles that he'd shown Aaron where they were heading. He'd be convinced that he was a spy of some sort.

'He can't just leave us here surely. It's midday. We'll die in the sun or from thirst.'

'You're the one who insisted on coming along. If you walk back towards Valencia you can probably catch a lift somewhere.

'I will do no such thing. No. We'll just have to walk along and hope that somebody stops and offers us a lift.'

'Come on.' Tom held out his hand to help Maria up from the grass. 'We should probably start walking.'

The only response he got from her was a deep sigh and a despondent look as she took his hand and got back up on her feet.

'How far is it?' she asked.

'If we'd been in the car, I think we'd have been there by this evening but maybe not until tomorrow morning if the roads were bad. Walking, it will obviously take a lot longer.'

'Oh good.'

'Sorry. It's not too late for you to go back home you know. If we go back up the road we came down, we should be able to get you a lift back towards Madrid. It will be eas-ier getting a lift inland than down south.'

'You know I'm not going back so why are you trying to get rid of me?' she asked glaringly.

'I'm not, you know I'm not. I just don't want you to do something you'll regret later.'

'Well, now that subject is closed.'

'Ok.'

They walked along the dusty road in silence. Charles led the way in a full suit and looked upon Tom with pity when he suggested he took his jacket off. 'Standards Tom. Standards.'

Tom was starting to have doubts about them actually reaching the airfield at all and had no idea how long the plane would be there waiting for them. There was no point asking Charles about it because he wouldn't know either.

He had not expected Aaron to drive off like that, but he was hopeful that there maybe somebody further on that would be willing to give them a lift. He had some French money to pay them for their troubles. They were still on a relatively small road but at some point this would join up with the main road going south. If anybody asked, they would stick with the journalistic reasons they had already decided on, reporting on the human aspect of the war, but their car had broken down a few miles back. That was him and Maria sorted out, what the hell was he supposed to say that Charles was doing with them.

It had been over two hours since Aaron had left and even though their feet had started hurting and the sun was at its highest Maria's mood had improved and they walked along chatting of little things. There had been a couple of cars and one army lorry going past them but none of them had stopped. If anyone of them felt unhappy about the situation they found themselves in, they kept quiet about it.

'Aha, there's another car coming down there.' Maria turned around and pointed.

'Let's just wait and see if it is an army one before we try to stop it,' Charles said cautiously.

'It looks like your friend's car.'

Tom squinted his eyes a little to get a better view of the approaching vehicle. It was indeed Silke's car coming towards them with Aaron in the driving seat and a wave of relief came over him. He slowed down as he approached and came to a halt by the side of the road, covering the three of them in white dust.

'I'm still not happy with you Tom. I expect a lot of favours for this one,' he said from the car window.

'See Aaron, I knew you wouldn't let the side down.'

'Sod the side, this is me collecting brownie points for later, and you better remember it.'

He got out of the car and threw a bag at Tom containing some of the clothes from his abandoned hotel room, and having spent the night with Louise, he'd stolen some of her clothes for Maria. Not having actually ever met Maria he'd taken a chance on her size and she near enough drowned in them. Not caring about the clothes, just relieved that she wouldn't have to walk the whole way, she quickly changed back to her old clothes.

'I should have realised they'd be too big. Louise used to be in the Polish Athletics Team. What a woman.' This was said very matter of factly and looking at Aaron's rather large frame Tom couldn't help a little snigger.

'You dirty sod. Poor Jacqueline,' he said whilst trying not to laugh

'Who is Jacqueline?' Maria asked.

Tom waited for Aaron to answer, but he didn't. He just had an indignant look on his face and started going back to the car.

'It's his fiancée.' he explained. 'She's still in Paris.'

'Oh.' She shook her head whilst getting back in the car. 'You should be ashamed of yourself. What if she did the same?'

'That's different,' he started the car up. 'I'm a man. It's expected of me'

Tom just shook his head when Maria looked at him to confirm that it was not something that he'd ever do. Aaron raised his eyebrows at him and started the engine.

'Can we stop this conversation now and be on our way. We've lost time already.' Charles said angrily.

It was the first time Tom had seen him show any kind of emotion. Maybe this trip would be good for him after all.

The sun had reached its highest point and as they drove on the fragile conversation died out.

A few miles down the uneven road they were stopped by a checkpoint, and after having queued behind another vehicle which they had taken their time over, it was a surprise and a relief that they let them through with just a glance at their papers and a couple of quick questions about where they were going.

One of the soldiers was very young and had a red neckerchief which had seen better days and a new looking rifle over his shoulder. He glanced back over his shoulder towards a Spanish man in slightly tattered civilian clothes leaning on an old pine tree smoking a cigarette, watching them through narrow eyes.

The soldier warned them to not drive too far as the front line kept on changing all the time and it was very easy to get lost. They assured him that they would take care and he sent them on their way. Tom was surprised and relived that they had got through it so quickly when the two vehicles in front of them had received the full treatment. It would be silly to ponder too long on why things went easier than expected today when you didn't know what tomorrow would bring.

After the checkpoint, the road was so bad that they would never reach the airfield before nightfall, and so they decided to stop somewhere for the night. Aaron was telling him about the journey back towards Valencia in great detail and how he'd got to the outskirts and felt guilty for leaving them in the sticks because of something that was indeed rather petty. Tom wasn't listening to him however as he was keeping an eye out for somewhere to stay that had a proper bed. He didn't want to spend the night in the car and he tried to stifle a yawn as they drove into a small town.

There were white houses along the main street which had once had little window boxes outside filled with bright flowers or herbs brightening the otherwise dreary street. You could see the sea in the distance and Tom assumed there would be militia or some such guarding the shoreline from seafaring fascists.

'There's a Pension just there' Tom said excitedly and pointed at a large white house down the road with an old "Pension La Casa del Mar" sign dangling precariously from an old iron bracket.

'What are the chances they are still open?' Aaron asked sarcastically.

'We'll just have to see, won't we.' Tom answered annoyed. 'It's probably our only chance to sleep in a bed.'

'I agree with Tom. I'm sure they'll let us stay the night.' Charles agreed from the front seat.

'I didn't say I didn't want to sleep in a bed.' Aaron said. 'Just that it was unlikely that they are still open.'

There were a few people wandering around the main street, mostly women and children as their husbands, fathers and brothers were away fighting. There were also militas about and being strangers in town the four of them automatically drew their attention.

The front door to the Pension was open and they walked in and rang the small golden bell on the front desk. It was an old desk and there was dust on the room keys which hung on gold coloured pegs behind it. The building itself looked like it would have looked before the war with unbroken glass in the windows and a vase of flowers on the table, but there was a distinctly musty smell overhanging the old furniture that cluttered the reception area.

There was no sign of anybody having heard them arrive so they rang the bell again, and finally an old woman came out from another room at the end of a long corridor. Her hair pinned back and still dark but with large streaks of grey cutting through it. She wore an old faded black dress and it looked like they had woken her up as she shuffled slowly along the corridor towards them.

'Sí, puede le ayudo, Compañero' She looked at them with dark curious eyes.

'Yes, Señora. We were wondering if you have rooms available.'

'We are not open anymore.' She came up to the reception and threw her hands in the air. 'There is nobody to help and I can't do it by myself. I am old now and all the rooms are dirty. I wouldn't let my dog sleep in them. I'm sorry.'

'Please Señora, we have nowhere else to stay tonight. We would really appreciate it.' Tom tried to persuade her, but she would have none of it. In the end it was Maria who got her on their side.

'I will clean the rooms first Señora,' she promised. 'If you could show me where I can find some soap and water, I'm sure it will take no time.'

The old woman looked at all four of them and the money Tom held out to show that they could pay their way.

'You have convinced me,' she agreed shrugging her shoulders 'but they will have to stay here until we are finished,' she said looking at Tom, Aaron and Charles as if they were not fit to clean. They didn't need convincing and the two women went off in search of water and soap and Charles went for a walk around the small town.

Tom and Aaron sat down on a hard sofa in what Tom guessed used to be the lounge area. Now it was a storage room and they squeezed themselves in between an old mattress and a pile of old towels that were none too clean.

'So you and Maria are together now?'

'Yeah, I guess so. Not the best of places for a budding romance, is it?'

Aaron laughed which was nice to hear, he hadn't laughed too much since he got here. In Paris he had been a very different person, the life and soul of any party and why he had attached himself to Tom and his less than positive outlook on life was beyond him. Here he had been miserable for most of the time; maybe Spain didn't agree with everybody.

'Mmm, it's not Paris is it, but it's different and quite exciting.' He looked at the mattress he sat next to, made a face and moved closer to Tom's side. 'And if anybody asked how you met, it will be more interesting than "our eyes met across the room at Le Bar Rouge.'

'That is true, but maybe a little less excitement would be good right now. She's the reason I'm back here.' It felt strange talking about it to someone else but at the moment

Aaron was his closest, or rather only, friend and he had to say it out load. 'And I thought I'd never see her again. All those nights in Paris when you asked what I was thinking about, it was her. It was always her.'

There was a pause as Aaron probably felt uncomfortable with his emotional outburst and then he changed the subject.

'I know you don't want to talk about it, but how were you injured.'

'It's a long story. Too long for tonight. Enough to say that I was chasing a story and someone didn't like me sticking my nose in. I should have let it go, but you know what it's like when something doesn't sound right, it sticks in your head and you just have to do something about it. Besides, I needed to get some good stories in so that I didn't look completely incompetent, especially with all the annoying top journalists coming to Madrid and all the officials falling over themselves to make sure they had all they needed.'

'Also, I was just about to join up and do my bit for the Republic, but thought I'd just have a little look at this story first. My friends, Bea and Eduardo, came with me and to cut a long story short, they were both killed and I'm not sure why, but they let me live and I was lucky to get away with a gunshot wound in my shoulder, broken bones and bruises.' He took a deep breath and continued.

'Then it gets a bit weird. Someone saw Bea alive and well in Madrid and in Paris for that matter and it turns out that

Maria has been in contact with her too. Unfortunately, the bastards that sent me on my way last time have somehow found out that I'm here and are now intent of getting rid of me again. Not sure why exactly but I'd like to know, especially as I have now dragged poor Maria away from her home and family. I can't allow anything to happen to her.'

'What was the story about? It must have been something big.'

'It was all to do with the Spanish gold reserves being shipped off to Russia and some of it being stolen whilst in storage. I don't know why it was done, but Maria's cousin saw them do it, and a Russian I used to know was somehow involved too. I know that because he was there that day we got caught and he's the one to blame for at least Eduardo's death. Anyway, turns out that the Russian chap, Pietr has changed sides and is now fighting alongside Franco. I'll find him once the war is over - for Eduardo.'

'You could have told me earlier you know'

'Maybe, but it's all very private and I didn't want all of Paris knowing.'

'I wouldn't have told anyone if you'd asked me not to. Anyway, it's done now.'

'What's done now?'

'Paris. I'll probably be as miserable as you when I get back there after this.'

One of the doors in the corridor shut with a bang and Maria and the old woman whose name was Agueda came over.

'The rooms are clean now. Agueda says there is a small restaurant open down the road and that they do generally have fish available.'

Tom asked if the Señora wanted to come with them and she said yes. They'd leave a note for Charles.

They went in to one of the two rooms that had been cleaned. He had assumed that he would be sharing with Maria but it turns out that now there was another Spanish woman around, and an older woman at that, it would not be seemly for Maria and Tom to sleep in the same room. Therefore she took the small room for herself, leaving him to share with Aaron and Charles.

It would not be quite the night he'd hoped for.

They sat looking out over the fields leading down to the sea and the air smelled of fish, grilling over an open fire. Fresh fish, not the old 'don't ask if you don't want to know' fish they used to get in Madrid. Charles had joined them and was in a reflective mood, concentrating more on his fish than on the conversation.

Agueda had taken of her cleaning apron and put on her winter coat even though it must still have been 20 degrees outside and she was chatting away. She'd taken a liking to Maria who looked very prim and proper sitting there listening to Agueda, like Tom was sure she would have with an old grandmother. It was difficult to tear his eyes away from her. Agueda must have asked Maria when they were cleaning what we were all up to and why she was travelling along with two men all on her own. He wondered what she had told her.

Aaron was in a world of his own and only answered direct questions, and even then they had to be repeated. If this was how often his mood changed normally he felt sorry for Jacqueline, in more ways than one. Agueda told us about her life whilst they were eating and drinking the local wine in rather large quantities and it was a pleasant atmosphere, almost like Spain had been before the war had come along.

She had grown up in this small town and married Manolito, the son of the Hotel owner when she was 15. He had died of tuberculosis many years ago, but her five sons had kept her busy. Sadly only two of them still lived. Three had died in the war already and she was worried that the same fate awaited the other two. They wrote her letters but she could not read them and she didn't want anyone else in the village to know her business and therefore wouldn't ask anyone else to read them for her. It made her happy just having them and as long as they kept coming, she knew they were alive.

Night time came quickly once the sun had set and they retired for the night.

~ 26 ~

Once they were on their way again they drove through little villages, which this close to the front, had almost been abandoned by villagers fearing the worst. The first one they drove through looked deserted to the world and empty of life until they drove around the corner and there was an old man, sitting on a chair outside his whitewashed house, watching the world go by with bright begonias on the windowsill and his front door wide open. Tom guessed he hadn't wanted to leave his home and decided that if the fascists came, it would be better to die at home. There was a smell of garlic wafting through the open door as they drove past, maybe his wife was indoors cooking lunch, like she probably had done most days since they got married. Tom hoped for their sake that Franco and his savage soldiers would not come here.

'I have got to get the car back to Silke again by tomorrow at the latest. It'll be a long drive back but I didn't tell him I'd borrowed it. Something told me he wouldn't approve, and you said that it was only a short drive.'

'It's all relative. Considering where we're actually going, it is a short drive. I expect he'll still be in bed and not even know it's been gone. You can always blame it on me, he'll know that I'm the one who talked you into it anyway. Stay with the old lady again on the way back.' Tom suggested. Aaron hadn't let him near the driver's seat since they set out. Tom wasn't sure what he thought he'd do to it.

'No, I'll just drive straight through on the way back. It'll be ok. Without the extra weight of you I'll probably drive faster.' He grinned now.

'Thanks. I meant to ask you, weren't you going off out and about with Johnny and co? You have hardly taken any photos at all since we got here.'

'I know but I wanted to get my bearings first and something in my head is telling me to go to the Madrid front first. Once I've dropped you guys off and taken the car back to Valencia, that's where I'm heading.'

'Why Madrid. Why not Barcelona or one of the northern fronts'

'I don't know. I was talking to some other press people in the hotel a couple of nights ago and they said that if I hadn't been I should go. The town will go down in history for its resistance to fascism and I'd be a fool to miss recording some of it.' He paused for a moment. 'I think I'll go. Where would one stay? Any suggestions?'

Tom saw Charles sigh deeply in the front seat. 'It's not a bloody holiday destination. The press office will find you somewhere. I'm sure it'll all be fine when you get there.'

Peering out of the window Tom continued. 'You need to turn of this road here I think.'

It was the only road taking them towards their destination and he hoped it was the right one.

'Please don't get us lost in these parts. I have no wish to die just yet.'

'I hope we're on the right track,' he said looking at the map whilst catching Aaron glancing over with a worried look on his face. The map was old and showed a United Spain of years ago but the roads would surely be the same. 'It'll be fine.'

It should only be another mile or so now along this road and then they would have to walk the rest of the way as the airfield was in a small valley surrounded by mountains and trees on all sides.

There was no sign of any battles going on and the only noise that could be heard was the odd vehicle driving to or from one of the towns along the main road they had just come off.

Tom leaned back and continued to worry about the flight over to Morocco. They, the insurgents that is, would surely see them and at least try to shoot them down. If they by some chance made it over the waters, they were highly likely to have been spotted landing and soldiers would be there ready to arrest them shortly afterwards. Tom had never flown before either and if the circumstances had been different he would have been really excited at the prospect, but as it was, he would rather not go.

The landscape hadn't changed significantly since they left the village and the hills at the bottom of the mountains showed signs of landslides where the melted snow and ice from the previous winter had briefly, and intensely, flowed down earlier in the year. The dry ground was covered in tuffs of rough grass patches here and there and pine trees swept across the higher areas where it would be cooler in the summer months.

As the car spluttered along he wondered how Aaron was going to make it all the way back to Valencia on the petrol that was in the tank and quickly decided that his problem was smaller than theirs so he could sort it out on his own. They got to the base of the hill and after a few minutes up-hill drive they saw a path continuing upwards through the pine trees where they could not take the car. Aaron pulled over and they climbed out onto the rough grass at the edge of the road.

'Take care Tom. Charles.' Aaron said and shook their hands vigorously and nodded his head to Maria. 'It's been an absolute pleasure meeting you. I hope we'll meet soon.'

'I hope so too. I hope all goes well for you in Madrid.'

Aaron just smiled, and eager to get back to Valencia, he got back in the car and they started their trek up the steep path.

They were all out of breath as they clambered up the pine needle strewn path to the top of the hill and even when they got there, there was nothing to see.

'What if this is the wrong place.' Maria worried.

'It can't be. This is where it's supposed to be according to the map. It must just be very well hidden amongst the pine trees down there. Any thoughts on the matter Charlie?' Tom asked.

'No. I don't normally go out on activities and I'm not sure what we're supposed to be looking for.'

'A plane and a runway.' Tom said sarcastically.

'What if it isn't there. What do we do then?'

'Let's worry about that if it happens, eh?' Tom smiled confidently at Maria and took her hand as they walked down the path on the other side. He hoped he was right and even if he was there was no guarantee that the plane would still be there waiting for them. He had toyed with the idea of asking Aaron to wait for a little while before setting off just in case this was not the right place or if something went wrong, but he would rather put up with fascists than risk another one of his bad moods.

It was more difficult going down the hill than up as it was easy to slip on the thick rug of pine needles and they almost slid down the path a couple of times.

It was only when they reached the end of the path at the bottom of the hill that they saw the small forest green airplane hiding at the end of two flat tracks in the grass and they stepped out from the trees and walked closer.

It was a very good place to have an airfield, which he assumed was used for moving high level politicians and other dignitaries. Tom could only see one clear way in, which was the one they had used, but there may well have been others hiding along the edge of trees.

'Thank God it's there. I have never been on an airplane before Tom. Have you?'

'No. It'll be a first for me too. There used to be an airfield near my school and me and my friend Edward would sneak out on a Saturday afternoon, if we weren't going home, and watch them. That was about 15 years ago though, and they looked nothing like this one.'

The wings were staggered and he didn't know if it was supposed to be that way or if it had been badly patched up in the past.

They looked around for a pilot as they went closer to the plane but there was no sign of anybody.

'Hello. Is anybody in there?' Tom knocked gently on the door, but there was no reply. He knocked again and this time got rewarded with a grunt from inside the plane and the small window above the door filled up with the face of a bushy haired, red faced man who had just been about to have his siesta inside the plane before they interrupted his lifelong habit.

'What do you want?' he asked in a harsh voice as he opened the door, gun in his hand.

'I'm sorry to bother you Compañero, but I think you are to take us over the water to Morocco. I'm Tom Lancaster.' Charles had asked him earlier to keep his name out of any conversations along the way.

The pilot looked at him blankly for a moment, and Tom wondered if he was drunk, but then suddenly he remembered.

'Ah, the English. Sí, sí.' There was a moment's pause, and then he scratched his head with his gun and yawned before continuing in a typically Spanish way. 'Of course I will take you over, but first I need to sleep. After a good lunch a man needs his sleep, no? How can I possibly fly without my siesta.'

He was about to make his way back inside the plane again laughing to himself about the stupidity of foreigners when Tom tried to appeal to his professional side.

'I'm sorry Senior, but can you please have a siesta on the other side?' He couldn't be serious.

'Do you really want me to fly without being able to concentrate properly? No. It will only be a couple of hours and you could have a sleep too. Have some food.' He pointed over to the pilots seat where there was a basket with, what Tom assumed, the garlic infused meal that he had just eaten. 'It's very good food, my wife makes the best cured..,' his voice trailed off as he saw something behind them and the trio turned around to see what had distracted him.

At the end of the field, where they had just come from, was Aaron running for his life towards them.

'Get the plane going. Get the plane going,' he shouted as he got closer.

The pilot just stared at him for a couple of seconds, but at the first sound of guns firing he jumped into the front and started the engines. Maria, Tom and Charles jumped in and the plane started moving slowly forwards, away from Aaron.

'Run faster.'

There were now guns firing from the path they'd come down and from further along the runway. Tom could hear the bullets hitting the metal and shouts from the soldiers shooting them. Aaron, running as fast as he could, his face getting redder and redder finally managed to get close enough to grab hold of a small handrail and this way he partly pulled himself on board. His legs were still dangling outside and Tom grabbed hold of his arms and dragged the rest of him onto the plane. He lay there panting on the floor for a few moments before Maria helped him up onto one of the one small crème leather seats.

'Shit, that was close.' He was trying to catch his breath and Tom struggled to close the door whilst not falling out. The plane was tugging in every direction and it was still being shot at when he finally managed to slam the door shut and sit down.

'It's taking too long, we must be at the end of the runway by now.' And judging by the new kind of bumps they felt Tom guessed they had over run it already. He got up to speak to the pilot just as the plane took off and he promptly fell back towards Aaron and Maria. Still on the floor one last bump told him they'd only just lifted off in time as a fir tree had nudged the bottom of the plane. And they were in the air.

'Oh God. Are you ok?' Maria helped Tom back up to his seat.

'I'm fine. Just a little hit on the head that's all.'

'My poor plane,' the pilot was wailing from the front. 'Who are you people? No, no I don't want to know. It will all be fine.' The pilot continued to mumble loudly to himself.

'Now what was all that about?' Tom asked Aaron who glared at him whilst rubbing one of his arms that had got squeezed in between himself and the plane as he tried to get on.

'Why are you asking me? How would I know why they were shooting at us. I don't understand. Why are they trying to kill us? Why did they come for you at the Pension? You must know what they want Tom.'

'I've told you before, I don't know. There's your answer Aaron, I have no idea.'

'Don't look at me, I don't' know what's going on.' Charles sat back in his seat, visibly shaken. This was the kind of event he normally only heard about from agents, not actually anything he'd ever been involved in.

'I think the fascists must have known about the airfield and just waited for someone to show up. They wouldn't have known who we were, but they would have thought that if we were important enough to go on this flash plane, we were important enough for them to catch or kill.' Aaron added whilst nodding in agreement with himself.

'That theory falls down with the fact that we were still in Republican territory.' Tom said rubbing the little bump on his head. 'But then again maybe the front's moved. We have been saying how easy it would be to get lost.'

'They were Republican soldiers. I saw the uniforms, and even without specific markings they are very different to the rebels.' Charles said.

'We all know that Charlie.' Tom said with an edge.

'Stop calling me Charlie. For God's sake, my name is Charles.'

Tom looked surprised at Charles before ignoring him and Maria took his hand just as the plane went sharply upwards.

'I was going to have a word with the pilot but probably best to leave him to it for the moment.' Tom said and leaned back whilst holding on to his seat.

The plane was obviously used for ferrying passengers with money and power around. It smelled of petrol and leather, and if you looked out of the dirty window, you could see the Mediterranean glittering below in the afternoon sun. There was smoke rising from ships in the harbour at Ibiza and planes circling above. He had no idea who was bombing who and even though he felt bad about it, he didn't care, he just wanted them to reach Morocco alive.

It felt like they were going much too slowly, although he knew they were moving faster than any of the boats below, towards an unknown country where he had no idea where they were going or what to expect. His plan of finding Bea and getting out of Morocco with Maria seemed quite simple considering everything that had already happened. Then when the war was over he'd take her back to Spain, to Madrid and Auntie's Café Rosa. It was easy to see how unsure of all this she was, not just having to leave her home and being shot at, but most of all not being able to tell her family what had happened. He'd make sure a message was sent as soon as they were back in a city. She was sitting looking out of the window and turned towards him with a smile when she felt him looking and he smiled back.

Aaron rolled his eyes before actually throwing up.

The Port of Tetuan, Morocco

The Major stepped off the ship and inspected his welcoming committee of three Nationalist officials. They had been standing in the burning sunshine for over an hour waiting for the ship to dock and unload all its passengers before Major Peter Alexandrow finally disembarked. He had changed his name almost the minute he reached fascist lands as his home country was so hated by the fascists that even Franco could not bring himself to say his real name out loud.

The last couple of months he had spent debriefing them on every single little thing he knew about the Republicans and the situation in Madrid as well as convincing them that Enrique was to blame for the missing gold. In the end they had believed him. This was in no little way due to the priest having vouched for him before his capture, confirming that it was indeed Enrique who had betrayed them.

Pietr knew better though, he knew who it was who had stolen it. It was more by luck than anything else that he had found out the location of the thieves and if this report was correct, they were all once again in the same area. Just thinking about it made him angry, He took a deep breath of the hot humid air and calmed down as the officers came walking towards him with their hands outstretched, ready to greet the Major who had given them such valuable information of the enemy.

The officers lead him quickly towards the mess and ordered some cold drinks from the Moor who appeared within seconds at their table. The bar was cooled by two fans whirling around loudly and the waiter behind the bar poured the drinks over a lot of ice which cracked as the glasses filled up.

The three officials introduced themselves and Pietr's crash course in Spanish paid off as he understood the conversation. He would much rather be taken to his residence and have a chance to clean up, but thought that he might need these people to be on his side so he took his drink and smiled.

'Welcome to Morocco, Major.' One of the officers held up his glass to him. 'We are honored to have you here.'

'Thank you.'

'May I ask why you wanted to come out here. Most officers want to be on the mainland.'

The Majors eyes narrowed for a moment before he smiled down at them.

'I always wanted to see Morocco. They say that the mountains here glimmer like gold in the morning sun.'

~ 27 ~

The Rif Mountains, Morocco, May 1937

The plane landed with a few bumps and a hair raising screech, but stopped relatively safely at the south western base of the Rif mountains. The city of Tetuan, where the uprising had started, was the stronghold of Franco and it was less than 40 miles north of their landing spot. They must have seen them come in to land.

'All of you out of my plane.' The pilot shouted in a neutral manner, no doubt glad to be rid of them after missing his siesta and nearly losing his plane at take-off.

The four of them jumped off the plane and onto dry hard soil. A warm, sweet smelling breeze from the mountain side where deep red bougainvillea and hibiscuses scented the air hit them as they drew their first breaths of Moroccan air. In essence they had only flown across a short stretch of water, but the smells and the feel of the sunshine was quite different to where they had come from. Of course they were in Spanish Morocco and therefore hadn't left the war behind, but as there had been next to no resistance there to the rebellion Tom hoped it would be calmer than mainland Spain. That just went to show that he had never been to Morocco before.

The plane ride had been a rather rocky journey. They had been hit by a few bullets as they sped down the runway for take-off but the air raids over Ibiza had at least served as a distraction to both Republicans and Rebels who had both ignored them in the air.

None of them had been on a plane before, and whilst Maria and Tom had found it exciting, Aaron had had his head in a bag feeling sick for most of the short journey. Charles had been quietly looking out of the window. All of them were relieved to get off in the end.

The pilot walked around the plane inspecting the damage done by the shooting and that last fir tree whilst quietly cursing to himself.

'Well, I need to get back to Spain,' said Aaron looking rather peaky. 'How the bloody hell am I to get back to Valencia? They will have taken the car from the airfield and how do I to explain that to Silke? I blame you Tommy boy for dragging me into this, and I haven't even got my bloody camera with me, it's still in the car.'

Tom almost expected him to start stamping his feet like a child who doesn't get his own way.

'Just go back to Spain with the pilot and try to get a lift north when you get there. The worst thing that can happen is that they take you prisoner and send you back home,'

Tom said grumpily, now getting tired of Aaron's whining and added. 'Unless they shoot you first of course.'

'Ha bloody ha. It'd be funny if it wasn't so true.' He went to have a word with the pilot and left Tom and Maria standing there, looking up to the craggy tops of the Rif mountains that surrounded them.

'I have never been abroad before. What will they be like? The people I mean.' Maria looked around her.

'I'm hoping we can avoid 'the people'.' He smiled whilst taking her hand in his and starting to walk towards Aaron and the pilot.

He didn't have a plan as such, this whole thing had been thrust upon him by the realisation that Bea was alive and apparently didn't want anyone knowing about it. He had only really wanted to see Maria and now here he was, leading her further away from home and without a plan to get out. The only good thing was that Madrid was probably as dangerous as any place was right now and therefore, Morocco could not be that much worse. Charles was sitting on a stone in the shade looking at a map.

The pilot and Aaron's voices grew louder as Tom and Maria approached them. Aaron turned around showing them that he held a gun in his hands. Tom's gun.

'He's not going back Tom. I have to get back right now.' He pointed maniacally towards the pilot. 'I saved your behinds over there, the least you can do is get me back to Spain.'

They had slowed down when they saw the gun and instinctively Tom edged forward in front of Maria, just in case he was to fire. All three of them were keeping their eyes on the gun and wondering what had gotten into Aaron. Charles lifted his eyes from the map to see what was going on.

'Alright. Put the gun away now, I'm sure he'll take you with him when he goes back.' Tom looked over to the pilot for confirmation to this and he nodded in agreement. Where had Aaron got the gun from? It was Tom's gun, how had he got hold of it. 'Now stop being an arse and give me my bloody gun back,' he said with authority and held out his hand towards him whilst still keeping his distance.

'Stay where you are Tom. He's not going back for a couple of days. Says he has business here, probably fancies a bit of a holiday or maybe a bit on the side.' Aron said as he moved backwards so that the gun was now pointing towards all four of them.

The pilot shrugged his shoulders.

'I can't take the plane back straight away. They will be waiting for us on the other side and also I need fuel. I cannot fly anywhere without fuel. I will stay with friends here for a couple of days until it all calms down. If your friend wants, he can also stay with them. They are very friendly, Moroccan people,' he said looking at Tom.

'Enough of this bloody nonsense. Put the gun down before someone gets hurt,' Tom said. He had enough to worry about without Aaron delaying him.

'It'll be me who gets hurt. Wake up and smell the coffee Tom. How do you think they knew where you were in Madrid, eh? How do you think they knew you were about to catch a plane? Where it was leaving from?' he shouted whilst waving the gun around.

'They could have taken you at any time whilst we were driving down to the airfield but they wanted to see what you were about to do, who you were seeing. I'm telling you, you have made some enemies somewhere and I saved your life on that mountain. Now do the same for me and get me back to Valencia.'

He'd lost his marbles.

'What are you talking about.' Suddenly the penny dropped and it must have shown on Tom's face but he just couldn't bring himself to believe it. He had wondered how they had known that he was in Madrid or indeed that he was at the Pension, but he had assumed that they, whoever they were, had been keeping the Pension under surveillance since the autumn, knowing he'd go back. He hadn't had time to think properly about how they knew where to find them when they were getting on the plane.

That also explained why Aaron wanted to know his plans for going to Madrid on his own and momentarily Tom was lost for words. 'What have you done. Why...'

'Does it matter?' Aaron sighed. The maniacal ranting and gun waiving had stopped and he sat down on a rock biting his lips, looking beaten.

'It bloody matters to me, it matters to Maria. It matters to poor Pabla and little Alejandro who will now grow up without a father.' The feeling of betrayal was never very nice and this one hurt because he had thought of Aaron as a friend and to find out that he had betrayed them, that he would happily have seen them dead, was quite a blow.

'I had nothing to do with the deaths of you friends.'

'Why did you do it? I know we weren't old friends, but I thought we got on and I trusted you. I didn't realise that you were spying on me, and was willing to see me dead. What has Maria done to you to deserve that?'

Tom walked up to Aaron slowly and sat down next to him. He was normally a calm person, not easily agitated but the anger and grief of the last six months were bubbling under the surface and he took a deep breath to keep his temper under control.

There were birds in the trees watching them and singing sweetly in the silence that had descended. The pilot and Maria had relaxed a little where they stood and Tom nodded for them to move further away just in case Aaron decided he was better off just shooting them all. Tom saw Maria still looking over, no doubt wondering what that was all about. God alone knows what the pilot thought. Charles was nowhere to be seen.

Aaron seemed to have calmed down, but it would be bad to assume he wouldn't try to shoot them all and fly the plane back himself.

'Why?' Tom asked yet again and there was a moment of silence as Aaron stared into space before speaking.

'It started back in Paris when this woman I'd talked to on a couple of occasions asked me if I would help the fight against fascism. You must remember that my whole family had been made to leave their home country some years earlier and it broke my mother's and father's hearts as they had to leave everything behind, and I said yes. I guess I was flattered that she'd asked me, good looking girl too.' He looked at Tom briefly.

'I had no wish to die in a rain filled ditch in a field somewhere in Spain, but I still wanted to help. She set up a meeting with one of her friends and that was the last I saw of her, I only dealt with the new chap after that. Her name was Vivian and I have no idea where she went, she just disappeared. - This new man told me that you were an English fascist spy, playing your republican role very well, pretending to be on our side. I just had to keep an eye on you, become your friend, you know. I had already met you down La Bar Rouge a few times and I guess they had noticed that.' He pulled back his shoulders, sat up straight and took a deep breath he continued.

'You would have done the same Tom. You were always acting strangely, like you had something to hide. And you'd obviously been injured somewhere, but never talked about what had happened. And I did ask you several times but you always brushed it aside. You talk about friendship, but maybe you weren't such a great friend either. If you had told me what happened back then instead of in the sodding Pension yesterday everything might have turned out differently.'

'So what? You're trying to ease your guilt by blaming me for your unscrupulous actions?' Tom shook his head unbelievingly. 'The least you can do now is tell me what you know.' He waited a couple of seconds. 'Go on then, who was this guy?'

'I don't think he told me his real name but called himself Jean-Paul and he had a slight foreign accent - could have been Spanish I guess.'

'They were very friendly to start with and I didn't mind it in Paris, it was easy and nobody was getting hurt. I really did intend to go over to Spain with Cloudy and leave you and them behind. Photography is my great passion in life and I'm good at it. It's probably the only thing I am good at. Besides, there was never anything to report on you. Your life was boring Tom, but Jean-Paul didn't agree to me leaving and when I told them I was just going to go anyway, all the niceties disappeared and they beat me up. - My leg wasn't broken by jumping out of a window, Jean-Paul's lackeys broke my leg by stamping on it. One of them holding me down, not that I was in any state to move anyway, and the other one just stamped and stamped and stamped until it cracked.' He had put the gun down and pulled two cigarettes out of his pack offering Tom one of them. He took it.

'Fuck knows what'll happen to me know.' He blew out a cloud of smoke into the sunshine. 'I'm so sorry Tom. I wished I'd just said no to start with or lied about where you went, but I didn't and now it's too late - for both of us.'

He picked up the gun and gave it to Tom.

'Go on. Just be quick about it please. I've never been good with pain and I'm an eternal coward.' He looked straight ahead, the cigarette glued to the corner of his mouth and it crumbled into his face as Tom hit him. He fell off the stone they had been sitting on and Tom threw the gun off to one side, jumped over and hit him again.

He couldn't control himself as the last six months anger finally came to the surface and the only outlet for it was Aaron. Tom saw his mouth move but didn't hear what he was saying through the buzzing noise that was filling his head. His fists hurt as they hit him anywhere they could until he was pulled away by the pilot and heard Maria shouting for him to stop and only then did he realise what he was doing. The calmness that Tom had prided himself on for so long was gone and he was breathing heavily as he watched Aaron sitting up. His nose running with blood which he wiped off with his shirtsleeve before crawling back on to the stone. Tom's anger was slowly giving way and he walked over to where he'd thrown the gun earlier and picked it back up.

Aaron was sitting on the stone, no doubt feeling more sorry for himself than anything he'd done to them. But what was done was done and they couldn't change anything now, and he had saved their lives in the end. Stupidity should not be confused with viciousness, but at the same time there was no excuse for it either. Tom lit his cigarette and walked up to Aaron with the gun in his hand, and could see in the corner of his eye, Maria and the Pilot watching his every move, in case he would do something stupid.

They need not have worried, the moment had passed and Tom sat back down next to him.

'So,' Aaron said with his eyes on the gun. 'Are you going to finish it now?'

'Don't be stupid man. I'm not going to shoot you. I'm not a killer, although maybe I should be.' Tom took a deep drag and blew the smoke towards the blue sky. He wanted Aaron out of their lives, but he knew very little of why all this had happened and maybe it was better to keep him close.

'Being a stupid cowardly arse doesn't generally deserve a death sentence. Although, if anything had happened to Maria, I would have filled you with lead and sung the 'International' whilst doing it.'

He stood up and figured that the devil you knew was better than the devil you didn't and continued;

'It seems like none of us can go back to Spain for the time being so you might as well come with us. You can try to make up for all the trouble you caused.'

Holding the gun in his hand he looked down on it. It felt very light so he opened up the barrel and it was empty. He looked at Aaron.

'I tried to get some more ammunition, but it's apparently in short supply,' Aaron shrugged his shoulders.

Tom wondered what had happened to the bullets that were in there when he left for Madrid.

'Is everything ok?' Maria asked looking at both of them.

'Yeah, I think so.' Tom answered and Aaron nodded, finding it difficult to look Maria in the eyes.

Charles had appeared as the fighting stopped and now came up to them with the map.

'All done?'

'Don't piss me off Charles. I'm really not in the mood.'

'No, of course you aren't, but we should get moving.'

The pilot who looked keen on leaving showed them where they were on the map and told them to head towards the twin mountain peaks in the distance, but to stay away from the blue town itself. The offer of a bed for the night had vanished with the threat of death and relived he'd done his duty he sauntered off down the hillside singing to himself and left them to it.

'So, what are we doing now. What is our plan?' Maria asked keenly

'We have to find the Moor's village which is around here somewhere.' Tom pointed on the map and Maria looked. Aaron was still sitting on the stone looking unsure what to do.

'It seems quite far away. How are we going to get there'

'I don't know. We'll just have to start walking and hope that some kind of transport presents itself. I guess we should stay clear of the roads but I don't want to get lost in the wilderness so maybe we just have to extra careful and keep an eye out for anyone approaching. We have our papers in order, but Aaron has only Republican paperwork.'

'Look, I'll try to get back home from here. I've caused enough problems for you.' He got up from the stone and winced with pain as he did so. 'You throw quite a good punch for a journalist.'

'Oh, stop feeling sorry for yourself. I'm bloody pissed off with you but I have more important things on my mind at the moment. If you stay here on your own you're likely to get shot. You know I said earlier when you wanted to go back that they would probably only send you back home?'

'Yeah.'

'I was lying. Franco would see you as a spy and shoot you on the spot like a dog. Your best bet is to come with us and find Bea and then over to the French side. We can get to the consulates in Casablanca once we've found her, but it's entirely your choice.'

Without waiting for a response, Tom took Maria's hand and started walking in the same direction that the pilot had taken, followed by Charles and a hesitant Aaron.

How would they get to the village? He had no idea, but it would be bad to stay too long with the plane as there must have been a fair few people who saw it come in to land.

There was a dusty white road leading up the mountain and according to their map, this was going in their direction. They had probably no more than five hours before dark and Tom wanted to get as much distance between themselves and the plane by nightfall. Maria was walking alongside him and Charles, and he could hear Aaron dragging behind as they made slow progress in heat.

The mountain road seemed to never end, and at every bend there was a new stretch and then another bend whilst they were trying to be alert and listen for anyone approaching. Twice they had to duck into the spring green bushes and trees lining the road as local farmers passed them in their wagons.

Darkness started to fall and it looked like they would have to spend it out in the open. Although it was still warm, Tom wasn't very keen on the idea of sleeping without any kind of protection at all. Suddenly, around a corner, a shepherds hut appeared and on closer inspection there were no shepherds. They decided to take advantage of this bit of luck.

Maria had some bread left in her bag and had taken the Pilot's leftover lunch from the basket in the plane before they left. They shared that with a generous helping of wine, also stolen from the pilot. Maria had presented the stolen food and wine whilst laughing happily at the surprise showing on their faces. Tom hoped they'd never meet that pilot again. The night was warm and the dark sky clear with myriads of bright stars twinkling against it.

Aaron had kept himself separate from them and after they had eaten Charles had fallen asleep on the mud floor. Tom and Maria went outside and sat themselves down on a rock, leaning against a large tree. They watched the silhouette of the shepherds hut and the mountains in the background magically lit by a slither of an orange moon. A slight breeze made Maria shiver and Tom put his arms around her to warm her up. All seemed calm and serene with only the odd animal sound to be heard from the mountains.

'Do you think the wild animals here are dangerous?' she asked.

'Not as dangerous as me,' he joked 'I'm sorry for all this you know. I've put your life in danger and dragged you far from home.'

'I'm glad you came. This is a walk in the park compared to Madrid. Twenty hour days at the hospital and falling into bed, cold and hungry, worrying that Franco will break through our defenses or that you'll get hit by the shells and bombs. Now, I'm with you so I know everything will turn out alright.'

Tom smiled at her, and he too thought everything would be fine because they would make it so.

'How long do you think it'll take us to get to the village?'

'I don't know. It didn't look too far on the map the way the crow flies, but we're in the mountains and we have to be careful. I'm not even sure we're going in the right direction.' Tom took her hand and kissed it. 'We'll be fine though.' He paused for a moment.

'I love you Maria.' Tom still looked at her hand, her nails short and somehow still clean, he didn't dare to look up.

'Let's get married. When we get back home. If you want to.' It had all sounded better in his head.

He knew she'd mentioned it earlier, but maybe she hadn't meant it and maybe just like Bea she'd say things, not taking them seriously.

'Not very romantic, but yes, of course I will.' She put her hand on his cheek and pulled his face towards hers and kissed him. 'I love you too, but you knew that already. It's only ever been you.'

'I wish I had a ring to give you.' Pulling out a few straws from the straggly grass tuft next to them, he twisted them together and put the temporary ring on her finger. It didn't stay on.

'I'll get you the most beautiful ring you ever saw when we get to Paris. With a big diamond.' He grinned and she laughed.

'I like this one, but it doesn't want to stay on. I wish auntie was here so we could share this with her. It is a big thing and I think auntie and my mother have worried that I would never get married. Maybe we can get married in the village when the war is over. I know my mother would like to be there too.'

'By the looks she gave me at the farm, I think you will have your work cut out for you convincing her I'm not a good for nothing foreigner.'

'And I get to meet your mother. What is she like? Do you think she'll like me?'

'How could she not love you. I have told you before that my mother is Spanish, and I know she'll be really pleased that I'm marrying a Spanish girl'

Tom wasn't too sure about that last bit as his mother already had a picture in her head of the woman he should marry. It was more of an English rose than a Spanish nurse, but once she met Maria she'd change her mind.

'I look forward to meeting her. Do you think we will live in Paris or London?'

'Where would you like to live, querido? We can live anywhere you want.'

'I have never been to France or England. Apart from this trip I have never left Spain and even that I haven't seen much of. I think I would like to be in the countryside, our children could run around and play and learn to ride and go to school. They can go to school and become doctors and lawyers and journalists. Women can do that in England, yes?'

'Of course they can. I hope you are a good rider because I'm rubbish at it. Must have fallen off the old horse they tried to teach me on at least a dozen times and then I refused to get back on. I don't know which one of us was more relieved, me, the instructor or the poor horse.'

'I can ride a horse. Our farm was very small but when my father was there, before the war, we used to have horses and he taught me when I was little.' She snuggled up to him.

'I think this evening is special. Look at the mountains and the stars. Are they not more beautiful than anything you have ever seen before. The stars, I think, see everything and watches over us, makes sure we're ok.'

Tom nodded.

She was leaning her head against the tree, looking up at the stars and smiling.

'We were always told by the church, before the Republic, that we would go to heaven if we were good, but now that we can make our own minds up, I'd like to think we become stars and that the ones who are good are the ones that shines brightest.'

'I suppose that is why there are fewer of the really bright ones, eh?'

'I've been having a few problems with religion lately though.'

'Why?'

'It doesn't matter. I've decided to believe in God like before but also believe in the stars. I'll keep quiet about the God part until I know what I should do, I don't think he will mind with the world being the way it is.'

'I don't think he'll mind either.' She made him smile.

'Do you think Aaron is alright? What happened up there?'

'He's fine. Just feeling a bit sorry for himself and guilty for what he's done.' Tom gave Maria a short version of Aaron's story and heard her gasp in surprise.

'I wonder how guilty he would have felt if we had both got arrested and either put away somewhere where the sun doesn't shine or been killed. He would probably have wiped the whole thing from his mind and got on with his own life, leaving us as an unwelcome memory when he had a few too many drinks.'

'Do you not think that he is genuinely sorry?'

'Oh he's sorry alright and I feel sorry for him. He's a useless toad and if I had any sense, and bullets, I should have shot him up there by the plane.'

'No you wouldn't. Even if you had the bullets you would never have shot him. You have too much kindness in you to do that. That's why I love you so.'

'Oh, I thought you loved me because of my rugged good looks' He joked when her longed for words tingled his senses.

'You don't look rugged, but very handsome and lovable.' She kindly agreed but Tom would rather have been rugged.

'Well, you're right, I wouldn't have shot him but probably should have. Our papers might be able to get us through a check-point, but his are Republican and will get us all into trouble if anybody finds them. They should really be burnt and he'll just have to get along with his French passport. Come on,' he got up on his feet and held out his hand to help her up. 'We should try to get some sleep.'

'I'm not sure I can sleep. We're getting married.' She smiled as they got back to the hut where they found Aaron asleep in a corner and quietly made themselves as comfortable as possible on the hard mud floor and tried to go to sleep.

~ 28 ~

Full of aches and pains from the previous day's fight, and from a night spent sleeping on the hard floor of the shepherd's hut, they started walking again at sunrise. It was not difficult to get started as their stomachs were growling with hunger and longing for this journey to come to an end.

The four of them must have looked a state, Aaron's face was now coming up a lovely variety of shades with both bruises and sunburn from the day before, Tom, Charles and Maria were in filthy clothes and warily limping along the road on blistered feet. All of them hoping it wouldn't be too far to walk. At least Aaron had cheered up a little and was now partaking in the odd bit of conversation along the road and by lunch time they were within sight of a town.

The town spread along the bottom of a mountain like a figure eight and the pale blue painted houses and streets could be seen for miles in the clear air. It was the town mentioned by the pilot. They sighed with relief that they had walked in the right direction. They still had to find the village Bea had supposedly gone to, but now they felt a little more positive about it.

Tom was very aware that they needed food and drink or they would collapse by the wayside, and the urge to go into the town was almost overwhelming, but along the blue tinted streets you could also see the odd military vehicle and that was enough to make them steer clear. They walked past the town, throwing only the odd longing glance towards it when, not more than ten minutes further on, there was a man with his family by the roadside trying to get a wheel back on their wooden cart. It had fallen off and now didn't want to go back on.

The man wore a jellabah with its pointed hood off and resting on his back and the woman was dressed in a multi coloured, and what Tom assumed, traditional, dress with a straw hat decorated with colourful balls of yarn that dangled around her head when she moved. The baby in her arms was screaming and the man stopped and looked up as they approached.

'Bonjour,' Tom said tentatively, hoping he spoke French.

'Bonjour,' he replied whilst his dark squinting eyes looked at them curiously.

The baby stopped screaming and the other two children were sitting quietly watching the strangers with interest.

'Vous faire nous aime vous aider?' Tom offered. He looked harmless enough and Tom figured if they helped him maybe he could tell them how to get to their destination, and maybe even sell them some food and drink.

'Ah, oui, merci, the wheel is a little bit heavy. Are you French?'

'No. We're English and Spanish' Tom replied, ignoring Aaron's nationality. It was tempting to pretend that they were all French but there was no mistaking Maria for anything but Spanish.

'Ah.' The man nodded knowingly whilst his leathery hands stroked the nose of the donkey that very calmly stood there watching and waiting.

The family got out of the cart whilst Aaron and Tom lifted it and the man pushed the wheel back in its place.

Maria stood off to one side, not understanding the conversation and a little wary of meeting new people in a foreign area held by Franco.

'Merci, merci. I thought for a moment that we would have to leave the cart here and walk back home. My name is Karim and my wife is Cherifa,' he smiled at them, 'And my three sons.'

Tom introduced himself and his friends and explained where they were going. He showed Karim the map but he ignored it.

'The village you are after is about half a days walk from here, not far. I know it well, I was born there. You will come to my house and eat and stay the night, it is a couple of hours away and then tomorrow it will be easy for you to reach the village.'

Not waiting for an answer he gestured for them to get on the cart and it was with little reluctance they did so. The only one who didn't want to go was Charles. He whispered to Tom that he didn't trust them and that they should make their own way. The thought of food was tempting and Karim and his family seemed very nice and friendly, but still, they didn't know these people. They could take them straight to the Fascists or some local thugs.

As if he heard the conversation, Karim slapped Tom on the back and laughed.

'Do not worry my friend, there are not a lot of military or police out here and you are quite safe.'

'I never thought we wouldn't be.' Tom lied. 'It is a curious colour of that town there.' He changed subject and could not help but smile a little back.

'The town is Chefchaouen. It means 'look to the horns', the two mountain peaks behind the town.'

Tom looked behind him and saw that the twin peaks were what they had used to navigate thus far.

'It is a holy town founded by the descendants of the prophet Mohammed a long time ago. It is very beautiful.'

The journey to Karim's house was bouncy to say the least, and Tom thought on more than one occasion that the wheel would come off again, but by some stroke of luck it stayed on and soon Chefchaouen disappeared from view and was replaced with the green hillside scenery they had seen a lot of so far. In the back, Cherifa and Maria tried to communicate using Aaron as a translator. Maria seemed more relaxed now, but Aaron, being in the middle of two women chatting, was getting grumpy yet again.

Tom enjoyed the ride and the impressive softness of the mountains melting into fields and farms headed by small flat roofed whitewashed houses and the conversation with Karim was pleasant.

'So, what are you doing here in Morocco?' Karim asked whilst trying unsuccessfully to get the donkey to move faster. 'I am only asking because it is not every day one meets strangers such as yourselves on the way home from the market.'

Tom did not answer straight away.

'You don't have to tell me.'

'No, it's ok. We are here to find someone, a girl, who's gone missing. The last time she was seen, she was setting off for this area together with a man whom she thought herself to be in love with. Maybe it is actually love but her father wants her back home.'

Karim nodded as he drove the mule onwards.

'Girls are very difficult and I am very pleased that I have three sons only. I would like to have a daughter but they are a worry to a father. Have you got any children?'

'No,' he laughed. 'There will be plenty of time for that later.'

They continued with some general chitchat, mostly about his little farm which was harmless conversation and Tom's whole body was happy to sit down. By the time they arrived at the house he was struggling to keep his eyes open.

It was a small but clean house and the smell of food cooking slowly through the day breezed along to the veranda where Charifa lit lots of lanterns as the daylight started to fade. They were invited to sit on the veranda with their host. It overlooked the mountains and they were treated to some beautifully sweet mint tea whilst Charifa and an older woman, whom they were not introduced to, prepared the evenings food. The tea and sugar revitalised them, just like a cup of sweet English tea in Tom's childhood had been the general remedy for most things.

'I am the youngest of twelve children, you know. My older brothers and sisters still live in the village.'

'How come you decided to leave?' Aaron asked.

'I wanted a little adventure and was going to go to a big city and make my fortune when I fell in love with a girl from this area.' He swept his arms out towards the lush valley in front of them. 'My father did not think she was good enough for our family,' he snorted. 'My family is large and important and they were making life very difficult for us there. It was easier to leave, and we have everything a man could possibly need here.'

He once again swept his arms towards the surrounding scenery as though he would embrace it if he could.

'The mountains, enough food and lots of laughter what more could anybody want. Our sons will grow up to be good charitable people, good Muslims.'

'It must be a hard life though.'

'Is not everything in life hard one way or another? Besides, if it wasn't hard at times, how would you appreciate the good times? You have just come over from Spain yes?'

'Yes. From Madrid.'

'I assume that you are not on Franco's side so you must appreciate that if something is worth having, it is worth fighting for. We hear that it is only a matter of days before Madrid is taken, they might be there already, no'

'They will not take Madrid. The whole population is fighting in one way or another.' Tom said whilst glancing over to Maria who didn't understand any of the conversation, but now paid attention as she recognised her home town being mentioned. 'There are volunteers from many countries there who have come to help the Republic fight.'

'And the Nationalists have the Germans and Italians yes? Sometimes travellers come by here on their way back home from the coast and they tell us of Germans arriving by boat and by plane. They are officially here for the mining, but everybody knows that is just lies.'

'Mmmm... I remember, back in January, the French being very uneasy about the whole thing and asking Herr Hitler for an official explanation as to why hundreds of Germans were here in Spanish Morocco, so close to the border of French Morocco. The 1914-18 war is still alive in every French man's memory, and I guess it's understandable that they should be worried.'

'So what did Herr Hitler respond?' Karim asked.

'That the Germans in Morocco were simply there for the mining. All civilians. It's obviously just lies, and the French and English must know it. I mean, we've seen the German and Italian planes swooping over and bombing Madrid and that scene will have been seen in every other city taken by the Nationalists and by every soldier fighting for the Republic.'

Tom looked over to Charles who must have been holding his tongue over this conversation. He smiled though and joined in as if he was a freedom fighter himself.

The conversation then reversed back to local matters, and general chit chat about his little farm until the food arrived. Tom was hungry and by the time the lamb tagine was on the table, his mouth had been salivating at the aroma of it for some time. The three of them tried to eat slowly and politely but did not say no to second helpings. The food was so much more than the war fare they had had in Spain that even Aaron looked happy and content afterwards.

Maria insisted that she help Charifa clear up whilst the rest of them had some more tea to finish the meal off. Tom thought that she was just bored of a conversation in a language she could not understand

'Do you ever go back to see your family?' Tom asked Karim as he lit a cigarette.

'Not since my mother's funeral. That must have been about five years ago now. Only one of my brothers spoke to me. We were always close Saïd and I. He is still there and he will help you find this girl you are looking for.'

'That would very kind of him.'

'Just tell him to come and visit us sometime. I still remember the mischief we used to get up to, me and Saïd. Being the youngest we used to get away with a lot as we were forgotten about most of the time.' He smiled at the memories as they finished their teas and bid each other goodnight.

There was only one room in the house to sleep in and therefore they had to share the barn with the donkey. The smell in there was unpleasant, but they were all tired and with full stomachs they drifted off to sleep quickly.

It was a very light sleep, as even though he was tired, Tom kept on waking up expecting to hear army vehicles and voices outside. There was no other way out of there and if anybody came for them, they were trapped. Luckily, the night passed peacefully and the next morning they were woken up early by the sun shining in through the small barn windows.

They went in search of some water to wash with before cups of tea together with some kind of deep-fried pancakes appeared on the terrace where the old lady from the night before was gesticulating that they should eat. There was no sign of Karim and the old woman made digging motions with her arms to show that he had gone out to work the farm earlier in the morning.

They said their goodbyes to Charifa and the old woman, and left the farm.

At least now they knew where they were going, all of them were more cheerful than they had been since the start of the journey.

Grab Bea and get the hell out of there was the plan.

They took the route suggested by Karim and by the afternoon they saw what must be the small town they were after. There were houses spreading out across the hillside from the main street, all different shapes and sizes and all of them white washed as the pueblos blancos in Andalucía. Karim's brother's house was on the outskirts of the village and it was easy to spot as it was situated just below a very grand house with balconies overlooking the sweeping valley below.

Cautiously they walked in to the village and along the almost deserted, narrow main street. There were a couple of shops which were closed and a few old men that were sitting outside the only café they could see. Dressed in their Jellabahs, they stopped talking as the four strangers approached and looked upon the newcomers with suspicion. Not having expected a trip to Morocco they had only French and Republican money in their pockets, but thought they'd try to buy some tea and possibly something to eat from the uninviting dark café. Avoiding the intense staring eyes of the old men outside, they made their way into the small gloomy place and sat down at a table by the window in silence.

It smelled of mint tea and spices in the now hot still air and they ordered tea from the europeanly dressed young barman who without a word went to get their order.

There were pearls of sweat trickling down Tom's back as the sweltering heat of the still air started to affect them. It would have been preferable to sit in the shade outside but there they would just draw attention to themselves, and besides, the stares of the old men would no doubt sour the tea. Tom guessed Maria was used to extreme heat as she showed no sign of overheating like the rest of them.

The barman brought their drinks and Tom asked if he knew where a blond English woman by the name of Bea was staying. She would have arrived a couple of weeks ago.

He wasn't much help and only shrugged his shoulders and said there were no foreigners in the village apart from themselves. Tom then asked if he knew where they could stay the night. Again, he shook his head in a non caring way and went back to whatever he spent his busy days doing behind the empty bar.

'He's a helpful chap. Now what do we do?' Aaron asked.

'I'm sure Karim's brother will help us. And if not, we'll just have to find someone else to ask.' Maria answered.

'Ok, that's easy. The streets are thronging with friendly people just waiting to help us.' Aaron said sarcastically and drank his tea. 'They all look quite unfriendly; the guys sitting outside. I wish this bloody heat would ease a little, and who in their right mind drinks hot tea in this heat?'

Tom was looking out of the dusty window. At the end of the street there were people getting into a proper motor car and it was coming their way. As it got a little closer to the café he could clearly see the Nationalist flag attached to the front and a smartly dressed uniformed man driving slowly past.

His friends were chatting in the background but Tom wasn't listening, because sitting in the back of the car, clearly outlined, was Bea laughing at something someone had said.

Tom felt like he had been hit by a bomb as his eyes incredulously followed her until the car had disappeared down the street. Everybody had told him she was still alive and well, but to see her was something quite different, and in a fascist car to boot. He suddenly felt lightheaded and found it hard to breath. He had to have some air and so got up from his chair and stumbled outside. Behind him he could distantly hear the others scrambling to their feet and following him outside.

The slight breeze helped, and a few moments later he had composed himself enough be aware of Maria's arm around him.

'Tom, what's the matter?' Maria asked anxiously. 'Are you ill?'

The old men sitting outside the cafe were unashamedly staring at them, but soon enough started chatting amongst themselves in a language none of them had ever heard before.

'Did you see the car that went past?'

'No, I heard it but...,' she shook her head and so did Aaron. 'Why? What was it?'

Tom looked at Charles who nodded. 'I saw it too.'

'Well, I think we have found the right village. That was Bea sitting in the back,' he said looking in the direction the car had gone.

Both Maria and Aaron looked there too even though the car was by now long gone.

'Are you sure?' Aaron asked.

'Yes. I'd know her anywhere, besides, there are not many blonde women around here, in fact not a lot of women full stop. And Charles saw her too.'

'What do we do now.'

'I think we should move ourselves away from the High Street. That car had Nationalist flags showing in front and there might be more of them here.' Charles looked up and down the street.

'She wouldn't have changed sides, would she?' Tom asked.

Maria shook her head. 'Never.'

Aaron went in to pay for the teas which were still only half drunk on the table. They walked down the road and turned a corner into a small street with some low terraced houses on each side, all white washed and giving heavenly shade from the heat of the sun. At the end of the street there were some children running around playing, but apart from them it was quiet.

'I think I should go to Karim's brother's house. Hopefully he will know what is happening in the village,' Tom said and lit a cigarette.

'Yeah, good idea. Those old men gives me the creeps,' Aaron agreed quietly.

'I don't think Bea would ever cross over to the Nationalists. She was passionate about our cause. I think this just proves that she is being forced into something. Our problem now must be, how do we get her out,' Maria said.

'I said that I should go. On my own. You two take Maria over the border to France, I don't think it's very far.' Tom looked to Aaron and Charles for confirmation that they agreed because he knew that Maria wouldn't.

'If you really want me to I will, but I think we'd do better sticking together. For now at least,' Aaron replied.

'Well, they can go if they like, but I'm here to bring Bea back. I won't leave without her.' Charles pulled his tie looser.

'Oh, just ignore me. What am I? Thin air? I'm coming with you.'

'Look, I don't know what Bea is up to and I don't want anything to happen to you. Coming to find her was my choice, not yours or even Aaron's, and I'd feel happier knowing you two were safely away from here.' Bea was his problem now and he would find her and drag her over to the French side of Morocco and then back home if he had to. There was still a little niggling feeling in the back of his head that maybe she had got herself involved in something she couldn't get out of.

He didn't want to have to worry about Maria at the same time, because if something happened to her he didn't know what he would do.

'I think it is a little late to say that after having dragged us all the way here. I'm staying, Aaron can go if he wants to,' she looked at Aaron for his response.

'I said we should stick together, I never said I should leave.'

This argument went on for a little while and in the end they decided that as the car she'd been travelling in was fascist they would have to take more care, and after some further discussion it was decided that Tom would go up and see Karim's brother on his own at first. If all went well, he'd come and get the rest of them.

They would be waiting for him on the hillside, halfway between Karim's brother's house and the village out of view from the road in case of soldiers or overly alert locals.

Tom walked up the steep hill to the large white washed house where he hoped to find Karim's brother. There were no houses opposite but the front was dominated by a large modern motor car and chickens picking at its tyres. He had to use the brass door knock several times before somebody opened. Karim's brother wasn't at home but his smartly dressed son was and he asked Tom in. The room was again rather basic and there were two small children running around chasing each other loudly and Karim's nephew told them be quiet and go to their mother. As they quietened down and slunk away from the room, Tom could hear what he assumed to be the wife, or maybe aunt making tea or some such like in the kitchen.

Karim's nephew excused himself for a moment and left the room, but he returned moments later with a big smile on his lips. It smelled of spices and herbs and after the heat outside, the coolness of the house was welcome. Tom followed him out to a shaded courtyard where they sat down at a stone table.

It was surrounded by three walls and on one end there was a green mosaic water fountain and its falling water enrobed the courtyard with calm. Karim's brother's son, whose name was Bilal, looked at him curiously whilst enquiring about his father's brother.

Tom assured him that he was very well and that he sent his regards.

'We don't see him very often now. He doesn't like the town, which is difficult to understand as he grew up here. But some people are like that, they don't care about family, obligations and loyalty,' Bilal said drily. He sat very straight backed on a wooden chair and looked at Tom as if his uncle was a traitor of some kind.

'Well, he seemed very happy with his farm and family. He did say that he wished your father would visit him.'

'Yes. My father does talk about visiting him quite often but somehow there is never the time. You seem to be a man of the world Monsieur Lancaster, so you understand this.'

A short woman, Tom presumed she was some kind of relation, poured tea into two glasses and then left the silver pot on the table together with some sweet cakes.

'Now, what can I do for you. It is not often we see European people here and it intrigues me.' Bilal looked at Tom with an air of superiority which annoyed him, in fact the man had annoyed him since he came to the door but he smiled and explained his reasons for the visit.

'I am looking for an English girl, blonde hair medium height by the name of Bea. She's disappeared and her father is worried about her. He thinks that she might be staying in this village.' Tom drank his tea and continued. 'I was hoping that you might have seen her here. As I said, her father is worried about her and just wants to know that she is ok.'

The incident in the village, the nationalist flag on the car carrying Bea made him feel uncomfortable mentioning her to a total stranger, but he didn't have a choice if they were to find her. There was quite a difference between this man and his uncle who had been so helpful and friendly to total strangers. Tom wondered what his father was like.

He looked like he was thinking, scratching his head and looking towards the blue sky in an exaggerated way and Tom wondered if he was a little mad. This was getting them nowhere. He'd leave as soon as he could.

'No, I'm sorry.' He shook his head and looked sad. 'There has been no strangers here, well apart from the odd Spanish military band, and you of course. No, apart from you and the fascists I cannot think of anyone fitting this description. I can understand a father's worry about his daughter though. Maybe he should have kept tighter strings on her, no?'

'Yes, maybe he should,' Tom answered feeling light-headed. He took a deep breath to bring himself back to normal, but his vision was blurring, making it difficult to focus on anything. Why was Bilal staring at him with that stupid smirk on his face?

Then it dawned on him. The bloody tea. Tom looked down on the table and noticed that Bilal had not touched his cup.

'Why...' The tall silver teapot and the glass cups went flying off the table as Tom tried to stand up, but his legs would not carry him. Everything blurred and duplicated, and in slow motion he crashed towards the hard stone floor.

~ 30 ~

Voices from far away whispered, but were too quiet, too mumbled, and too unimportant for Tom to open his eyes. He was comfortable in his darkness, and once again he drifted off into pleasant dreams which he was in no hurry to leave. When he woke up the voices had gone quiet and he slowly opened his eyes. His mind was foggy and he struggled to remember who he was, never mind where he was, or why he was there.

It was a strange room, one he had never seen before with deep red and gold throws and ornate mirrors on the walls. It smelled odd too. This was not Paris and he felt confused and nauseous. He was lying on a sofa, fully dressed in someone else's clothes, and slowly he started to remember bits of what had happened.

He closed his eyes again and heard the door open and light steps coming towards him. Still a little groggy, he opened his eyes, and there she was. She was just sitting down next to him with a bright copper bowl next to her.

She saw the surprise in his eyes and smiled.

'Tom, darling. I'm so glad you're awake, I could just hug you.' She took his hand and squeezed it.

'Is this still a dream? Was all of it a dream?' Tom asked hopefully. 'All that happened before.'

She picked a small sponge up from the bowl and started cleaning his face. The water felt cool and he closed his eyes again. She was safe, it had all been a bad dream, he knew it had to be, because it was too awful to be true.

He could feel himself drifting off again, but when she spoke Tom opened his eyes and tried to concentrate.

'For you it was sweetie. I can't tell you how lovely it is to see you, I've thought about you almost every day since you left Madrid.' She took a deep breath. 'Now, we have to get you cleaned up. You hit your head on the stone floor when you fell and there is a nasty cut to your head, but don't worry, I'll fix you darling. When I'm finished with you, you will be as good as new.'

Only just noticing that he had a sore forehead his hand went up to it. Then little streams of memory came back to him and he struggled a little to get them into the right order. He remembered the journey through Morocco to find her, the tea and Maria.

The fog cleared his head almost instantly, the past was no dream and he felt heartbroken with the realisation that Eduardo was still dead and reality had come back. Where was Maria.

'Where's Maria?' His voice low, he grabbed her wrist and pulled her towards him.

'Let go, Tom. I'm so happy to see you, don't spoil it.' She steadily held his eyes and he let go.

She sat up straighter and there was something hard showing in her eyes, something that had not been there before.'

'Your friends are fine. They were picked up quite easily, well, Maria was, your other little friend kicked up a little bit of a fight I understand. Maria's making a lot of fuss about not being allowed in here to see you, but I wanted to see you before she did.'

Bea leaned her head to one side, then the other, like she had sore shoulders.

'You must be rather surprised to see me, darling.'

'You could say that,' Tom answered.

'I'm so glad you're here. It would have been better if you'd waited for a few days until everything has blown over.'

'Strange, I never thought of drugging someone as a 'I'm so happy to see you gesture'.'

'I never meant to get you involved,' she continued, 'but you just wouldn't let go. Asking questions, drawing attention to us, talking to people you shouldn't have, and I don't think you even knew what you were getting yourself into.' She put the bowl away and lit a cigarette whilst Tom sat himself up.

'I assume the gold is at the heart of this. And what people are you talking about?'

'People you shouldn't have spoken to, like Charles and that over efficient Captain Santos you asked about Blackstone. It all got back to Pietr and you were getting your friends involved too.'

'By friends I suppose you mean Eduardo?'

'Yes. And that awful American, whatever his name is.'

'So what are you saying? That you were in on Eduardo's murder?'

'It's really not that simple. They wanted to take you in to the nearest cheka and have you executed and dealt with in minutes. And they would have if I hadn't saved you. You would just have disappeared and your friend Eduardo would have done the same. So you see, this outcome was better, not ideal because I liked Eduardo, but better than the alternative.'

Tom's head was spinning from the heat in the room and together with the cigarette smoke and Bea's story he felt nauseous again.

'You're looking ever so tired Tom. Shall we continue after you've had a rest? It's nothing that matters now anyway.'

'No, you'd better tell me.'

Silence filled the room before she continued.

'Very well. It all started when I met Pietr. He came to the hospital to visit someone and he fell head over heels in love with me. We went out a few times and I think he was looking to impress me. He told me about all this gold he'd got hold of. I later found out that he'd helped General Andriev steal the gold from Cartagena, killed the other men who were in on it and taken the gold for himself. That's General Andriev, head of NKVD in Spain and the man put in charge by Stalin and Negrin to transport the gold safely onto the ships at Cartagena. I guess Pietr planned to put the blame on someone else and be gone before Andriev found out the truth. - He did try to convince me that he was only holding onto the gold for the good of the Republic and for a little while I actually believed him.' She shook her head at this. 'Andriev's cover for transporting the gold from Madrid to the coast was as an American banker called Blackstone.' She watched Tom close his eyes. 'This is the man you were asking questions about. The head of the Russian secret police.'

'How do you know about all this?' Tom opened his eyes and looked at her.

'I have contacts Tom. People tell me things. Maybe they think I'm just a blonde airhead but that suits me to the ground. Anyway, it was only when I overheard a conversation I realised that Pietr was a spy for Franco.'

She paused whilst a girl came in with some tea and sweet biscuits.

Bea had a sip of her tea and looked amused when Tom left his untouched.

'Oh, Tom. It's all quite safe and will do you good.'

'So, what was Pietr planning to do with the gold then?' Tom said, ignoring the refreshments.

'Hold on, I'm coming to it. Just before all this started to go wrong, I met Muhammad. He was from this village and forced into Franco's army. To cut a long story short, he'd been left for dead on a battlefield but was found, quite by accident, by an IB ambulance who reluctantly brought him into the hospital. I looked after him and slowly I found myself in love with him. You will really like him too.'

Bea lit up another cigarette and offered one to Tom which he accepted.

'Well you see darling, his family is an old part of the Rif. They never gave in to the Spanish and about fifteen years ago they set up an independent republic here, in the Rif Mountains. They even sent diplomatic convoys to England and France,' she smiled. 'They were ignored of course and then Spain and France beat them. Both using German chemical weapons. You just can't get away from those Germans can you.'

She leaned back on the sofa and continued.

'If Pietr had found out about us he would have killed Muhammad, and I think he would probably have killed me too, so I had to do something about the situation. Whilst I was trying to keep everything together you were just causing problems. I heard about you from Pietr who wanted you shot and from Charles who wanted you out of the country.'

'I didn't realise you had any contact with Charles. Why did he want me gone?'

She ignored him. 'Your anarchist friend was trying to tell people there was a secret communist base somewhere south of Madrid full of stolen Spanish gold and it all went on and on.'

'Why couldn't you just have told me about it instead causing all this misery.'

'I had to make a decision Tom, and I would make the same one again if I had to. I managed to talk Pietr into scaring you off instead of shooting you. My death was just to stop you coming back.' She paused. 'How did you get back into Spain?'

'Your father.'

'Ahh. That makes sense. I won't enquire about his health.' A shadow came over her face briefly and then she continued. 'You must believe me darling, I didn't think that Pietr would be that brutal with you. I nearly cried when I saw you and the state you were in. I didn't even think that you'd actually make it back to France. I knew after that, I had to get rid of him. It was the right thing to do, he was a spy for Franco all along.' Her voice trailed off.

'How do you know?'

'Never mind that. It's not important.'

'Then, shortly after you left, the gold vanished and the only people who knew where it was kept was me, Pietr and Charles.'

'Charles again?' Tom interrupted. ' You mentioned him earlier. How did Charles know?'

'I don't know, but he did. I didn't tell him if that's what you think. Dear Charles, I hurt him a lot once you know, but still he wanted to marry me. I called him boring at a dinner party. Embarrassed him in front of people. Not the done thing, is it?'

'I don't care about you and Charles. Did you take the gold then?'

She shot him an annoyed glance.

'Well, I'd taken a few bars earlier, more than enough for what I needed, and hidden them away. I knew that Pietr hadn't moved the rest of it because when he found out he went mad, but for some reason he refused to believe that I had anything to do with it. It was only when I actually told him that I had proof of his activities and that soldiers were waiting outside his flat to arrest him that he must have realised what had happened. The look he gave me before managing to escape... I'll never forget it and I hope I never have to see him again.'

'So where was the gold? Where is the gold?'

Bea shrugged her shoulders and laughed a little.

'I'm not really sure. I had a word with Charles even though I didn't think that he'd stolen it. He strongly suggested that it was with the rest of the gold on its way to Russia. I guess he is more involved with the Republic than he likes to admit.'

'Hang on a minute. I tried to tell him about the gold and he wasn't interested.'

'I know you did. He told me.'

There was nothing Tom could add to that. The list of questions he'd ask Charles as soon as he saw him was growing though.

'Anyway, I had to travel to Paris for various reasons and left Muhammed at Maria's house until I got back.'

'I know what you did there. Your father has pictures of your meetings.' She'd been in Paris whilst he was there, not contacting him at all. Maybe seeing him in the street and hiding behind a corner so that he would not spot her.'

'I thought I was doing so well.' She laughed. 'I didn't use my name. I borrowed a passport from one of the nurses at the hospital and called myself Vivian for a little while. It wasn't a pleasure trip.'

Tom recognised the name but could not place where he'd heard it.

'You're not just here for a cosy get together with his family are you.'

'No, you silly man, although they are lovely people. The money was to buy arms for Muhammed's family to get at the Nationalist army here in Morocco and also to get France involved in the war.'

'I'm not sure the French would be up for bribing so I'm assuming you have something else in mind'

'We need strong countries like Britain, France and America to help us, but they are all looking the other way whilst Germany and Italy are helping Franco to bomb and kill us. - I always hoped that one day there would be some help coming, but there has been nothing so far, as you well know. Russia's help is very much appreciated, but it is just not enough.'

'Then one day, after I had met Muhammed, it came to me, we had to make France enter the war, break the non-intervention pact. And we had to make sure it was on our side and an act of aggression towards France from Franco would see to that, wouldn't it? France has been on edge ever since the Germans started arrived here posing as mining engineers. Well, we all know they are not engineers and I figured that France, who wanted to help the Republic to start with, could do with a little bit of a push in the right direction. Besides, the Republic would give Spanish Morocco its independence in a jiffy if France had not been so worried that their Moroccans would want their independence too.' She paused. 'So, what do you think?'

She looked rather smug as she sat there with a smile at the corner of her lips waiting for his comments.

'Well, you have been busy,' he said drily. 'So are you telling me that you are invading French territory? Are you talking of parading into Paris with guns, tanks and Franco's banners flaying?' He looked at her and said slowly. 'Or is it just over the border, here in Morocco?'

'Paris, eh. I would if I could darling. What I wouldn't give for a decent meal at La Baroque, but no it's your second guess. - Quite simple really, tomorrow evening we bomb the French part of Morocco with Fascist weapons and show people that fascists were here preparing for it. France might be a little woolly minded with a lot of things but it won't stand for an attack, and they will break the non-intervention agreement. Voila.' She threw her hands in the air. 'Do you see now why I could not have you nosing around making a nuisance of yourself. This is important.' She sighed and looked at Tom for his response.

He was surprised, he had not expected this. Little Bea, stealing gold, committing murder, by association maybe but still murder of poor Eduardo and God knows who else.

'It's a lot to take in.' He said slowly lighting a cigarette from her box. 'Where are you bombing? Will there be deaths or are you just trying to make a point?'

She smiled at him like he was a child who didn't understand the grown up world.

'There has to be a lot of deaths, Tom. Enough deaths to make France very angry and not accept some story from Franco, and angry enough to stand up to Britain who told them not to help Spain in the first place. I know it sounds bad, but think how many people have died in the trenches and been bombed in their homes and all the mass murders on Franco's side. How many have been shot for even the slightest connection to the left in the areas he's already taken. Officially sanctioned death, rape and destruction is all that awaits Spain if he wins. And if that was to happen, don't think that the rest of the world is safe because Franco, Hitler and Mussolini won't stop of their own free will. - I don't want anyone to die at all, but needs must and this is the way it has to be, because if we don't, there will be no Spain left.'

She stood up. 'Do say you agree with us Tom. Maria did and I think she is rather keen on the idea, and I have always known you'd do anything for her. Not for me, but for Maria. Have a little think about it whilst you bathe.'

'Bathe?'

'You smell, and also, you couldn't have dinner with Muhammed and his family looking quite as in need of a bath as you do. Besides, I think you will like it.'

She smiled as he took the hand she held out and they walked in silence along a walkway, open to the courtyard on one side, and vaulted archways leading to, he assumed, the rest of the house on the other side. He had seen buildings like this in Andalucía, but not on this scale and he tried to take in as much of it as he could. He knew that they'd need to know the layout of this place if they were to get out.

It was still light outside but the sun was low, making the heat more bearable and the scent from the near apricot trees lingered in the still air. The brown wide trousers Tom was wearing were too long, and dragged along the tiled floor.

'Bea, I need to see Maria. I can't think about anything until I know she's safe.'

'I've told you that she is fine. What kind of person do you think I am.'

'Can I see her then.'

'Of course. She's not a prisoner, I'll let her know you're cleaning yourself up and then she can go and see you. I was never going to keep her away from you,' she said as though he'd hurt her feelings as they continued walking down some stairs at the end of the walkway.

This seemed to be what he had to settle for and a wash might clear his head, although he doubted that any amount of baths could possibly make sense of all of this.

'This is as far as I can go. There will be someone out here to take you back to your room when you are done. Don't be too long, as you don't want to be late for dinner.'

'I'm assuming Aaron and Charles will be there too. I've got quite a list of questions for Charlie.'

'Charles isn't here.'

'But you said Maria, Aaron and Charles had been picked up.'

'We only picked up Maria and your foreign friend. Is Charles here with you?'

'Well, he was.' Tom wished he'd kept his mouth shut. He hadn't realised that Charles was still out there.

'I'm sure he'll show up. He always does.' She started walking back up the stairs and turned back. 'I am truly sorry for what happened last year you know. Don't think bad of me Tom. Not you.'

And with this she walked up the stairs and Tom opened the heavy ornate door in front of him and went in.

The large, blue and green tiled room was gloomy, and the only light came from some lanterns scattered around the sides of the small sunk marble pool in the middle of the floor and from an small barred window at the end of the room.

On a chair beneath the window Tom saw his old clothes, now clean and neatly folded up. The air was heavy with rose scent and he quickly removed his borrowed clothes and walked into the luke warm bath. The water, even though it was not hot, irritated his sunburnt skin as he submerged himself in it before sitting down on the bottom step leading into the bath. He sat like this for a few minutes, feeling strangely invigorated, before using one of the soaps provided and dipping his head under water to remove the bubbles. He sat back up again and closed his eyes. How had this happened.

She'd only been in Madrid since August last year, and here they were, ten months later, and she had turned into a terrorist. He knew that she had been affected by the deaths and misery of her work but never thought her capable of stealing, killing and kidnapping. He guessed that makes the lie of her death rather insignificant. But she was part of the murder of Eduardo, and Tom could still see his lifeless staring eyes in the corner of that house and it was her fault.

He was just about to get up and dry himself when the door opened and a woman, carrying a tray of mint tea and biscuits, came in and placed the tray on a small table by the side of the bath. Not having ever been in a situation quite like this, Tom sank deeper into the bath, hiding beneath the bubbles, and thanked her as she left whilst wondering whom the other glass of tea was for. He was sick to death of mint tea.

Quickly washing the last soap off, he got out of the bath and was just wrapping a towel around him as the door opened once again and a man came in. He looked like he was in his late twenties, Tom's age, and his build was slight as he smiled awkwardly at Tom.

'I am Muhammed. Please do not let me disturb you.'

Tom nodded in response, wanting to get dressed and out of this room and its thick intense air.

He sat down, poured some tea in the two glasses and continued. 'Bea told me that she had explained everything to you.' He indicated for Tom to join him at the table and he slowly walked around the bath and sat down on a chair more suited to a Parisian café than here.

'She explained some things,' Tom said neutrally

'Bea is a remarkable woman, without her I would be dead. She doesn't think you approve of what we are doing, so I have come to explain to you, maybe in a different way to Bea, why this is so important to us. - I think you are a fair man Tom Lancaster and your opinion means a lot to Bea.' He smiled and ate a biscuit whilst waiting for Tom to agree to listen.

Tom just wanted to get out of there, to make sure Maria was safe and to take her, Bea and Aaron away from there. He didn't care about their reasons, maybe he would later but right now getting out of here was the most important thing.

However, he was hardly in a position to refuse and so he nodded whilst drinking the tea, wishing it was something stronger.

'It is difficult to know where to start, but I come from a family who has been fighting for our independence for centuries. Ever since the Romans there has always been some foreign power here to suppress us and take advantage of our people and natural resources. Iron, copper and coal have together with our location by both the Mediterranean and Atlantic seas been the main reason for our troubles through the years.'

'For a few years, in the twenties, one man, his name was Abd el Krim, united us all and the Rif became an independent state which, if it had been properly recognised, could have united the whole of Morocco and retrieved its freedom and independence. You understand the words freedom and independence? It is exactly what the Republic in Spain are fighting for is it not, to regain the country for its people.'

'I do understand your situation, but you shouldn't have got Bea involved. She's a nice girl with no experience of these things. Even though she likes to think that she can do anything, she can't. - Send her back home, and then, when your wars are over, you can go to London and do things properly.'

Tom looked to see if his reasoning had had any affect but Muhammad's face didn't show anything.

'This whole thing was not my idea. I was just glad for the possibility of getting back home again after everything. Bea came up with the plan. She knew where there was gold, she knew how to move it and buy arms which is quite a feat on the Republican side where there are not a lot of weapons or ammunition around even for their own troops. This plan seemed to work for what she wanted, which was for France to enter the war on the Governments side, it worked for me as a way of getting our independence and a way back home.'

Tom wasn't surprised that it had been Bea's idea but there had been no mention of love here, maybe it wasn't a very manly thing to do.

'Do you love her?' Tom asked

'Love? What is love? Love is for fairytales, Monsieur Lancaster. Common goals, bravery and respect is what counts, and I think, in those terms, we are very well suited.'

She loved him though and Tom guessed she was doing a lot of this to make herself indispensable to him, perhaps to make him love her. It wasn't important right now and he didn't want to provoke him in any way whilst here.

'I feel better now, having explained this to you. Can I tell Bea that you understand what we are doing?'

'Yes, you can tell her that. Also tell her I'm looking forward to dinner.' He smiled. It wouldn't hurt to get on his good side for now. Muhammed nodded and left.

Tom got dressed in his old clothes and felt a little better. That chap seemed reasonable enough. How could he not be, he'd deserted from Franco's army because he wanted to go home.

Tom was escorted by a short miserable chap who carried a gun over his shoulder and didn't smile or attempt to talk on their way back upstairs.

He could hear him locking the door securely behind him and he had only just gone over to the window to look for escape possibilities when the door opened and there was Maria. She closed the door behind her and rushed up to him.

'Tom, are you ok? Bea said you'd hit your head when they brought you here.'

'I'm fine.' He assured her. 'Really, I am.' He touched her face with his hand and she looked up. 'How are you? Did you get hurt?'

'No. I was daydreaming when they snuck up on us so I didn't have the chance to do anything. Aaron got himself bashed up a bit but he was alive and swearing at them as they brought us here. Charles went for a walk and wasn't with us when they came.'

'Thank God you're all alright.'

'Has Bea told you?' she asked whilst holding on to his arm as they went to sit down.

'If you mean, has she told me about her big plan, then yes, she has,' he nodded.

'I want to go home Tom. Home to where I don't know, but I really don't like this.'

Those words tore at his heartstrings because he'd known all along that he should have made her go back to her mother's and he pulled her close and kissed her forehead.

'I know darling. We'll try to get out of here tonight and we'll to bring Bea with us, but if that doesn't work, we'll just leave her here. This is the bed she made for herself and if her father wants her to come home, he can come and get her himself. We need to raise some sort of alarm, they can't be allowed to go through with their plan.'

'Do you think they'll do it without her? She said that a General Carlos had helped her put it all together on the Spanish side. Maybe he will still go ahead with it.'

'Maybe, I don't know. I guess it must have been General Carlos who ordered the raid on the Pension and who asked Aaron to spy on me.'

'He said it was some woman. I guess she was just acting on someone's behalf.'

Tom suddenly remembered where he'd heard the name Vivian before. It was the name of the woman who'd asked Aaron to spy on him. Bea kept on popping up everywhere. It couldn't be her who got Aaron involved. Still, she was in Paris at the time and she did call herself Vivian.

'Are we in that palace like building we saw when we arrived?' Tom asked her as he had only seen the view from his window which showed a wide view of mountains ahead and a sheer cliff falling below it.

'We are in that house yes, just outside the village, on the cliff above Karim's brothers house. I would tell you it is very grand but you have obviously seen some it.'

She looked suspiciously at his clean appearance and nodded to herself before continuing.

'There are smaller buildings scattered all around on the other side from here. It belongs to Muhammad's family.'

'What about guards, are there lots of them.'

'There are some armed men around yes, but if we are careful I think we can get past them. I know where Aaron is kept, or at least I think I do, there is a guard outside the door but I don't know how he is.'

'Bea told me he was fine, but we'll need to get him out too. I have no idea what Charles is up to though. Without us he's probably trying to make it across the border on his own.'

In hushed voices they continued to plot their breakout and felt better by having a plan.

If it would work was anybody's guess.

~ 31 ~

The late dinner passed in an uneventful way and Mohammed's father was a good host making sure they all had enough food and kept the conversation going. There was no mention of what they were planning, nor any talk of politics or war. It was surreal.

Once back in his room, Tom took the long red rope holding the thick wall curtain in place and attached it securely to the iron hoop drilled into the wall by the window and sat himself down to wait for the call to prayers.

It was due, according to Maria who had noticed it the night before, a couple of hours before dawn and they would use this opportunity to escape. His stomach was full and he felt his eyes close several times whilst waiting for the hours to pass so he got up and stood by the window. The sky was clear and he looked at those brilliant stars. Maria's theory on what happened when you died made him smile and he spent the remainder of the night pacing the dark room from the bed to the window until it was time. The prayers took place just outside the main building facing east, away from the house but they would still have to get past them somehow to leave. Maria had caught a glimpse of the main entrance to the house where there had been several cars parked, one of which they intended to steal.

Tom opened the window and looked down, his stomach tied itself in knots at the prospect of climbing out of it. There was nothing below but a great fall onto rocks a hundred meters below, but the open walkway outside his door extended all the way to the end so all he had to do was tie the rope to his wrist for safety and climb out onto a few iron bolts sticking out from the wall.

They looked robust enough to hold him for the one step along he needed to jump onto the wall of the walkway.

Knowing they had very little time, he tied the rope to his right wrist and climbed onto the windowsill facing outwards and whilst not looking down, he put his right foot onto one of the bolts, took a deep breath and grabbed another one with his hand and he was on the wall.

He could hear the blood pulsing through his head and kept repeating 'don't look down, don't look down' to himself. His left foot scratched around for the edge of the walkway wall whilst trying not to panic. His heart was beating fast and the wall scratched his face as he finally felt a flat solid surface underneath his foot.

Grabbing onto another bolt with his hand he swung around and landed with a thud on the walkway. He felt dizzy with relief and rested his head back on the chiseled stone wall.

'You are going to have to be more quiet than that.' Maria whispered as she emerged from the shadows and he got up on his feet.

'I'm glad that's done.' He looked at his hands that were shaking.

'Here, have this.' Maria held out a modern looking gun

'Where did you get this from?' He took the gun and checked for ammunition which, unlike his old gun, it had lots of.

'I've been walking around for a little while.'

'You could have got caught' He said disapprovingly. 'Now, let's get Aaron.'

Hunched down below the walkway wall they hurried along, Maria showing the way, until they got to the lower level. There they could see a man with a rifle thrown over his shoulder leaning against the wall looking bored.

'Right,' Tom whispered, carefully glancing around the corner at the guard. He'd had some military training in school, and he'd handled a gun before, but apart from his experience on the front the previous year he'd never actually used one.

The only light came from a flickering lantern further down the corridor and Tom quietly approached the guard and hoped he wouldn't turn around. He was just going to threaten him with the gun and make him open the door, but quickly decided that it was better to hit him over the head instead. The butt of the gun crashed down with force on the man's head and he fell soundlessly to the floor. As he laid out cold on the stone floor, they went through his pockets trying to find the keys to open the door.

'They're not here,' Maria whispered nervously whilst her hands went through the pockets again. 'What shall we do, they're not here.' She leaned back against the large oak door behind her and sighed.

'They must be there. Go through them again.' Tom looked up at her and in the faint light from the lantern, a key reflected it's light. He laughed quietly. 'It's in the door behind you.'

'They obviously don't take us for the adventurous kind then,' Maria said as she stood back up and turned around.

She turned the key and quietly opened the door. The room was dimly lit and bare, and the smell of damp hit them instantly.

'Aaron. Are you there.' Maria's voice softly echoed over the bare walls and across the darkness.

'You took your bloody time.' Aaron came towards them. His face that was bruised before now looked positively awful and Maria gasped at the sight of it. He had been gone over properly, but was still be able to walk.

'What happened to you.'

'Your friends happened to me, that's what. Although I can tell that you two seem to be ok. I tell you what,' he wagged his finger at Tom in the semi darkness. 'Ever since I met you there has been nothing but problems for me. Once we're out of here, that's it. No more.'

'Good, good. Let's get to work.' He ushered Aaron out of the way whilst dragging the guard in there and locking the door behind them. Tom hoped he would stay unconscious and quiet long enough for them to get away.

Once out of there they told Aaron the plan which he readily agreed to, apart from the fact he thought they should leave Bea there.

Tom gave them the rifle they'd stolen from the guard and he kept the gun Maria had given to him. Whilst Aaron and Maria went off to find a car, Tom went to find Bea. His conscience nagged him that they should also get rid of the explosives, but there was not enough time to find out where they were kept and if indeed they were kept there at all. They'd have to leave that to someone else.

He knew from Maria where Bea's room was and really hoped her new man was honorable and would not be anywhere near her.

He needn't have worried. Her room, in the grander part of the house was dark with only the moonlight slipping in through the ornate shutters showing her asleep in bed.

Tom walked up to her and wished he had some chloroform or something like it, but he didn't, so he took a deep breath and put his hand over her mouth to avoid her screaming. He'd expected her to struggle but she didn't. Instead she opened her eyes and pointed a gun at him through the bed cover. Tom removed his hand and Bea put the light on with her other hand whilst still pointing the gun at him.

'For God's sake Tom. I knew you would do this. Couldn't you just play along a little longer. Get this done and then gone off to wherever you want to go.' She got out of bed fully clothed. 'I've got to tell them' She seemed troubled as she walked over to the door.

Tom assumed she was about to call out for help when shouting and gunfire came from the other side of the estate. For a couple of moments Bea lost concentration, and he knocked the gun out of her hand. He had seconds to grab her and run for the car which he hoped was waiting for them outside. This meant wasting no time struggling with her so he hit her hard on the side of her face and she went out like a light. Second time he'd done that this evening.

He must have been full of adrenaline because Bea felt light as a feather as he carried her over his shoulder towards the back of the house. As they got closer to the noise he saw the outline of nationalist soldiers in the dark, shooting at the guards of the house.

They must be the fake fascists that were supposed to carry out the bombing and he briefly wondered why they were shooting at their own. He didn't have time to think about that as he could see Aaron and Maria starting up a car at the back of the house and urging him to run faster. He heard footsteps behind him, getting closer and closer but with Bea over his shoulder he couldn't stop to shoot. He threw her in the back of the car before turning around. It was Charles who'd been running after him.

'For God's sake Charles. How did you get here.'

'Through the gates. I'm not going back without her.'

'Well, get in the car quickly then.'

Aaron was staring thoughtfully at Bea for a second before noticing that Charles had a gun aimed at Tom's back.

'Once you're out of the car I'll get in. Come on. Hurry up or I'll shoot the bloody lot of you.'

Aaron and Maria got out of the car whilst not taking their eyes of Charles.

'What are you doing? We've got to get out of here quick.'

Charles backed himself into the car and smiled.

'Sorry chaps. You'd better hurry up though.' He pointed to something behind them and drove off down the road with Bea in the back seat. There was no need for the trio to turn around, they could hear them coming. There was nothing for them to do but to run for the village.

'We need a car.' Tom shouted as they almost flew down the hill towards the centre of the town. Suddenly he remembered seeing a car outside Bilal's house and changed direction suddenly. He knew that they couldn't drive after them because Aaron and Maria had let all the tyres down whilst he got Bea.

Bilal's house was dark and quiet. The car was still parked outside and they threw themselves inside. Mohammed's friends would be there any moment and they had yet to get the car started. Aaron got the car electricity on by using the old Talbot key he still had in his pocket and pressed the starting pedal. A low noise started up from the engine, increasing as Aaron pressed the accelerator and they were off. The men running after them jumped out of the way as the open topped car drove straight at them and down the hill, the way Charles had driven off minutes earlier. Tom glanced backwards, avoiding the bullets zinging past them, and confirmed that they were all wearing fascist uniforms. It was all rather odd, were they actual fascists or Bea's fascists? It didn't really matter now anyway. They sped along the rough road and were finally out of shooting range.

'Just drive as fast as you can Aaron. Word will be out in no time and we'll have half the town after us.' Tom shouted over the noise of the engine.

The mud road was dusty and bumpy. A closed top car would have been preferable, but they were away. What was Charles up to? It had happened so quickly. He was obviously more involved than Tom had realised. They drove towards the French border. They needed to get over the border quickly and that would also be where Charles was heading.

'Was that Bea you threw into the car up there?' Aaron shouted above the engine.

'It was.' Tom knew what he was going to say.

'That was the woman I told you about. Vivian, the one that asked me to keep an eye on you.'

'I thought as much.' Tom tried to see around the bends, to see how far ahead of them they were.

'It makes sense now.'

'I'm glad it does to one of us.'

If it hadn't been so windy he would have lit up a cigarette, instead he leaned back over the seat to give Maria a kiss and almost toppled out of the car as Aaron drove around a corner and came to screeching halt. Tom turned back in his seat and saw why. The road was blocked by an army van, and before they had a chance to re-start the engine and go around it, two very smartly dressed fascist soldiers appeared by the roadside, pointing their guns at them.

With no other option, the three of them put their hands up and were ordered out of the car as an officer stepped out from behind the van.

Tom wanted to put his hands over his face and cry. They had come so far only to be stopped now when the border was so close. There they stood by the side of the car as the first rays of the morning sun lit up the dust that was slowly settling back on the road behind them. The officer came closer and he smiled when he saw Tom's face change as he recognised him. Before them stood Pietr Alexandrow, alive and well and dressed in a pristine fascist officer uniform.

Tom could feel the blood rushing through his veins, hear it sing in his head and he threw a quick glance over to Maria.

'Tom, it's been a long time. How have you been? And Maria as well. I don't think I know this friend of yours.' Silence settled for a second. 'It's rude to ignore a polite question, is it not.' He walked up and stood in front of Tom.

'Fascist, eh. Well that makes sense. I always found it difficult to believe that an arsehole like you would be on the Republic's side.' Tom answered.

'That is not a nice way to greet an old friend is it? And to think how nice I was to you last time we met.' He shook his head as he stood in front of them, looking at them, one by one. Tom's throat tightened up by the mention of that last time. Pietr had won then. Tom's hate of the man mixed with embarrassment for how easily he'd been beaten and how they had laughed at him.

'It's funny don't you think. I'm collecting you all here. Maybe if I stand here for a while longer General Carlos will be in my possession also.'

Only then did Tom notice the car in the ditch a little further on.

'So where is she? What have you done with her this time?'

'Take it easy Tom. She's in the van with the balding man who was driving.' He said something to one of the soldiers who opened the truck door. She had a gash on her forehead but that was Tom's doing so he couldn't blame that on anybody else. He'd never seen her look scared before, but she did now. Hurried on by the soldier, she walked slowly towards Pietr. Charles trailed out after her and made a noise when he saw who was there.

'I haven't yet had the pleasure of, how do you say in English... ah, catching up with Bea yet. We have a lot of catching up to do.'

'Just leave out the dramatics Alexandrow. What do you want from us?' Tom stepped forward.

'I want payment for what you've stolen from me, and payment for the betrayal and life of a friend.'

'Don't we all. We haven't got the bloody gold. Would we be here if we did? None of us betrayed you and as for the life of a friend, I hope you remember mine.'

'One of your friends has the gold and if they speak up now I will follow my orders and let you go. If you don't, I'll shoot Bea here and now. Then I might as well shoot the rest of you.'

Silence fell once again over the little group.

'I took the gold.'

Everybody looked at Charles who stood, straight backed, at the back of the group.

'It's been shipped to Russia already.'

'I don't know who you are, but I know you haven't got the gold. Like everybody else you're just obsessed with protecting her.' Pietr pointed at Bea and then spat at Charles' shoes before moving back towards Tom. Charles' face went red with indignation. 'I'll have you know I work for the British Government. One of my closest assets was Andriev and he knew what you were up to. That's how I got my hands on the gold and how it was returned to its owners. Now apologise for calling me a liar.'

A hint of a doubt showed on Pietr's face. The mention of Andriev had made Charles' story possible.

Pietr lit a cigarette. 'You wouldn't do that Why wouldn't you take the gold for yourself?'

'Because some of us have honour and know the meaning of right and wrong.'

Tom was sure that Charles knew the difference, but he hadn't taken the 'right' path up at the house when he left them there to die.

'I will have that gold somehow.' Pietr mumbled to himself, stubbed out the cigarette looked back at Tom. 'You are so lucky today. I am under orders to let you and your friends go, that doesn't mean I wouldn't give a lot to keep you here and show you and that bitch,' he looked over towards Bea, 'the price you pay for trying to screw me over. I know that one of you did and I will have something for my troubles.'

He turned his attention back to Tom. 'As I said, I have to let some of you go but I'll have Maria and the spy master instead.' His eyes were still resting on Tom. 'I'm sure you have heard how friendly we are towards Republican whores.'

'Don't even think about it.' Both Tom and Aaron stood in front of her.

'The girl is Spanish and she's coming with us. You count yourselves lucky we're letting you go.' Pietr waved his hands at the two soldiers who pulled Maria away before Tom or Aaron realised what was happening. Stunned,

Maria walked with them quietly. Charles had gone pale but held his head up as he turned and followed them.

'You three get back in the car and go,' he pointed at Tom, Aaron and Bea. 'Now before I ignore my orders and say you tried to run.'

'No. Maria's coming with us or we all stay.' Tom felt the gun in his pocket and hoped that there were still some bullets in it.

The officer came up close to Tom's face and he could smell his breath.

'That can be arranged. I would like nothing better than to shoot some Republicans right here and believe me, I will. Now, for the last time, get in that car and drive.'

With speed and strength that Tom didn't recognise as his own, he pulled the gun out of his pocket. Whilst Pietr was looking towards where his two soldiers were dragging a now kicking and screaming Maria into the van, Tom pressed it to Pietr's face and grabbed the back of his head.

'Tell them to let her go.' Tom said slowly and when nothing happened. 'Let her go or I will shoot you and then I will shoot them. Now do it.' Tom shouted, and the two soldiers hearing the commotion, stopped and looked back their weapons drawn. Nobody held on to Charles and he took the opportunity to run into the forest. He disappeared into the lush greenness remarkably quickly. Not one single shot was fired after him as all eyes returned to Tom and Pietr.

'They'll kill her if you don't let me go.'

'You were going to kill her anyway and it's better she dies now. It's your choice Pietr, but you have to make it now because I have dreamt of putting a hole in your head since October.'

Still, Pietr kept calm and said nothing.

'Maybe this will make your mind up.' Aaron said calmly whilst waving the rifle they stole from the guard at the palace in one hand and a hand grenade in the other. The two guards lowered their guns and let Maria go. She came flying back towards the car and jumped in it next to Bea.

Tom dragged Pietr, still with the gun in his face, into the front of the car. He figured that the only way to get away was to take him with them for a little while up the road to discourage the soldiers from following them.

Aaron manoeuvred their car around the van and set off along the uneven dusty road towards the border.

'Are you alright, Maria?' Tom asked, wanting nothing more than be at the back with her, but with a great lump of a man squeezed between himself and the car door, that wouldn't be happening.

'I am.' She replied. 'I thought for a moment that that was it though.'

'Nearly safe now.' Tom promised. 'We've got to shift him, the bastard is crushing me,' he said to Aaron.

'How do you know him?' he asked.

'He's the one I told you about, the one that killed Eduardo and nearly killed me last year.'

'Just pull the trigger, Tom.' Aaron shouted over the loud engine. 'If anyone deserves it it's him.'

'Yes, Tom. Pull the trigger.' Pietr's voice was low, right next to Tom's head. 'Because if you don't, I'll find you and I'll find Bea and you will both wish you'd never been born.'

Tom pressed the gun harder into Pietr's ribs and ignored his words.

'I know I should.' Tom replied to Aaron. He wanted to kill him, to put a bullet in the head and make him aware that it was for Eduardo, but he couldn't do it. His finger was on the trigger but he couldn't push it. Bloody wimp he was. He'd regret not doing it.

'Let's just get rid of him, I can't feel my legs.'

'Ok, I'll slow down and you can just push him out I guess. As long as you are sure you don't want to pull that trigger. Just think what he did to you and your friend.'

'I just want to get us out of here.'

Aaron slowed down and there was a tirade of Spanish curses coming out of Pietr's mouth as he was pushed out of the car and into a ditch. Moments later there were bullets hitting the car. Tom was sure that they were out of range and wasn't overly concerned about it.

'You didn't take his gun?' Aaron asked sarcastically.

'Sorry. I only had two hands and they were busy.' Tom wanted to laugh. A few minutes ago it had looked like the end of the road for them and now it was all going to be fine again. He'd barely finished the thought before he heard Bea shouting in the back seat. Tom turned around to see what the fuss was about and saw Bea staring at her friend. Maria was still sitting up in her seat, but there was blood slowly dripping from the side of her head where one of the bullets had entered. One of the bullets he'd thought wouldn't catch them, had done just that.

'Stop the car.' Tom shouted at Aaron but his request was ignored and Tom jumped over to the back seat with the car still hurtling down the road.

Her beautiful brown eyes were still open, looking at him.

Was this it? This was what he'd done to her. What Pietr had done. His stomach felt filled with lead and his eyes with tears as he checked for signs of life, even though he knew fully well there would be none. His mind went blank and for a short while he could have been anywhere in the world looking at her, holding her hand.

'I didn't do it Tom. It wasn't my fault.' Bea kept on talking but he wasn't listening. 'I'm so sorry Tom, but you should have stayed with us.' Bea put her hand on his shoulder.

'How the hell do you justify this? She was a good, beautiful and kind woman who never did anything bad to anyone and you killed her. As sure as you put the bloody bullet in her head yourself. - And I loved her.' He turned to look at Maria and took her other hand.

He knew the future had seemed too good to be true. Having lived so long without realising he loved her, he now found himself thinking he could not live without her.

Bea had tears streaming down her cheeks and they annoyed him and he took a deep breath to calm himself down. It was all he could do to not hit her. Deep inside he knew it wasn't Bea's fault directly, but if it wasn't for her they would never have been there and Maria would still be alive, at home with her auntie, where she wanted to be.

~ 32 ~

French Morocco, May 1937

They managed to get over to French Morocco shortly afterwards and found Sir Arthur waiting for them at the border. There was a nationalist officer with him that left just as they arrived. Tom would never have expected it, but Aaron had taken charge of the situation and got them over the border and there was actually a lot to thank him for. These last few hours, he'd helped with protecting her and Tom had to let him know that he had forgiven him for all he'd done earlier and if he could ever help him with anything at all, he would. He would tell him that later because at this moment he couldn't talk. But he thought it was important that he should know.

It turned out that Sir Arthur knew where they were all along. Charlie had informed him of where they were going and the shooting at the house had carried across the mountains for miles.

Bea stayed quiet and didn't move from her corner of the car. Her face was still pale but now it was set sternly, ready to defend her actions, until her father came out to get her.

Tom couldn't move, he was still holding Maria's hand.

'Tom, you have to let go. She needs to go'

He looked up at Sir Arthur. 'I'll never get her back if I let go now.'

'But you know she's already gone.'

How had it come to this? He let her hand go and with a final kiss he left her and walked on unsteady legs towards the house. If he didn't have arrangements to make for her he would just have continued walking, not caring where. He would have found somewhere to sit down and look at the stars and she would have been there with him.

It was easy to blame people and there were so many of them to blame. Pietr for shooting her, Bea for getting them involved in her lies and deceit that lead to all this in the first place, her father for making it possible for Tom to go back. Tom knew he was being unreasonable, but Sir Arthur had got his precious, lying, deceitful daughter back and she was well. Apart from a small mark on her head she got away scot free. Even Aaron could go back to his old life in Paris and continue as normal.

Mostly Tom blamed himself, he's the one that couldn't keep away from her and subsequently dragged her away from the life she knew, even though he knew what could happen. Now she was dead, and with her gone, he had lost everything that mattered.

Later that afternoon, Tom was sitting in the walled garden, in the shade with a large whisky. He was trying to keep himself together, staring into nothingness. He had to make sure that Sir Arthur would do the right thing before he set off back to Paris.

Sir Arthur came and sat down next to him, squeezing his large frame into a small garden chair and put his hand on Tom's shoulder in a conciliatory gesture.

'I'm so sorry. I would never have asked you to go if I had thought the stupid girl had got herself into this much trouble'

'It seems to me that sorry is a word used by you and your daughter a lot. She got everyone into trouble. She got a good man killed last year, she faked her own death, she introduced Pietr to us and she was planning to kill hundreds of people over on this side of the border.' He couldn't bring himself to mention Maria.

'That's not quite the story I've heard from Bea, but we'll talk about that tomorrow when you're feeling better'

'I don't care what you heard. You know I only went to Madrid to see Maria, I couldn't stop thinking about her, day and night she was always there, in my thoughts. Thanks to me she had to leave her home and family and go on the run, but it was ok because I'd keep her safe and we'd be together.' He took a gulp of whisky and stared into the glass, 'And thanks to your daughter she's now dead.' He wanted to add that they had plans, were going to get married and live happily forever, but he didn't. Those plans and dreams belonged only to them.

'You will have to arrange for her body to be taken back to her family for burial. I don't care how you do it but you owe her that much. You owe me that much'

Sir Arthur was looking at Tom with concern.

'Of course Tom. I will make sure she goes home, and I will make sure they know how much you cared for her. Bea is another problem. I'm sending her to Scotland for a few months to stay with relatives to see if they can get her back to normal again. - You know her mother didn't die from TB as we told you and Bea when you were little. She had become mentally unstable and couldn't cope with life anymore, and so she committed suicide when Bea was only two years old. I made the mistake of trying to keep the truth from her, but somehow last summer, she found out and she felt hurt and cheated by all of us who knew. Mostly she felt cheated by her mother for not considering her worth enough to stay alive for. That's what the argument was about before she went to you in Madrid. I guess she felt like you were the only one she could trust. I'm not making excuses for her Tom, but you can see how this kind of thing can change a person.'

Well, that made sense, Tom had wondered what that argument was about and funnily enough, now that he finally found out, he was past caring.

'I don't want to talk about her anymore if you don't mind.'

'We haven't had any news about Charles either. Your friend said that he ran into the forest and I think we have to assume that he's dead. What I don't understand is why he was there with you.'

'He said it was you who told him to come with us. If he brought Bea out he'd be brought back to London.'

'Well, I said nothing of the sort. He was going to be posted back to London within the month anyway and he knew that. I guess we'll just never know his reasons.'

'Do you know why they broke up? Charles and your daughter?'

'I think she was bored with him. Well, he's not the most exciting man in the world is he?'

'When we arrived at the border, there was a fascist officer there with you...' Tom let that hang in the air

'I had to call in a big favour to get you out of there. If you had just waited at the house they would have escorted all of you here. It took a lot of persuading to make them agree to this as you were all, according to them, Republicans on Nationalist territory.'

'Are you telling me that all the shooting at the house was fascists coming to our rescue?' He looked at him disbelievingly.

'Well, almost. They were going to raid it anyway for reasons of their own, but they would have let you go. If I hadn't arranged it you would not have cleared mainland Spain before you were shot down on your journey over here.'

That explained Pietr's orders to let them go he guessed, but if he hadn't stopped them and tried to take Maria away, they would have cleared the border alive anyway, all of them.

'They were the ones that shot her so don't give me any of that grateful rubbish.'

Tom finished his drink and left Sir Arthur sitting there. He didn't want to hear any more. It didn't matter anyway, it would change nothing.

For Tom, Spain and the war was over.

Canouan Island, St Vincent, Eleven months later

'Your guest is here, sir.'

'Thank you, Lakitia. Show him down to the pool and prepare some afternoon tea. He's had a long journey.'

'Are you sure you wouldn't prefer some ice tea in this heat.'

'Quite sure, thank you.'

He went over to the window and looked out over his secluded part of the island. Light blue sea and lush green mountains meeting with every wave along the shoreline. And he was still in Britain, well in the empire anyway. His guest had sat himself down by the pool under a parasol and removed his jacket. More used to the weather in Belarus, he looked hot and uncomfortable. He tightened his college tie and went down to greet his guest.

'Andriev, welcome to the island. I hope your journey wasn't too uncomfortable.'

His guest stood up to shake his host's hand.

'Your plane was quite comfortable thank you. When I get my affairs in order I will repay the favour.'

They both sat down and Lakitia served the tea together with a lemon cake.

'We'll have a gin and tonic after this I think,' he smiled. 'Let's get the business part of this visit over with first, shall we.' He pulled out an envelope and handed it over.

His guest put it away in his briefcase and smiled.

'It is the whole amount?'

'Of course. Less the commission I had to pay on the sale of the gold, but that was shared between the two of us. There is more money there than either of us could possibly spend in several lifetimes.'

A parrot landed on the pool house roof and Andriev smiled.

'It all went rather well, don't you agree?'

'You didn't spend days wandering around a forest trying to get out, but yes, in the end it all went quite well.'

'I don't understand what you were doing there in the first place. We had the gold, all you had to do was to get back to London and organise the sale.'

Charles drank his tea and asked Lakitia for a couple of proper drinks.

'For a moment something, or someone, mattered more than the gold. I had to prove something. It was a rash decision and all dealt with now.'

'You managed to prove this 'something'?'

Charles pondered the question for a while and smiled.

'You know, I think I did.'

HISTORICAL NOTES

These historical notes are more difficult to write than the story itself due to having only a short few pages to write them on when there is so much to tell.

The history of the Spanish Civil War was mostly written and recorded by the losing side, by the writers and volunteers that flocked to the Republic's aid. Due to this one has to take great care when reading and researching this part of Spain's history. One of these writers, George Orwell, writes in Homage To Catalonia:

'... beware of my partisanship, my mistakes of facts and the distortion inevitably caused by my having seen only one corner of events. And be aware of exactly the same things when you read any other book on this period of the Spanish Civil War.'

This is obviously a fictitious story, but it is weaved around some actual events and some that could quite easily have taken place.

The bombing of the Plaza de Colón was the first attack on Madrid city centre. However, the planes were neither seen nor heard as they bombed the square killing 16 people and wounding another 60. It was the first bombing of a city, in modern times, for no other reason than to terrify its population. This would be followed by many more, including the bombing of Guernica in 1937.

Madrid came under siege in November '36 and by then the government, and most of the journalists, had already left for Valencia, convinced that she was lost. The Madrileños kept on defending their city and with the help of the International Brigades that came marching up the Gran Via on 8 November 1936, they kept the fascists out of the capital until the end of the war in 1939.

When the gold reserves were moved from Madrid to Cartagena and then onto ships bound for the Soviet Union, the man in charge was the NKVD liaison officer, Alexandr Orlov. He signed papers confirming that 7,900 boxes of gold had been loaded onto the ships at Cartagena, but when they were unloaded at Odessa there were only 7,800 boxes on-board. This may well have been due to paperwork or counting errors, they did after all load the ships under fire from the enemy, but there is always the possibility that the missing boxes, full of Spanish Government gold, were actually taken somewhere else.

Alexandr Orlov escaped to America in 1938 to avoid Stalin's show trials and possible execution in Moscow. He lived there for the rest of his life, and only came to the CIA's attention 15 years after he first arrived by publishing a book about Stalin's crimes.

His cover for the transportation of the Spanish gold was as an American banker by the name of Blackstone.

In 1921, Riffian tribesmen united under their leader Abd el Krim, defeated the Spanish army at Annual in Morocco and created the Republic of the Rif. This state only lasted until 1927 when the French, worried about their own Moroccan territory, joined the Spanish army and defeated Abd el Krim who went into exile and never returned to Morocco.

At this time in Spain, Miguel Primo de Rivera, declared himself a dictator, and with the backing of the generals and the King, he kept hold of that power until 1930 when he was forced to retire. With the constitution of Spain no longer valid, the people rose up and demanded that the King abdicated. In the end the King was forced to announce that an election was to take place in April 1931. When the victory of the second Republic was announced, the whole royal family left Spain that same day.

The workers in Spain were one of the most oppressed people in Europe. A lot of them were illiterate and had never left their villages and they were controlled by the landowners and their managers with brutality.

The landowners and the church had always ensured that there would be a government to back them, and now with a left wing government in place, they were worried.

During the next couple of years the new government tried to implement various reforms for the workers, but the trade unions expected these changes to happen overnight and when they didn't, they went on strike and declared that this government was no better than the previous one.

The Left lost the following election in 1933 to the Centre Right and a pattern of strikes and uprisings by the workers and violence from the police and army followed.

By 1936 the Left and the Centre Left had pulled themselves together and formed into a popular front party, and as such won the last free election to be held in Spain until after Franco's death in 1975.

General Franco had been posted to the Canary Islands to keep him from causing trouble. However, this didn't stop him, and on 17 July 1936 he started the uprising. The rebels took the Spanish part of Morocco quickly and easily, but the rebellion was quashed in most of the mainland. There it would probably have ended if Mussolini hadn't sent planes to Morocco to enable Franco to airlift his African army to the mainland and thereby starting a civil war which would last for three bloody years.

The Republican government had reassured people that the uprising would amount to nothing, but the people still retrieved arms hidden away from previous uprisings and formed themselves into militia groups under their trade unions.

Equipped with Italian and German weapons and soldiers, General Franco moved inland from the south and General Mola from the north. It was plain to see that no matter how enthusiastic the workers of Spain were, they had no experience of modern warfare and no proper equipment with which to fight back.

France at the time had a popular front government and its first instinct had been to help the Spanish Republic. There are several reasons why France retracted their offer of help, but there is no doubt that the main reason was that they would lose the support of Britain if they did so. Britain was determined to keep peace in Europe and was willing to sacrifice Spain to do so. The Non-Intervention agreement was developed by both France and Britain to justify their unwillingness to help a democratically elected European government in trouble. The agreement of non-intervention was signed by all the members of the League of Nations including Italy and Germany, both denying any involvement in Spain. The Soviet Union who had also signed the agreement, finally declared themselves no more bound to it than Italy and Germany and started sending essential food and equipment to the Republic. Together with this help came the darker side of Communism, their advisers, their secret police tactics and their grip on Spain tightened as the Republic came to rely on them more and more.

The Soviet Union did help to form the International Brigades through the Comintern and channel ordinary men and women from all over the world into Spain. All these normal people from all walks of life had one thing in common; they hated fascism and believed that if it was not defeated in Spain, it would be on the streets of London, Paris or Warsaw next. With hindsight we now know that the same year that Franco won the Spanish civil war, Hitler invaded Poland and so started world war two.

The Republic never stopped hoping that Britain who had a reputation for standing up for the underdog would see what Franco was doing and come to their rescue, but they never did. For whatever reason, Britain kept out of Spain and the enormousness of the Second World War ensured that the Spanish war would forever sit in its shadow.

Both Mussolini and Hitler lost their wars and their lives, Franco on the other hand stayed in power and kept Spain under his tight control, killing more people in revenge after the war than he did during it, until his death in 1975. In 1977 the first free elections to be held in Spain since 1936 took place and a pact of forgetting 'el pacto de olvido' agreed to help send Spain on a calm road to a modern democracy.